508
3

BAD BEHAVIOUR

Also by Cheryl Mildenhall in Headline Liaison

Bad Behaviour

Cheryl Mildenhall

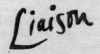

Copyright © 1998 Cheryl Mildenhall

The right of Cheryl Mildenhall to be identified as the Author
of the Work has been asserted by her in accordance with
the Copyright, Designs and Patents Act 1988.

First published in 1998
by HEADLINE BOOK PUBLISHING

A HEADLINE LIAISON paperback

10 9 8 7 6 5 4 3 2 1

ISBN 0 7472 6051 6

Typeset by CBS, Felixstowe, Suffolk
Printed and bound in Great Britain by
Mackays of Chatham plc, Chatham, Kent

HEADLINE BOOK PUBLISHING
A division of Hodder Headline PLC
338 Euston Road, London NW1 3BH

Bad Behaviour

Chapter One

The passageway outside the library was silent, save for the insistent clunk-clunk of the grandfather clock as the pendulum swung back and forth with metronomic precision within its mahogany carcass.

With a fresh wave of trepidation, Charlotte Hetherington shifted her gaze to the face of the clock. She felt almost catatonic with panic as she watched the brass hands move inexorably toward the ultimate moment. At nineteen, she was waiting for her life to change irrevocably. And she knew the moment would soon be at hand. All she could do to mark the agonising minutes was wait, with as much patience as her impetuous soul could muster, until the door to her father's study was finally flung open and she was invited inside to be told of her fate.

At twelve o'clock precisely, the clock chimed the hour. Each chime rang out sonorously from within the eighteenth-century long-case. On the ninth chime, Charlotte heard the sound of a heavy tread behind the study door.

All at once she was gripped by the jitters. She felt far more nervous than she had before. More nervous, in fact, than she had ever felt in her indulged, highly charmed life.

Without thinking, her hand flew to the silken cap of gold-blonde hair, styled in a fashionable jaw-length bob, that framed her delicate features. Her cornflower blue eyes, usually bright and alive with inquisitiveness and mischief, widened with apprehension in her pale-complexioned face. Her short, slightly snub nose was her pet hate, though it was a feature which everyone else who laid eyes on her found particularly endearing. But the most seductive feature of her fine-boned countenance had to be her wide, full-lipped mouth. Though painted girlishly with blush-pink lipstick at the moment, they were undoubtedly the lips of a woman. Wanton in their lushness, they habitually formed a natural pout that suggested bruising, passionate kisses and barely restrained sensuality. It was a mouth no man could resist.

The rest of Charlotte was damningly irresistible too. Her limbs were strong and well-toned, though her torso was far too sinuous and full-breasted to be truly *à la mode*. Current fashion trends dictated a boyish figure with flat chest and bottom and narrow hips. Consequently the straight tube '*flapper*' dresses that her peers favoured looked totally wrong on her. Her figure belonged to a decade or two earlier, when waist-nipping corsets had been the order of the day.

Having given up trying to look like everyone else, Charlotte did what she could to make the best of her natural assets. Today she was dressed from shoulder to toe in the most delicate fabrics: pale blue crêpe de chine for her morning dress, which was cut on the bias and hinted seductively at the rounded curves of her breasts and hips; finest oyster silk for the stockings which graced her shapely calves and ankles; and softest pale cream kid for her indoor shoes.

Although she was far too modest to admit it to herself, Charlotte was a delight to behold.

Such a sentiment was agreed upon wholeheartedly, but only in the private thoughts of the two men who were revealed as the study door swung inwards. To each man, similar in age and broad-shouldered, prosperous in stature (one her doting father, the other her just-agreed-upon fiancé) Charlotte – or Chattie, as she was known to her friends and family – was indeed as lovely a vision as one could imagine.

At least, on the outside.

Of the two men, only Charlotte's father, Alfred Hetherington, was aware that Chattie's demure, exquisitely feminine frame concealed the heart of a rebel. And it was to his profound relief that this was something which, as of ten minutes ago, had finally ceased to be his problem. Now it was up to Cadell Fox-Talbot, an old business acquaintance and a man of particularly successful means, to try to tame the headstrong young woman.

'You may come in now, Chattie,' Alfred Hetherington said,

pushing his guilty thoughts firmly aside as he swung the door further open to admit his daughter.

He did so in a way that was intended to be inviting, yet to Charlotte was an indisputable command.

Looking as hesitant as she felt, Charlotte stepped forward, the soft leather soles of her shoes sinking into the luxurious depths of the hand-knotted, elaborately patterned Aubusson carpet.

Not for her parents the clean lines and almost austere minimalist style of the current era, she mused fondly as she entered the dark wood-panelled lion's den that was her father's study. A relic to the past, the Georgian house occupied by the Hetheringtons was large by urban standards but appeared much smaller than it should, crammed as it was with heavy pieces of seventeenth- and eighteenth-century furniture inherited from the estates of various long-departed members of the family.

With a sweep of his hand, Alfred gestured toward one of the olive leather wing chairs that stood before his desk; itself an imposing monstrosity of carved oak. 'Sit here, Chattie dear. And Cadell, old chap, why not sit beside your future wife?' His voice boomed with unnatural bonhomie and a smile, rarely glimpsed by members of his family, curved up to meet his usually sombre grey eyes. 'In view of the circumstances, I would say it is high time the two of you became better acquainted.'

The idea of becoming more familiar with the virtual stranger who took the seat next to her sent a fresh wave of trepidation through Charlotte. As her father went on to offer both herself and Mr Fox-Talbot pre-lunch drinks, she felt compelled to drag her gaze unwillingly in his direction. With a churning sensation in her stomach, Charlotte charted the unfamiliar territory of her newly betrothed.

She could only assume by her father's words, and his unusual attempt at levity, that somehow the threatened deed had been executed. Clearly a deal had been struck between the two men. From now on, she realised, her palms dampening automatically at the perception, she was no longer the highly eligible Charlotte Hetherington, débutante, but the future Mrs Cadell Fox-

Talbot. And the virtual stranger seated beside her was now her fiancé.

Which meant she had been pushed across that invisible barrier into full-blown womanhood and all the responsibilities that entailed.

Adventurous though she was by nature, it was a difficult transition for Charlotte to make mentally, particularly as it dashed all her hopes of going to university. Or perhaps not, she thought in the next instant, embracing her characteristic optimism. It could be that her future husband was, despite at thirty-eight being twice her age, a forward-thinking man.

This was something, she knew, she would have to discover for herself as soon as possible and, as she had no option but to accept her fate and get to know this man better, she decided. The sooner she got started, the sooner she'd know where she stood.

As Charlotte's mind whirled, she hardly realised she had already begun her visual assessment of her future husband. He was not bad-looking. A little paunchy, perhaps, but his frame was so large and broad that the excesses of his prosperous lifestyle hardly showed. His dark mohair and silk-mix suit and leather shoes were obviously expensive and handmade, while the black opal cufflinks that fastened the cuffs of his cream silk shirt doubtless equalled her clothing allowance for a year.

At least, she thought, feeling avaricious, her future husband was capable of keeping her in the manner to which she would like to become accustomed.

Unwilling to let him know that she was appraising him, she left his face to last. But when the moment came, as her eyes flickered over the thick head of dark hair feathered with distinguished silver, slipped down the high, proud brow and slithered over the craggy terrain of his countenance, she was surprised to find her gaze arrested suddenly by twin pools of deep blue.

Profound and unblinking, his eyes were framed by thick black brows and lashes. They gazed straight back at her, transmitting a new, exciting message which sparked the strangest of tingling sensations in her lower belly. Charlotte was too naive to translate the meaning in his gaze automatically

4

but, as she continued to challenge him with her eyes, she realised the suggestion he conveyed was a most exciting combination of intimacy and interest. It was as though she and the man who sat no more than a finger-length away from her shared something akin to a private, rather racy joke.

This was the first moment that Charlotte acknowledged the prospect of intimacy between the two of them. Not just intimacy of thought and shared goals, which was how she viewed the marriage pact, but the other sort: the veiled, slightly sinister threat of physical intimacy that, she was ashamed to admit, she knew nothing about.

Out of the blue, the full realisation of her fate hit her with such exhilaration that it set her whole body tingling. The idea of sharing such intimacy with the man seated beside her, of presenting herself to him naked and allowing him to look at and touch those secret places which she hardly dared acknowledge herself, was too shaming to contemplate.

As she fought to contain her blushes, Charlotte became dimly aware that her father was speaking to her again. Feeling ashamed, she glanced up at him and accepted the sherry he handed to her with a mumbled word of thanks. Then she dipped her head to consider the pale Amontillado in the glass and was immediately grateful for the way her hair fell forward, concealing her burning cheeks.

'Having vulgar thoughts, my darling?' Cadell Fox-Talbot's teasing whisper made Charlotte's humiliation increase a thousandfold. 'Don't be embarrassed,' he went on relentlessly, 'we all have them. It pleases me to see you are as human as the rest of us. I admit, I was beginning to wonder . . .'

'Wonder about what?' Charlotte's head snapped up.

Quick to erupt, she felt immediately enraged by his teasing. Her hot temper and the unfamiliar excitement his mockery induced made her eyes sparkle with barely restrained passion. The impudence of the man, she fumed inwardly, trying desperately to quell the impulse to slap his cheek. Never mind that he was older than her and was her future husband: how could she possibly be expected to show respect and deference to someone who so blatantly insulted her? And in front of her own father, of all people.

5

It angered her even more when she realised that Cadell Fox-Talbot was amused by her display.

'This is the third occasion that we have met, my dear Charlotte,' he said smoothly, sitting back in the wing chair and crossing his legs casually at the ankles. 'And never once have I seen you lose your composure, nor show any kind of emotion whatsoever. I was beginning to think of you as the archetypal ice-maiden.'

'And you think I am being emotional now?' Charlotte demanded, her eyes still blazing as she met his unremitting gaze. 'Or that I have the capability of being vulgar?'

His azure eyes locked with her bold stare, becoming warmer, more insistent, as they probed her remorselessly. 'Yes, I do,' he replied smoothly before pausing, as if for effect. His eyes left hers to flicker over the rest of her for an electrifying instant. 'But I confess, I am attracted to vulgarity and equally to a fiery spirit. I am intrigued by these glimpses of you and looking forward to discovering everything there is to know about you.'

Charlotte felt as though she were rooted to the spot. He spoke to her with a terrifying degree of intimacy, as though they were alone. And the way his gaze returned to hold hers, once he had finished his frank appraisal, made her feel as though he had her bound and gagged.

After a long, drawn-out moment, during which Charlotte held her breath, he put down the brandy glass he had been cradling and stood up. She shrank back as he seemed to loom over her, her eyes widening as she wondered what he intended to do next.

'Come with me, Charlotte,' he said, in a tone that brooked no argument. 'I think a walk before lunch would do us both good. I have an urgent need to become better acquainted with the real you.' He held out a hand to her.

Automatically, Charlotte flashed a pleading glance at her father. To her surprise, he appeared unconcerned by Cadell Fox-Talbot's suggestion. She had been hoping he would pick up on the tone of the conversation and offer some objection. She told herself her unwillingness stemmed from the fact that she was not dressed for the outdoors, no matter that it was early summer and the day pleasantly warm. However, there was something in the challenge of her fiancé's broad hand and the commanding yet seductive timbre of his voice that compelled her to stand and nod her agreement.

'Very well,' she agreed, pointedly ignoring his proffered hand. 'Though I fear I am not dressed for such an exercise.'

She regretted her words and was forced to knock back the rest of her sherry in a single indecorous gulp as Cadell Fox-Talbot swept her body with a bold glance that was at once appraising and assessing. It seemed, she realised, forcing herself to maintain her usual proud, shoulders-flung-back stance, as though he were evaluating her as an animal: a prize head of cattle. The idea inflamed her even more.

Despite her misgivings and the trembling in her knees, she agreed to accompany him. But by the time she and her loathsome companion had stepped through the side door that led from her father's office, their feet crunching on the wide strip of gravel that surrounded the house, Charlotte felt more angry and humiliated than she had ever felt in her life. And she owed it all to this man. The one who let go of her hand to take her by the elbow to guide her on their walk and whose fingers seemed to sear her pale bare flesh with the intensity of a branding iron.

The man she was destined to spend the rest of her life with.

All at once the full force of Charlotte's fate hit her. It dealt her such a powerful blow that she reeled from it. Only the light yet insistent pressure of his hand cupping her elbow stopped her from crumpling to the ground.

'Is there something the matter, my dear?' Cadell's face was grave with concern. He was bothered that the girl had not offered up a single word since they had left her father's study. Now he wondered if she was perhaps sickly and that her father had cleverly concealed the fact. Or could it be that she was pregnant with another man's child?

The possibility horrified him so much, he had to blurt out the question. It was not unheard of, unfortunately. Since the Great War had ended, a good number of single young women had greeted the war's returning heroes with indecorous passion, with many a liaison bringing forth disastrous results. And since that time, it seemed, a new immorality had become the norm.

Was that possibly the reason why the Hetheringtons had acceded so readily to his interest in Charlotte? Could it be they were anxious to save themselves and their daughter from utter disgrace?

Although she still felt slightly woozy, Charlotte whirled her head around to look at him, her bobbed blonde hair flying, the blunt-cut ends grazing her cheekbones before resettling just above her jawline.

'Am I what?' she demanded, unable to believe he had just asked her such a vile question.

'I asked if you were pregnant,' Cadell said, forcing himself to keep his voice even, as though it were the most natural question in the world to ask. 'Being in such a delicate state often makes women feel faint . . .' He was surprised to find himself stumbling over his explanation. Though perhaps the realisation, brought on by the look of shock and disbelief in Charlotte's eyes, that he had made a mistake was reason enough. 'I'm sorry,' he murmured with genuine regret. 'That was very crass of me.'

He tried to grip her elbow more tightly, to force her to turn around and look at him so she could see the sincerity in his eyes, but Charlotte would have none of it. She shook him off angrily, stomping across the gravel and cutting across the carefully tended lawn at a furious rate.

Cadell managed to catch up with her at a charming Japanese water garden, which comprised a small lily pond with a wooden bridge over and a tiny pagoda large enough only for two or three people. Unfortunately, he was too intent on Charlotte to notice the carefully contrived beauty of their surroundings.

As she leant over the bridge, studying the darting bodies of the koi carp below, Charlotte sensed rather than heard him come up behind her. When he reached her, she heard him panting with exertion and a moment later felt his breath, irregular and warm, on the exposed nape of her slender neck. Even so, she refused to turn round and acknowledge his presence and merely continued to contemplate the pool below.

As his hands gripped her shoulders fiercely, so her breathing increased to a rate that matched his.

'You insulted me,' she said, dulling the accusation with her obstinate refusal to look at him. 'If I were to tell my father, Mr Fox-Talbot . . .'

'Cadell. Please, call me Cadell.' He laughed then, briefly, apologetically, the unexpected sound easing the tension in Charlotte's body. 'If we are to become man and wife,' he continued, 'I don't think it is fitting for us to continue to behave so formally.' There followed a long pause, then, 'Please, Charlotte won't you turn round?'

Charlotte hesitated for a moment, then did as Cadell bade her. It took a long moment for her to meet his gaze. For a while she stared at the blank wall of his chest, she tried desperately to hang on to her anger, but to no avail. All her senses felt consumed by his closeness and the heat and scent of masculinity emanating from him.

All at once, her gaze took in the fact that one of the tiny pearl buttons that fastened the collar of his shirt had come undone. Without thinking, she moved her hands up to his throat to fasten it. And it was as the button slid smoothly through the hole that she happened to glance up.

His sudden smile melted her from the inside out and once again she felt like swooning. But this time she maintained her composure by placing her palms flat against his chest, her elegant fingers splayed. She blushed again as his eyes bored into hers.

'I take it you are a virgin?' he said gently, understanding now.

Blushing more furiously than ever, she nodded.

'Well, that is good, I suppose . . .'

Charlotte was amazed by the hesitancy in his tone. It made her speak up. 'What do you mean, you suppose? Doesn't every man wish his bride to be a virgin on their wedding night?'

Though she acknowledged that, nowadays, girls her age took far more sexual liberties, it had never occurred to her to be anything less than virginal. The retention of her chastity was something she took very seriously indeed and had 'repelled all those trying to board', as her father might have put it, vehemently denying the young men she met anything more than a chaste kiss.

She hardly dared even touch or look at herself in anything

9

more than a detached, clinical way. It was too dangerous. Too exciting. Especially if she were to contemplate the sensations roused by the glance of a hand across her breasts. Or that of a finger sliding along the groove which separated the unsullied lips nestling between her thighs. Just thinking about the way her body seemed to respond so readily to such careless caresses, usually made during bathing, gave her cause for concern. And extreme embarrassment.

Without realising it, she shivered.

'Oh, my darling, are you cold? I am so thoughtless.' Cadell immediately began to berate himself.

'No, not at all.' Their earlier argument all but forgotten, Charlotte was anxious to reassure him. 'Shall we sit inside the pagoda?' she suggested, taking a step back from him and dropping her hands to her sides. 'It will be a little warmer in there and it's quite comfortable.'

Without waiting for his reply, she led the way across the bridge to the red and gold painted pagoda, which was hardly more than a gazebo. It was a clever work of carpentry, wrought by a local man to one of Charlotte's mother's own designs. The rest of the water garden had been similarly fashioned by the Hetheringtons' own gardeners. Inside, the pagoda was secluded from prying eyes and comfortably furnished with a banquette seat, deeply buttoned and padded with red and gold satin. Charlotte sank down onto the seat gratefully, feeling her feet tingle with relief as she did so, though she resisted the urge to slip off her shoes.

Cadell appeared strangely ill-at-ease as he sat down next to her. His frame was so large and the confines of the pagoda so small that they were forced, by circumstance, to sit very close together. So close that Charlotte could feel his body heat even more keenly than before and, without meaning to, allowed herself to become intoxicated by the very masculine scent of him. The combination made her senses reel, causing her to fan herself with her hand.

'Gosh, it's much warmer in here, isn't it?' she commented, trying unsuccessfully to inch away from him. The heat from his thigh pressing against hers seemed to sear her flesh through the thin fabric of her dress. And the fine material of his jacket brushed her bare arm in such a way that it caused the fine blonde hairs on her arms to quiver, like blades of grass disturbed by a breeze.

'I suppose it is,' Cadell agreed. 'Do you mind if I remove my jacket?'

A lump formed in the base of Charlotte's throat as she shook her head dumbly, then watched him as he stood up to shrug off the jacket. When he sat down again, draping the jacket neatly across his lap, Cadell turned his head to smile at her.

'You really are very beautiful, Charlotte,' he said. His eyes, deep and warm like the ocean, crinkled endearingly at the corners. 'I count myself a very lucky man.'

'You really think so?' Charlotte was at once pleased and flustered by his unexpected compliment. It wasn't that she was unused to receiving such positive affirmations of her good looks, but they usually came from much younger men who displayed all the eagerness of puppies.

For some reason, the fact that it was Cadell who paid her such a compliment mattered a great deal more. In an automatic gesture, Charlotte patted the sleek cap of her hair, though naturally there wasn't a single golden strand out of place. All at once, as her eyes slid slyly sideways to glance coquettishly at her future husband, Charlotte realised they were actually flirting with each other.

'Yes, I do think you are beautiful,' Cadell said, reaching out and taking her hand, which still hovered by the side of her face. He turned the hand so that it rested palm upwards then, to Charlotte's surprise, he raised her arm to his lips and began to lay a trail of featherlight kisses from wrist to elbow.

Charlotte was stunned for a moment but, when his mouth touched the sensitive flesh at her inner elbow, she let out a low, involuntary moan. His touch was soft and seductive, kindling a slow-burning sensation deep within her womb. The feeling was unfamiliar, yet seemed entirely natural and, for once, Charlotte felt unafraid of her bodily responses. Perhaps, she mused, arching her neck as Cadell transferred his kisses there, it is because we are engaged. How could something this delightful possibly be sinful?

Cadell moved his hand slowly across Charlotte's thighs as

11

he continued to kiss her. It was taking every ounce of restraint he possessed not to give into his passion and ravish her. The tautness of her thighs and the heat emanating from between them, combined with the way her body trembled and her ecstatic whimpers, told him his desire for her was reciprocated. Even so, he knew he must proceed slowly.

Used to women who were completely in touch with their sensuality and gave freely of themselves, Cadell found the situation with Charlotte frustrating yet perversely arousing. It would be a novelty to bed a virgin after so many years, he thought. It was only a pity that he did not have enough free time at his disposal to teach her everything properly from scratch.

It was then he decided what must be done. The school at Bad Alpendorf had served him well before, with his first wife. Hopefully, Charlotte would benefit just as greatly from the Swiss school's special curriculum.

While he was showing great restraint, Cadell had to remind himself that however naive his future bride might appear, at nineteen she was hardly a child. Nor did she look anything like one. With her lush breasts and rounded hips, she was every inch a woman. Only a few intimate caresses and an even more scant membrane of flesh separated her from the full delights of full-blown womanhood.

The thought of being the one to instigate Charlotte's completion of her education made Cadell smile and, in so doing, he found his lips curving around the underside of her right ear. Taking the lobe between his lips, he nibbled it, delighting in the succulence of her flesh. To his pleasure, he heard her moan once again and felt her thighs slip ever so slightly apart beneath the fragile and slippery fabric of her dress.

With acute sensitivity, he ran his fingertips lightly over her lap, over one thigh and up and over the other, before skimming lightly around her hip and across her belly. When he did so, he felt her stomach muscles tighten and then quiver as he slid his fingertips lower down. Ever so carefully, he began to slide his fingertips between her thighs, his senses tingling at the way the delicate crêpe de chine of her dress slithered over silk panties, a curly fleece and the soft hot flesh beneath.

He risked a glance at her face, half-expecting to see an expression of shock and reproach. However, to his pleasure, he saw her delicious lips were slightly parted, emitting short, sharp gasps, while her eyelids flickered under the heavy toll of voluptuousness. There was no doubt she was enjoying his caresses, as if the way she squirmed upon the padded banquette as he dared to slide his fingers lower, cupping her sex, were not proof enough.

Then, all at once, she was furious. Sitting bolt upright, she dashed his hands away from her, her face livid with anger. 'How dare you?' she spluttered, struggling to right the hem of her dress and smooth it as far over her knees as possible. 'Fiancé or no, I hardly think it proper for you to take such liberties. And at my father's house!'

Her outrage was such that Cadell felt compelled to laugh. 'If it is simply the location that bothers you, I would be honoured if you were to agree to accompany me to my own house, after lunch. As it is to be your home, too, it would be –'

'Go to your home – are you mad?' Charlotte stared at him, wide-eyed.

All trace of humour wiped away in an instant, Cadell narrowed his own gaze. 'No, Charlotte, not mad,' he said, shaking his head in disbelief. 'If anything, I must be mad to think of marrying such a silly, featherheaded, tight-laced –' His insult was cut short by the sharp slap of Charlotte's palm as she swiped his cheek.

'How dare you?' She seemed to blaze with self-righteous indignation and stood rubbing her palm, which glowed as hotly as her eyes.

Now it was Cadell's turn to feel enraged. Grasping Charlotte by the wrists, he dragged her across his lap and held her, kicking and squirming, as she protested vehemently.

'What do you think you're doing, you fiend? Let me go . . . let me go, damn you!'

'You would dare to damn me?' Cadell thundered, pressing the heel of his hand into the small of her back to keep her still.

He could feel her lush breasts crushed upon his right thigh and the rapid pounding of her heart beneath her ribs. Despite his best efforts to hold her, she still bucked and fought, her movements exciting him, daring him to teach her a lesson and, at the same time, slake a little of his rising desire. Without hesitating, he used his free hand to pull her dress up over her hips, exposing a deliciously rounded bottom clad only in a pair of écru silk French knickers. The fabric was so fine, and clung with such fluid ease to the contours of her buttocks, that the intriguing dark shadow of the cleft between them was clearly defined.

Pausing only to draw in his breath, in an effort to quell the thunder of excitement that ran through him, Cadell grasped the waistband of her knickers and ripped the flimsy silk down to her knees.

Chapter Two

The constant plop-plopping sound of fish coming up to the surface of the lily pond to feed, together with the occasional chirrup of grasshoppers in the long grass that surrounded the pagoda, were the only things that reminded Charlotte that she hadn't suddenly been whisked off to a different dimension. Yet the very normality of her surroundings only served to heighten the awfulness of her predicament.

In reality, it beggared belief.

She could no more believe what Cadell had just done to her, than accept that she was to spend the rest of her life welded to this man by matrimony. Only her horror at the prospect served to keep her sanity intact as she continued to squirm under the heavy pressure of his hand on her lower back and kick and thrash about with all her might. Her overwhelming desire was to get away from this monster. As far away as possible. And stay away.

It took some time before Charlotte came to the sorry conclusion that her efforts to fight Cadell off were all in vain.

Though it went against her instincts she tried pleading with him instead. 'Cadell, for goodness sake, this is most unseemly. I beg of you, let me go.'

Cadell's response to this new tactic was an infuriating chuckle and the gentle yet possessive caress of his hand upon her bottom. He moved his hands, switching their position quickly, before Charlotte could take advantage of his movement, to grasp her hair and drag her head back so that he could look, upside down, into her shocked eyes.

'Save your breath, my darling, for your screams of ecstasy,' he said mockingly. 'I have absolutely no intention of letting you go until I have properly taught you how to behave.'

Charlotte's immediate urge was to wriggle furiously and glare at him with all her might. 'Hah! Teach me how to behave,' she crowed, fighting desperately to inject as much venom into her voice as possible. 'I know very well how to behave, *Mr Fox-Talbot*.' She stressed his name with as much of a sneer as she could muster. 'Clearly, it is you who does not. Is this how one normally behaves in polite company?'

'If you were polite, my dear girl,' Cadell countered thinly, 'I would have no difficulty treating you with the respect you so clearly believe you deserve. However . . .'

With the realisation that she was getting nowhere with him, Charlotte let out a howl of frustration. She was acutely aware of the fact that her bottom was as naked as the day she had been born, she felt a cool wisp of a breeze snake across it and through the slight gap at the apex of her thighs. It was acutely stimulating, as though the draught of cool air were a finger, insolently investigating the places where no other finger had ever dared. Her pretty face burned with fury and humiliation as she switched tactics again.

'My father will be furious when he finds out about this. Have you thought about that?' she said, sounding haughty now and not a little over-confident.

'Your father?' Cadell laughed. 'How little you know the man with whom you have hitherto spent your whole life.'

Charlotte was shocked. 'What do you mean?' She shook her head, forcing him to release his grip on her hair. To her mortification, Cadell immediately moved his hands again and went back to caressing her naked bottom. 'My father is the most upstanding of men,' she insisted, trying desperately to ignore his caresses. 'He is a respected –'

'Upstanding, yes, I agree totally,' Cadell interrupted her. He paused to slide an assessing finger down the cleft between her tightly clenched buttocks and smiled as she tried to wriggle away from his touch.

Charlotte winced at the insolence of this new caress but said nothing, merely waited for him to continue with his explanation.

'There are many women in our respected circle who could vouch for your father's ability to remain upstanding,' Cadell

16

said; his words sounded mysterious to Charlotte's ears.

She shook her head again; this time she raised it and turned to look at him of her own accord. She was surprised to see such a degree of amusement dancing in his sea-blue eyes.

'I don't understand,' she muttered crossly.

To her surprise, Cadell gave her a gentle, almost sympathetic smile. 'Of course you don't, my dear, naive little Charlotte. You have no idea at all of the games grown-ups play, do you?' When Charlotte remained mute and simply gazed at him with incomprehension, Cadell continued, 'While some people prefer to go to their marriage bed as virgins, they do not stay that way for long. Many, admittedly the more intelligent of our class, soon discover the pleasures of the flesh and the delight in sharing those pleasures with others. They discover that marriage is the ideal foundation for exploring their sensuality and expanding upon their knowledge, either within the bounds of discreet little liaisons, or in a more open way. Exhibitionism becomes a new realm of pleasure.'

'Are you talking of orgies?' Charlotte found her voice, though she could hardly keep the incredulity she felt from it.

'So you have heard of such things?' Cadell's laughter was gently mocking. His hand continued to caress her bottom, his fingers alternately smoothing and squeezing the pliable alabaster flesh. His conversation with Charlotte had the effect of inducing certain memories: of wild, uninhibited parties, with men and women of all ages and sizes engaged in various acts. When combined with the sensation of her buttocks beneath his fingers, those memories invoked a keenly erotic stirring at his groin.

As she felt something begin to stir beneath her belly, Charlotte frowned. It couldn't be one of Cadell's hands, she thought; they were both engaged in either restraining or exploring her. All at once, the realisation that it was another, altogether more intimate, part of his body which caressed her from underneath made her cry out with alarm.

'You disgusting pig!' she cried. 'I can feel your . . . your thing . . .'

Once again Cadell uttered a chuckle. 'I confess, I am feeling a little emboldened by our predicament. What red-blooded man wouldn't be? Here I am, seated in secluded, delightful surroundings, with all the bounty of nature around me and a deliciously nubile nineteen-year-old woman spread across my lap. My hand is currently caressing her bared bottom and my thighs are taking immense pleasure in the heat and sinuous movement of her torso and the crushing weight of her breasts. How then, may I ask, am I expected to behave?'

Without meaning to, Charlotte let out a heavy sigh. It was true, she admitted reluctantly to herself, the situation did provoke a certain sensual pleasure. Try as she might, she could not deny it. Her own body felt heavy and warm: even her naked buttocks which, after a further moment, she forgot to clench with fury.

'If this is what pleases you, future husband,' she said wryly, 'I suppose I cannot complain. I daresay I will discover certain other peculiarities about you on our wedding night.'

Cadell kept his immediate response – that she would discover his peculiarities, as she put them, much sooner than she anticipated – to himself. 'You have made no comment about my disclosures concerning your father,' he said after a moment.

Charlotte considered this thoughtfully. 'Frankly, I don't believe you,' she said, pursing her full lips in such a way that Cadell felt the sudden urge to push his throbbing stem between them. 'I think you are trying to goad me. You like a woman with a fiery spirit. You said so yourself. No, Cadell, do not take me for a fool. I will not rise to your bait.' So saying, she shook her head firmly and went on to rest her chin on the backs of her folded arms.

When she did this, Cadell was unable to tell if she had ceased to care about the situation they were in, or was simply feigning nonchalance. There was only one way to find out. Raising his hand, he delivered a sharp smack across her buttocks.

To his delight, Charlotte's response was immediate and full of heated indignation. Her head shot up again and she managed, by speed of movement, to twist her body and raise one arm to rake her long, unpainted nails down his right cheek. His instinct was to raise a hand to his face and the minute he did so, Charlotte began to struggle to her feet.

'You animal!' she yelled at him, thrusting her indignant face so close to his he could feel the furious warmth of her breath and smell its sweetness. 'You will never, ever lay a finger on me again. I swear, I will see you dead first.' As she offered up the empty threat, her eyes blazed with indignation. Standing with her hands planted firmly on the lush curves of her hips, her feet apart, chest heaving visibly under the delicate fabric of her dress, she looked every inch a blazing inferno of passionate outrage. And never more desirable.

Quick to recover his composure, Cadell reached out and grabbed her by the waist, his large strong hands gripping her, his broad fingers and thumbs almost meeting around her narrow circumference.

Charlotte immediately began to fight him, her fingers grabbing at his wrists, sinking her nails into him painfully while kicking ineffectually at his groin.

Fed up with playing games and wholly aroused, Cadell stood up and lifted her with him, carrying her in front of him so that her feet dangled a few inches from the ground, to the broad semi-circular rail that fronted the pagoda. Lifting her higher, his heart beating fast, he set her down on the rail.

'Keep this up, and you will fall and hurt yourself,' he warned her, referring to the way Charlotte continued to thrash about wildly.

For a moment she hesitated and glanced down. The pagoda was set on a high plinth and, from her seat on the rail, it was a good four or five feet to the ground, which looked hard and uncompromising.

Seizing the opportunity, Cadell pushed the hem of her dress up to her hips, exposing the pale flesh of her thighs above her garters and the triangle of lush gold fleece at their apex. He pushed his broad body between her knees, forcing them apart and thereby urging the petals of her secret flesh to blossom unexpectedly.

'No!' Charlotte's single word of protest was a horrified scream. Her eyes widened.

Without an pretence at finesse, he thrust his hand between her legs and immediately sought the little button which would activate her pleasure. His fingertips ground remorselessly upon it, seducing her gently but with enough pressure to cause this secret part of her to swell quite speedily.

Almost beside herself with shock, Charlotte now felt a sensation of a different kind. The humiliation of being forced into such a predicament was far outweighed by the strange and not unpleasurable sensations coursing through her body. Of course, it was unthinkable that Cadell, a virtual stranger, should have such lewd access to her body. And yet . . .

She sighed as a tingling sensation began in her groin and flooded her pelvis with a sudden warmth. All at once, she felt like spreading her thighs wider apart. The thing Cadell was doing to her with his fingers, the part upon which he strummed so deliciously, was making her lose her senses.

'There, my little one,' Cadell murmured, slowing the rhythm of his fingertips slightly and adjusting their position so that he could sink his middle finger into her moist depths, while maintaining her arousal with the pad of his thumb. 'Isn't it more enjoyable when we are not fighting?'

'Mm, perhaps.'

With her eyes half-closed, Charlotte allowed a smile to flicker across her face. In truth, she felt suffused by sensuality. Between her widespread thighs she felt on fire, yet her body seemed to be creating its own dampness, as if in an effort to quell the heat. Little pools of moisture gathered in the hollows at the tops of her inner thighs. This in turn was caressed dry by the warm breeze which wafted between her legs and stroked her nakedness from time to time.

All her previous humiliation seemed forgotten as she strove to capture something indefinable: a goal which she sensed instinctively her body was capable of attaining. Feeling daring, Charlotte let go of the rail upon which she was balanced, and wrapped her arms around Cadell's neck. The skin on the back of his broad neck felt warm and slick with perspiration, the short dark hairs bristling under her exploratory fingertips.

Cadell felt his arousal soar. Without realising it, Charlotte had managed to discover one of his most erogenous zones. Perhaps the nape of his neck was not the most obvious pleasure spot, he mused, moving closer to her and surreptitiously unbuttoning his fly with his free hand, but her innocent caresses were definitely having the desired effect on other parts of his body. Not that he could deny the singular pleasure of exploring her secret portal. He was in no doubt now that she had not deceived him about her virginity. And she felt so hot and tight, not to mention moist, that he could hardly contain his desire to sink his throbbing prick into her to the hilt.

He had no compunction about deflowering her now and not waiting until their wedding night. When all was said and done, he reasoned, he could not send her to Bad Alpendorf with her virginity still intact. Even so, he couldn't help wondering what her response would be when he committed this final irrevocable act.

Cadell needn't have worried quite so much. Though Charlotte felt a quiver of trepidation when she first realised what he was about to do, her sensuality was rising on such a high tide that there was no way she felt able, or willing, to refuse him. Indeed, she whimpered with delight when she felt the unfamiliar sensation of the smooth roundness of his cock as it nudged her intimate lips apart and coasted inside her on a slick coating of her own juices.

Her pleasure soared when she realised the sublime way his hardness filled her. She felt stretched to capacity and yet, as she wound her slim legs instinctively around his hips and pulled him deeper inside her, the brief stab of pain she felt was immediately obliterated by the fierce bolt of fiery passion that engulfed her.

Her body arched as she felt consumed by the most indescribable voluptuousness, as though every pleasure in the world had been heaped upon her at once. And throughout it the darkest, lewdest of images galloped through her mind, propelling her toward new, previously unimaginable, heights of wicked desire.

She felt like Salome and Lucretia Borgia all rolled into one, such was her sinfulness and the pleasure she took from it. Spurred on by an incredibly mounting desire, she bucked harder, gripping tighter with her legs, rubbing her swollen feminine lips and the bud that protruded between them against his pubic bone. She could feel the rough rasp of wiry hair; she was sure that it was as dark as that on his head, though she hadn't dared to look.

But why not now? she asked herself, releasing her grip around Cadell's shoulders to glance down to point where their bodies were joined. The sight arrested her vision and she gazed in horrified fascination at the way her own body, previously so demure and compressed into its little pouch, now seemed stretched so wide open it appeared alien to her. It seemed as though this part of her belonged to someone else and yet she could feel the warm tremors and tinglings that coursed through her every time her body grazed his.

When he noticed Charlotte's fascination, Cadell eased himself out of her almost completely, then slid his hardness back inside her welcoming body. He repeated this action time after time, noting with pleasure when he glanced up at her face, how her eyelids seemed to widen with surprise, then flutter with the heaviness of desire as he plunged back into her again.

His powers of restraint were admirable but, all too soon, he felt her inner muscles contracting around him again; this time there was no possibility of him holding back. With a loud cry of ecstasy, he spurted into her, his fingers digging into her hips with such fierceness that afterwards he feared he might have bruised her.

Charlotte seemed not to care. She smiled at him with the beatific smile of a woman thoroughly satiated. Her eyes, he noticed, were hazy, their lids drooping with languor. And her body seemed softer and more pliable than ever as he slipped regretfully from her, righted himself, then carried her over to the banquette and laid her down gently.

There he covered her face and throat with kisses, punctuated with murmurs of approval and endearment. 'My darling Charlotte, you are perfect. Absolutely perfect. I knew . . . I hoped you would be like this. Oh, my love, we are going to have such a wonderful time. When we are married . . .'

Charlotte stopped him with a fingertip pressed against his lips. 'Don't talk so much, my darling,' she admonished him softly. 'I would prefer just to bask for a moment in the glow of pleasure I am feeling.'

'Did you truly relish it? You don't feel guilty for what we just enjoyed?' Cadell had been concerned that she might feel overcome with guilt afterward. It would be understandable, given her girlishness and naive nature.

To his relief, she shook her head slowly from side to side, a satisfied smile curving her full lips. 'Not a bit,' she told him. 'Although I'm not sure I won't feel a little guilty later on.' Her lips formed a slight moue for a moment, and she appeared to Cadell as though she were considering something. Then she laughed. Her laughter was not the light, girlish tinkle he had heard her emit before but was more husky. Without doubt, it was the knowing chuckle of a full-blown woman.

'What is it? Tell me,' he urged.

Instead of answering him straight away, Charlotte moved an arm behind her and nestled her head in the crook of her elbow. Then she gazed levelly at him. 'I was just imagining going back to the house and sitting down with my parents for lunch,' she said. 'Do you imagine that they will notice anything different about me?'

'They will see you are a woman in love, certainly,' Cadell assured her with mock gravity, 'but nothing more.'

'If they see me as a woman, then they will know what made me so,' Charlotte answered pertly. She treated him to an impish grin that restored her girlishness for a fleeting moment. 'But do you know what, Cadell, my darling?' she added, raising her head to run the tip of her tongue across his surprised mouth in a way that was sensual and instantly arousing. 'I really don't care.'

Two weeks later, Charlotte found herself once again seated in her father's study. She had a slight inkling as to why she had been summoned there and felt restless with anticipation because of it.

Cadell would be arriving shortly. That in itself was enough to spark certain tingles of excitement. But this time, she knew, Cadell was coming to talk to her father about something important. Something that her future husband had hinted at several times over the past couple of weeks: the continuation of her education.

Here Charlotte felt a little confused. She had not actually mentioned to Cadell in so many words that she wished to go to university. Indeed, she wasn't at all certain now that university was the right choice after all. It required a degree of dedication which she felt, as Cadell's wife, she couldn't properly apply. However, some kind of mind-enhancing course, such as art appreciation, or anthropology, might be a good compromise . . .

Her thoughts were interrupted by the arrival of Cadell, who looked as powerful and heart-achingly desirable as usual. Not surprisingly, Charlotte's body reacted with its usual response, tingling and moistening. Her heart began to race at the prospect of being alone with him again. Of the kisses and caresses she found so pleasurable that she had begun to crave them – him – like a drug.

She and Cadell had taken pleasure in each other's bodies many times during the past fortnight. Sometimes they were snatched moments, when he would drag her into an empty room, or a secluded corner, and ravish her as far as he was able with his hands. But on two occasions, they had managed to spend a couple of blissfully uninterrupted hours together. Once in Cadell's huge bed, during which he had pleasured her over and over and the other, a daring interlude in her own boudoir, where Cadell had shown her the delights of her own body in graphic detail, reflected in her cheval mirror.

Hardly able to contain her lascivious thoughts, Charlotte shifted deliberately on the leather chair. She had intentionally left off her underclothes and, when she sat down, had surreptitiously hitched up the back of her dress so that she could rub her naked sex upon the warm hide.

Apparently able to guess what she was up to, Cadell winked at her as he crossed the room to take the seat beside her. The situation was heavily reminiscent of that morning two weeks ago, when Cadell had asked her father for permission to marry her, Charlotte mused happily. And yet she was keenly aware of how much she had changed since then. No longer was she a naive little girl. Through his powerful seduction and persuasive charms, Cadell had turned her into a woman.

'Good afternoon, my love,' Cadell said formally, taking her hand and kissing it when he reached her side.

A slight flush tinted Charlotte's cheek as she acknowledged his greeting and dared to look into his eyes. They were deep and mesmeric as usual, but now also harboured the profundity of knowledge and shared secrets gained over the past couple of weeks.

Charlotte blushed harder as she recognised the intimacy in them. In a deliberate gesture, she licked her lips slowly, lowering her eyelids a little as she did so and pressing her thighs together tightly to assuage the throbbing excitement in her little bud. Moisture gathered inside her and trickled out of her, prompting the shameful realisation that her impulsive urge to gratify her sexual longings on the leather seat might well leave its own impression.

The idea of her father noticing and recognising the source of the resultant stain on one of his study chairs made her blush even harder.

Throughout all this Cadell was regarding her steadily, with amusement in his deep blue eyes. When her father turned his back to them to answer the telephone, Cadell reached out and slipped a hand under the hem of Charlotte's rucked-up dress, sliding it up higher and higher, past her garter, to the patch of silky skin above. This he began to stroke gently and rhythmically, his finger gradually slipping between her thighs to caress the warm moist purse of flesh nestling there.

With great difficulty, Charlotte fought to resist the urge to moan and to spread her legs wider apart. It seemed the most deliciously obscene pleasure, to be enjoying Cadell's intimate explorations of her body when her own father was a mere yard or two away from them. If he was aware of what was going on, he gave no indication of it. His telephone conversation seemed to be taking up all his attention. And this encouraged Charlotte to utter a tiny, stifled whimper and raise her hips to press her throbbing clitoris urgently against Cadell's rotating fingertips.

He had taught her the proper names for all the parts of her body, and had used some lewd descriptions of his own, which he insisted were a natural result of his passion for her. Furthermore, he had encouraged her to use her own pet names for his genitals and, after a little embarrassment, Charlotte had come to give his penis the adopted name of Freddie. This meant she could quite happily talk to Cadell on the telephone, or in mixed company, and enquire how Freddie was feeling today and if he was in high spirits, without anyone being any the wiser.

Their sexual games gave Charlotte a frisson of excitement hitherto unknown to her. She felt in a state of permanent sexual arousal. Like a common bitch in heat, all her thoughts were consumed by the recollection, or anticipation, of physical delights. Her body constantly blushed and tingled with desire; the pulsing between her legs was an almost permanent state of affairs. It was only while she was sleeping that she felt any release from it. And then this was only because her dreams were so extreme and erotic that she felt as though her desires were being assuaged in reality; the expected culmination of her passion invariably woke her and left her gasping and perspiring among the damp tangle of her sheets, her hand or a pillow clasped firmly between her thighs.

She quaked at the thought of her maid, or indeed one of her parents, coming into her room to investigate the reason for her cries and finding her in such a state. And yet this possibility had its own erotic merit. The ever-present danger of her truly lascivious and depraved nature being discovered was an added thrill.

The only person she could talk to about this was Cadell. Even now, she marvelled at the calmness with which he listened to her shameful confessions. The only indication that he felt in any way affected by her honesty was the bulge that invariably strained at the front of his trousers, disturbing their impeccable cut. When this happened, Charlotte would feel such a sense of responsibility for his predicament that it seemed only right that she should use her hand to make proper amends and restore Freddie to his former neat and tidy state.

With such delights at her disposal and such growing intimacy between herself and Cadell, Charlotte had every reason to doubt the advantages of going away to university. The academic life no longer held any interest for her. Since her betrothal to Cadell, she was far more preoccupied by the pleasures of the flesh and had no real wish to stimulate her brain any further.

So when her father finally finished his telephone conversation and turned around to find Charlotte seated, once more demurely, with her skirt pulled neatly down to her knees, and made reference to her continued education, she shook her head emphatically.

'I have decided, father, that the academic path is no longer one I wish to pursue,' she said firmly, risking a sideways glance at Cadell. He remained, she noticed with a wry smile of amusement, completely enigmatic. 'I realise now,' she went on, 'that my first duty must be to my husband and to creating a delightful and relaxing atmosphere at home. The wish to enhance my intellect was purely selfish.'

Her eyelashes fluttered as she glanced down, in what she hoped was a suitably demure gesture. If only he knew that her intentions were totally dishonourable and impure, she thought, aware that her father was smiling fondly at her.

'Then we are all agreed, in that respect,' her father replied, to her surprise. 'Cadell and I have discussed your future education at great length, and have come to the conclusion that some sort of finishing school would be the best option for you.' When Charlotte raised her head quickly, a protest springing to her lips, her father interrupted her with a stern look that brooked no argument. 'You need to learn certain skills, Chattie,' he went on, softening his tone slightly. 'As you are aware, your future husband is a powerful man and very well respected. As his wife, you will be expected to present an image of sophistication that you do not, as yet, possess. A finishing school would equip you with the skills and knowledge necessary for you to complement Cadell's standing in the community.'

'I have made a suggestion to your father,' Cadell said, before Charlotte could interrupt, 'of a school which I know to be of the highest calibre. It is in Switzerland and –'

'Switzerland?' Charlotte couldn't stifle her protests any longer. 'But that is so far away – from you. And my parents, of course,' she added hastily.

Cadell smiled. 'Not that far. Overseas transport is very efficient these days, my darling. And the course is intensive but fairly short. After a month or so –'

'A month!' Charlotte was horrified. Four whole weeks, maybe more, without any kind of sexual contact with Cadell, was unthinkable.

Reaching out, Cadell touched her arm lightly with his fingertips. It was supposed to be a calming gesture but his very touch electrified Charlotte, making her dismay at being parted from him all the more intense. 'Charlotte, calm down.'

'I won't calm down and I won't go,' she said stubbornly. 'You can't make me, either of you.' With anger flashing in her eyes, she glanced from Cadell to her father and back again. Her eyes locked with Cadell's steady gaze for a moment, her frown turning into a petulant moue.

Cadell suppressed a smile. Right at that moment, Charlotte appeared the embodiment of a spoiled brat. Yet the incomprehension and passionate outrage in her eyes made him realise that she felt hurt by this new turn of events and that he would have to word his explanation carefully.

'We wouldn't be able to be together anyway, my dear child,' he said, taking her hand and squeezing it. 'You see, I have to go away on business, to North Africa,' he improvised. 'It is unfortunate, but that is the nature of my professional life. And it does mean that I would be able to travel with you to Switzerland first and then collect you once your course is completed.'

For a moment Charlotte wavered in her disappointment. Then calm reasoning took over. If Cadell had to go away on business, it couldn't be helped. As his future wife, she knew she must learn to expect and deal with his absences. The bright light in the murkiness of her instant despair was the prospect of journeying with him to Europe. It would most likely involve spending several nights alone with him, on a sleeper train and on a boat. And then there was the possibility of a further few days . . .

'All right,' she conceded, still trying hard to appear reluctant, so that her father couldn't possibly guess the lustful turn her thoughts had taken. 'I will go. But only because you both think it best for me.' She shook her head vigorously, as if to deny outright the possibility of any other reason for her uncharacteristically easy capitulation. 'I do want to learn to be the best possible wife,' she added, before stopping abruptly when she realised her father might think she was gilding the lily rather too much.

As she lowered her eyes demurely again, she missed the look of complicity and amusement Cadell and her father flashed each other. They were both aware of Charlotte's naivety. Neither were fooled by her. Yet they were both keenly aware that she had a few shocks in store. Bad Alpendorf, the finishing school Cadell had in mind, was definitely not the sort of place Charlotte would be expecting.

Chapter Three

Charlotte's first impression of the school at Bad Alpendorf was as though she had just stepped into a scene depicted on the lid of a box of her favourite chocolates. The school itself was housed in a charming though deceptively large wooden chalet, typical of the region, which was set against an imposing backdrop of mountains and fir trees.

As it was already late evening when she and Cadell arrived, it was difficult to see much at all; but the crisp tangy air gave Charlotte the impression that the tops of the mountains, although presently shrouded by a cloak of encroaching darkness, were snow-capped. And she felt a keen sense of anticipation at the thought of waking up and witnessing the view in daylight for the very first time.

This went some way to assuaging her feelings of disappointment at the prospect of being parted from Cadell. He couldn't stay, he'd insisted, not even until the morning. At first, his response had provoked an angry response from Charlotte, which was gradually tempered to one of calm though frustrated acceptance.

On the few occasions Charlotte had tried to argue with Cadell during their journey, insisting that there was no need for her to attend a Swiss finishing school and that her mother and the family's housekeeper were perfectly well equipped to instruct her in such wifely necessities as flower arranging and such like, Cadell had put his foot down firmly. It was, he insisted, absolutely essential to their future happiness that she complete the course at Bad Alpendorf. And, as if to underline his unwillingness to give in to her increasingly inventive attempts at persuasion, he had put her over his knee and delivered the sort of reprimand that left her in no doubt as to who the master of the household was to be. Or that his command of her had already begun.

Despite her wilfulness, Charlotte conceded willingly to these moments of chastisement and, more grudgingly, to his wishes. Although, in more private moments of careful reflection, she felt shamed by her reaction to his powerful dominance, she allowed her excitement and arousal to overshadow her natural inclination to object to his treatment of her.

'Now Charlotte,' Cadell warned her as they walked up to the front door of the school, 'I want you to follow your instructions here to the letter. To the letter, do you understand me? Anything you are told to do you must obey, is that clear?'

'Yes, mein Kommandant,' Charlotte responded pertly, clicking her heels together and giving him a mock salute, 'I *vill* obey orders.' She was grinning from ear to ear, but her smile quickly wavered when she saw that her attempt at jokiness had no effect on Cadell, other than to make him frown.

'And you will keep that sort of behaviour to yourself as well,' he said, snatching her hand down and grasping her by the shoulders. His thick dark eyebrows beetled as he frowned down at her. 'These people are still sensitive to the Germans. Remember, they had to suffer the war going on all around them, unlike us on our sheltered little island.'

For once, Charlotte felt genuinely contrite. She hadn't intended to cause upset to anyone, and certainly wasn't happy about having made Cadell angry with her. Particularly not when they were soon to be parted.

'I'm sorry, I didn't mean to be flippant,' she said. She attempted to shrug her shoulders, which hardly moved at all under the weight of Cadell's hands. All at once, the pressure of his fingers eased.

'I am sorry, too,' he said. 'I shouldn't have snapped at you like that.'

They stood looking at each other for a long time, until their mutual silence was broken by the sound of the front door opening. The hinges sounded rusty and a blast of warm sweet-smelling air enveloped them as the door opened wider.

Charlotte glanced up automatically and gave an involuntary shudder when she saw who was waiting to greet them.

A woman stood on the threshold to the chalet. Dressed all in black, she was dark-haired, tall, very thin and yet incredibly imposing. Her carriage was excellent, Charlotte noticed with a kind of quaking envy. The woman's narrow shoulders were thrown back; her pointed and equally narrow chin was raised. And the coolly appraising look she gave Charlotte and Cadell had to travel the entire length of her straight nose to reach them.

After her scrutiny of them was completed, a flash of recognition suddenly showed in the cold grey pools of the woman's eyes. And in the next moment, her wine-coloured lips, which seemed to cut a vicious slash across her thin face, curved upwards at the corners into a semblance of a smile.

'Monsieur Fox-Talbot, you have arrived at last. I am so pleased to see you again. And this lovely girl must be your fiancée.' She sounded far more welcoming than she looked.

The woman turned her smile to Charlotte and, as Cadell nodded, there came a flurry of activity from behind her. Within moments, a group of young women were ushering a smiling Cadell and a slightly bemused Charlotte into the chalet.

Charlotte hardly had a chance to get her bearings. She and Cadell were shown through a maze of wood-panelled corridors into a wide square room, bounded on three sides by huge windows. The windows were unobstructed by curtains of any kind and one of the young women who guided them, a perky girl with a sleek cap of chestnut hair, was quick to explain to Charlotte that, during daylight, the windows offered an uninterrupted view of the alpine valley.

'This is a wonderful place,' the young woman assured Charlotte, who still felt ill-at-ease in her unusual surroundings. 'I take it that fabulous man with you is your husband?'

'He will be, soon,' Charlotte murmured, her eyes glancing automatically to Cadell. She noticed straight away that he had been commandeered by the woman who had opened the door to them. She had taken him aside, to the furthest corner of the room, and now they appeared in deep discussion, with their heads close together. Quickly pasting a smile on her face, Charlotte turned her attention back to the girl. 'I'm sorry, I didn't catch your name. I'm Charlotte Hetherington, by the way. But most people call me Chattie.' She held out her hand.

'I am Yolande. Simply Yolande,' the girl replied as she grasped Charlotte's hand and shook it briskly. 'We only use first names here.'

'How odd.' Charlotte, who had been brought up to believe in the social niceties, decided that this must be a peculiarity of the Swiss.

'Can I get you some refreshment?' Yolande asked. 'And let me take your coat. It is always very warm inside the house.'

As she obligingly shrugged off her long black velvet coat, Charlotte found herself sniffing the air. The sweetness she had smelt as the door opened seemed stronger now. All at once, her stomach growled.

'Ah, you can smell the pastries cook has just baked,' Yolande observed with a chuckle. 'If we are at home, we always have mulled wine and pastries at this time. Wait here; I'll bring some to you.' Flashing a careless hand at the nearest chair, Yolande scurried off.

As she was left to her own devices, Charlotte found herself looking around with keen interest. The decor was very simple: large, square items of furniture in natural light wood and neutral colours and a profusion of thick geometric-patterned rugs thrown about the hardwood floor. The most decorative objects in the room were the half-dozen or so young women milling about, chattering among themselves and occasionally flashing a look of interest in Charlotte's direction.

Feeling oddly overwhelmed by her circumstances, Charlotte risked a half-smile back at one of them, a slender ice-cool blonde, who was dressed most becomingly in a sheath dress of pale blue shantung. She was saying something to another young woman who was dressed in a red satin Cheongsam embroidered with gold dragons. She had rich black hair that cascaded unfashionably down her back, the tips reaching the uppermost swell of her buttocks as she threw back her head and laughed loudly at whatever it was the blonde had just said to her.

'Adèle and Sanchia,' Yolande murmured conspiratorially, as she reappeared at Charlotte's elbow. She leant forward and placed a tray of tiny bite-sized pastries and a glass in a silver filigree holder on the low table in front of Charlotte. Steam swirled up from the amber-coloured liquid in the glass. 'They share our dorm. Madame told me that you would be sharing with the three of us,' she added, when Charlotte gave her a quizzical glance.

'How cosy,' Charlotte remarked, trying to sound nonchalant. 'I have never shared a bedroom with anyone else before.'

Yolande's response was a girlish giggle. She circumnavigated the low table to sit down next to Charlotte. 'It is the first step toward losing one's inhibitions, or so Madame says,' she told Charlotte. 'And, believe me, we are supposed to shed them pretty quickly here.'

For some reason Charlotte found herself gripped by an ominous sensation. All at once, she felt quite nauseous and hastily put down the pastry that she had been about to eat.

'Not hungry? Oh, too bad. In that case I'll have that one.' The clipped and very English voice came from somewhere above Charlotte's head. A moment later, a slender white-skinned hand swooped down and delicately lifted the pastry between thumb and forefinger.

'Adèle, you greedy thing,' Yolande admonished the owner of the hand. 'These pastries are for our guest.'

As Charlotte's gaze swept upwards, she noticed the hand belonged to the blonde girl she had been staring at earlier. It seemed inconceivable that the owner of such a thin lithe frame should ever eat anything at all, let alone pastries, Charlotte thought as her gaze continued down, navigating the flat narrow plain of the young woman's torso. Even when standing, her stomach seemed to be practically concave and her legs appeared almost as slender as most people's arms.

In that instant, Charlotte decided that, whoever this Adèle was, she hated her.

Adèle however, appeared undaunted by Yolande's reprimand. She helped herself to the nearest chair and drew it closer to the table before resuming her inspection of the tray of pastries. 'Frankly, I couldn't give a damn what you think, Yolande,' she said in lazy drawl, as though the company she had chosen to associate with bored her to tears. As if in an act of defiance, she selected another of the pastries and popped it into her mouth whole. 'So,' she said to Charlotte after she had finished chewing and swallowing the pastry, 'who are you?' Dusting pastry crumbs from her fingertips, she fixed Charlotte with a penetrating gaze. Her irises were the same pale watered-silk blue as her dress, her lashes long and fair.

'This is Charlotte; she's going to be rooming with us,'Yolande chipped in eagerly, before Charlotte had a chance to reply for herself. 'That's her fiancé over there.' She glanced in Cadell's direction.

'Cadell Fox-Talbot. Very impressive.' Adèle's voice was still a drawl, but this time it contained a hint of interest. 'How did you manage to hook him?'

'He – er – he rather hooked me actually,' Charlotte stammered. She felt unnerved by Adèle's directness and her unblinking stare and was forced to glance down at her hands.

'Lucky thing; he's loaded and incredibly sexy.' Adèle's observation was at once envious and approving. 'No wonder you have decided to take this course.You'll need to know every trick in the book to keep him interested.'

'I don't know what you –' Charlotte's confusion was cut short by the merciful reappearance of Cadell at her side. He squatted down beside her and whispered in her ear.

'I have to go now, my little one,' he murmured. 'I have arranged everything with Madame, and she assures me you will be well taken care of.'

'Oh, no, Cadell; don't go yet. Don't leave me here!' Ignoring the fact that the other girls were staring at her, Charlotte turned and flung herself at Cadell. Trepidation gripped her harder than ever now at the thought of being left alone at Bad Alpendorf. It all seemed too strange.

For a moment, Cadell held her tightly, then he relaxed his grip. 'I have to go,' he said, gently but firmly. He kissed the tip of her nose, then her lips, just lightly. 'It is only for a month. Then I will be back and we will be married and –'

'If you don't take me with you, I'll run away,' Charlotte cut in stubbornly.

'No, you won't.' Cadell was stern, though his eyes were smiling. 'You'll have a good time here, you'll see,' he promised her. 'And I notice you have made friends already.' Glancing up, he smiled warmly atYolande and a simpering Adèle before reverting his attention back to Charlotte. 'Please, Charlotte. Please promise me you will stick this out. Believe me, I wouldn't ask this of you if it wasn't important. I want us to be happy together –'

'So do I,' Charlotte insisted, interrupting him vehemently. She wrapped her arms around his neck and kissed him hard on the lips. 'Oh, Cadell, so do I.'

'Then be a good girl and do as you're told,' he said. Gently disengaging her arms, he straightened up and looked down at her. 'I can't stress to you enough, my love, how important it is to me that you abide by all the rules here. Some things you will be asked to do may seem a little outlandish, but I am aware of everything on the curriculum and support the teaching methods here wholeheartedly.'

Charlotte frowned. 'That sounds a bit ominous.'

'I can't say any more,' Cadell said, smiling at her. 'But please don't worry.'

As Charlotte reluctantly bade him goodbye, she realised his entreaty to her not to worry just made her worry all the more.

Despite her earlier misgivings, an hour or so after Cadell had departed, Charlotte was already feeling much more relaxed. The mulled wine, which seemed to flow freely, helped to smooth her entry into the sequestered world of Bad Alpendorf. Though the friendliness of the girls, particularly Yolande and Sanchia – who turned out to be a lively and spirited young thing of Spanish parentage – also made a huge difference. Even the cool, laconic Adèle seemed to thaw out considerably as the evening progressed.

At ten-thirty, their lighthearted chatter was interrupted by a loud hand-clap by Madame. 'Girls, it is time for bed.' After she had delivered her general instruction, she came over and spoke specifically to Charlotte. 'I see you have already made friends with your room-mates. This is good. They will show you where to put your things and explain to you how we like you to behave here. Tomorrow morning, you will have a medical examination. Yolande will show you where the medical room is. Then you may join us for classes afterwards. Do you have any questions?'

37

Struck dumb by Madame's imposing figure looming before her and the brisk authoritative way she spoke, Charlotte could do nothing more than shake her head.

'Very well,' Madame continued, 'then to bed, all of you. We shall start bright and early tomorrow morning as usual.' Having delivered her instructions and treated the gathering to a tight half-smile, Madame swept out of the room.

'This way, Chattie,' Yolande said, jumping up immediately. 'Sanchia, could you take one of her bags? I'll take this one.' Snatching up one of Charlotte's cases with one hand, Yolande heaved it into her arms. 'This weighs an absolute ton,' she observed as she staggered toward the door. 'What a shame you won't be needing any of this stuff.'

Having given up trying to relieve Yolande of the case, Charlotte asked her what she meant.

'The school provides everything: clothes, soap, shampoo, even hairbrushes and eyebrow tweezers,' Yolande explained.

'I would really prefer to use my own things,' Charlotte demurred.

'No chance, darling,' Adèle cut in as she swept past them to take up the lead. Glancing back over her shoulder, she added, 'Madame is most emphatic. Here we are all equals.'

'It's just that some are more equal than others,' Yolande muttered cryptically, with a nod at Adèle's willowy back as she strode imperiously down the corridor ahead of them. 'If you know what I mean.'

Her cheeky wink sent Sanchia into a peal of laughter and, for the first time that evening, Charlotte found it easy to smile.

Her feelings of optimism and comradeship were soon dented when the four girls reached the room that was to become Charlotte's home for the next month. In comparison with the rest of the chalet, the bedroom was fairly spartan, with just four high cast-iron beds and four narrow wardrobes. Inside the wardrobe allocated to her, Charlotte discovered a selection of clothes and some toiletries on one of the shelves.

'The bathroom is next door,' Yolande told her, 'but we're not allowed to use it unaccompanied. If you need to use it at night, you must wake one of us up to go with you.'

Charlotte was amazed by this new revelation. 'Why – what possible reason could there be to –'

'To make sure you don't play with yourself while you are in there, darling,' Adèle cut in from across the room.

'Play with myself?' Charlotte frowned. What on earth could they . . . ? She suddenly realised what the other girls were alluding to and flushed bright crimson. 'I wouldn't – I couldn't . . .' she stammered hopelessly as she felt her cheeks flare hotter still.

'You haven't been here long enough to know,' Adèle assured her, unzipping her dress and letting it fall to the ground. 'We all would, given half a chance.'

Flashing a glance at Yolande, then Sanchia, Charlotte realised they were all in agreement. 'Well, not me,' she asserted firmly, pushing her suitcases under the bed at Yolande's instruction. 'I have never touched myself below the waist and I don't intend to start now.' She felt her piousness gave her an edge over the other girls, who were obviously either more ill-bred than they appeared, or were totally deranged, she decided smugly.

She tried desperately not to observe the other girls as they undressed and attended to their toilette at a small porcelain basin in the corner of the room. However, while Sanchia was washing, Charlotte risked a glance in her direction and was surprised to find her gaze riveted.

The young Spanish girl was standing before the basin completely naked, her thick dark hair cloaking her shoulders and the long sweep of her spine. Her figure was full and sinuous, with broad shoulders and ribcage tapering to a surprisingly narrow waist. Her hips were lush and ripe, her olive-toned skin seeming to gleam in the places where she was most fleshy. Her hips rolled as she moved, the full succulent mounds of her buttocks jiggling slightly.

Charlotte felt entranced by the sight and was embarrassed to find herself still staring open-mouthed when Sanchia happened to turn around. She blushed immediately and averted her gaze.

'You have not seen another naked girl before, have you?' Sanchia observed. Her tone held no rancour, only amusement. And her huge dark eyes shone like black marbles in the wavering gaslight. 'Come closer if you wish,' she added, assuming a bold demeanour.

Feeling thoroughly embarrassed and aware that the other girls were watching her, Charlotte moved hesitantly across the room toward Sanchia. As she neared the young woman, Sanchia moved her feet apart and scooped up her full breasts in her hands. She held them out to Charlotte like an offering, the nipples hard and round, jutting toward Charlotte, as tempting and rich ruby red as a couple of ripe cherries. Without realising it, Charlotte licked her lips.

Sanchia smiled in a way that was provocative and catlike, her eyes narrowing slightly, as though she were a party to the tumult of unfamiliar emotions churning away inside Charlotte.

'Mind you take care, Sanchia,' Adèle warned from the other side of the room. 'If Madame should catch you . . .'

Sanchia's eyes widened as she appeared to register Adèle's warning. She glanced up and flashed a look at Yolande. 'Keep lookout, would you?' she said. 'I am not planning to do anything other than let our new friend enjoy her fill of looking at me.'

Yolande frowned but did what the young woman asked, positioning herself by the door and occasionally glancing through the narrow panels of frosted glass. A dark shadow glimpsed at the far end of the corridor would be enough to alert them to the fact that Madame was on the way.

'Come closer, Chattie,' Sanchia meanwhile urged Charlotte. 'You have never seen breasts quite as magnificent as these before, have you?' She made it quite clear how proud she was of them and, for the first time that evening, lapsed into heavily-accented speech.

Not knowing quite how to reply to such a bold question, Charlotte cleared her throat. 'I – er – I've never seen another pair of breasts before. Other than my own, that is.' She gave a nervous titter. 'I was brought up to believe that the body is merely a vehicle to move one through life.'

At this, Sanchia threw back her head and laughed throatily. The abandoned gesture was becoming familiar to Charlotte now and she couldn't help but smile.

'This is true, but the body is also a wonderful instrument,' Sanchia assured Charlotte. She released her breasts to allow

40

her hands to follow the sinuous curves of her figure and come to rest lightly on her hips. 'There is so much pleasure to be derived from it,' she went on, idly allowing a hand to drift inwards, across her belly to the thick mat of glossy black fur below her navel.

Sanchia's pubic hair was lush indeed, Charlotte observed, unable to help her gaze following the path of the young woman's hands. It completely covered her mound of Venus and continued higher, some way up her belly and feathered across the join where her thighs met her pelvis.

'The others keep urging me to trim this,' Sanchia said, stroking her bush fondly, 'but I am quite proud of it. Many men find so much hair an attractive feature. And it is all the more exciting for them to burrow their way through, to discover the delights that lay hidden beneath it.'

'Many men?' Charlotte was unable to keep the incredulity from her voice. 'Do you mean you are not a virgin?'

This time Sanchia's peal of laughter was matched by the other two girls.

'Oh, my dear, how little you know and understand,' Adèle drawled. 'None of us are virgins, my innocent little chick. Are we to take it that you are?'

Blushing bright crimson, Charlotte shook her head. She didn't know if she felt more embarrassed by Adèle's mockery, or at her admission of having relinquished her chastity before marriage.

'Then you are already a member of our élite club,' Adèle responded approvingly. 'Particularly as your lover is Cadell Fox-Talbot.' She hesitated. 'I take it he is the one who –'

'Oh, yes,' Charlotte interrupted hastily. 'As we are to be married anyway, I thought –'

'You are quite right,' Sanchia cut in. 'It is important to sample the goods before you buy: is that not right, girls?' She flashed an amused glance around the room.

'But one man cannot tell you the whole story,' Adèle said. 'That is the beauty of this place. We are here to learn the art of love and to explore our sensuality, so that we may pass our expertise onto our future husbands.'

'Like a gift,' Yolande cut in, sounding wistful. 'Oh, I can't

41

wait until I am with Nigel again. He will be so pleased with me.'

'Yolande's fiancé,' Sanchia explained to Charlotte. 'He's an earl or something, isn't he?'

Yolande nodded eagerly. 'Yes, but not a bit old and crusty. I only hope he will prove to be a match for me, after the schooling I have had here at Bad Alpendorf.'

'He should be,' Adèle cut in. 'He has bedded over a hundred women, I hear.'

'But numbers mean nothing,' Yolande argued, looking not the least perturbed that her future husband was such a libertine. 'It is skill and imagination that counts. Remember what Madame has taught us.'

'Just a moment . . .' Charlotte shook her head as she tried to digest the conversation going on around her. 'Are you implying that we are expected to have sexual relations with other people while we are here?' Even the possibility, ludicrous though it seemed, horrified her. Surely the girls were only teasing . . .

'But of course; did your fiancé explain nothing to you?' Sanchia appeared genuinely amazed.

'He – he only said that I should obey all the instructions that I am given here,' Charlotte stammered. She felt a great slab of cold dread sink like a lead weight inside her stomach. Suddenly, her knees turned to water and she had to grip the edge of the basin to steady herself.

'Come on, you look as though you are in shock.' Sanchia reached for Charlotte and began to guide her over to her bed. 'We are being so thoughtless, keeping you awake with our chatter. You must be exhausted from your journey.'

Nodding wearily, Charlotte sat down on the edge of her bed. It was so high that her feet barely touched the floor. Her legs dangled, feeling light and insubstantial, though she stiffened immediately when Sanchia began to slide down the zip at the back of her dress.

'No, really,' she protested. 'I can undress myself.'

'All right.' Sanchia took a step back and gave Charlotte a rueful smile. 'Here,' she added, reaching under Charlotte's pillow and drawing out a flimsy garment, 'put this on and climb into bed.'

As the other girls resumed their night-time ritual, Charlotte considered the garment Sanchia had placed in her hands. It appeared to be nothing more than a gauzy chemise, hardly long enough to cover her torso. Keeping her back to the other girls, she undressed quickly and slipped the chemise over her head. She had been right in her assumption, she realised, tugging ineffectually at the hem. It barely reached the tops of her thighs.

As she risked a glance around, she noticed the other three were similarly attired. Not one of them was sufficiently covered, with pubis and buttocks left naked. And the fabric of the chemise was so fine that it hinted suggestively at the curves and contours of the girls' breasts, their nipples appearing as dark buttons which peaked their gauzy covering.

'Are we all ready for lights out?' Yolande asked cheerfully, reaching for the gas lamp on the wall by her bed. She glanced across at Charlotte, who had just drawn back the top bedcovers and was staring with amazement at the bottom sheet, which was not made of cotton but was a thick fleece of lambswool. 'It may feel a little strange at first,' she assured Charlotte. 'It's warm and comfortable. Oh, by the way, we are expected to sleep on our stomachs.'

'Why?' The question sprang to Charlotte's lips, although she was beginning to feel less surprised by the strange rules of this place.

'Madame's instructions,' Yolande said.

It was a phrase Charlotte would become used to hearing over the ensuing weeks and one which she quickly learn not to question.

Chapter Four

Halfway through the night, Charlotte awoke to a familiar sensation. Her bladder felt full and, as she was forced to lie on her stomach, the pressure on it was too great to ignore. As she moved, she became aware of another, more unexpected sensation: a fullness and throbbing between her thighs. Desperate to relieve the burden of the twin sensations Charlotte wriggled this way and that. Unfortunately, as she did so, she became aware of the beguiling caress of the lambswool. It tickled the cleft between her sex lips and sent unmistakable tingles of desire through her. Despite her best efforts, she knew sleep was likely to elude her until she had been to the lavatory.

She got out of bed and crept as stealthily as she could to the door. Just as she reached it, Yolande's voice whispered in the darkness, 'Chattie, is that you?'

'Um, yes,' Charlotte mumbled, immediately feeling guilty. She crossed her legs tightly, unable to bear the overwhelming need to relieve herself.

There came a rustling sound, then a moment later Yolande was at her side. 'Remember, I told you, you can't use the bathroom without one of us going with you. I'll come; I need to go anyway.'

'No, really.' Charlotte shook her head. She was aware of the heat that suddenly sprang to her cheeks. Then all at once her bladder screamed at her not to delay much longer.

Her anguished expression must have told its own story, as Yolande grabbed her by the arm, opened the door and steered her through it. Thankfully, the corridor outside their bedroom was empty and in darkness. Charlotte was only too aware of the shameful nakedness of her lower body and as she hurried down the corridor with Yolande, could feel a cool draught glance

45

across her buttocks and snake between her legs.

The bathroom, when they reached it, was cold and austere. The walls were covered from floor to ceiling in white tiles. Against the far wall stood a huge deep claw-footed bath with a heavy chromium shower attachment. At the foot of the bath stood an equally large pedestal basin and, in the opposite corner, a lavatory with a mahogany seat.

The lavatory beguiled Charlotte, luring her over to it, her bladder burning by this time. No matter how desperate she felt to use it, Charlotte still hesitated, eyeing Yolande warily. The other girl seemed frustratingly unperturbed. She lounged against the wall, her arms folded.

'Come on, hurry up; it's freezing in here,' she urged Charlotte.

Charlotte grimaced. 'I – I can't, not with you watching me.'

'But I have to,' Yolande protested. 'I do understand, really I do. I felt the same way, when I first arrived here, but look at you: your clitoris is so swollen you must be dying to touch it.'

'My . . . ?' Charlotte was too surprised by Yolande's observation to feel embarrassed. She glanced down automatically, her fingers fluttering to her pubis.

'No, you mustn't,' Yolande admonished her harshly. 'Madame will know if you do. Then we'll all be in trouble. Just please, for pity's sake, use the lavatory and let us go back to bed.'

Charlotte lowered herself reluctantly and was relieved when she saw the way Yolande took pity on her and glanced away. As soon as she was seated, the flow began; warm and continuous, it cascaded into the white porcelain bowl. With her legs parted, Charlotte was able to see how swollen and distended her clitoris had become and it was now she blushed, realising that the shameful proof of her inexplicable arousal must have been visible the whole time. She cursed the fairness of her pubic hair, which concealed hardly anything, and wished she had been born with a bush like Sanchia's to hide behind.

It surprised her to find herself thinking such intimate thoughts about another woman. And was even more surprised to feel her clitoris pulse hard as her mind recalled the image of Sanchia's lush body. She was so absorbed by her thoughts that she didn't realise Yolande was watching her again.

'All done?' she inquired, her gaze fixed to that exposed, intimate part of Charlotte between her spread thighs.

With cheeks flaming, Charlotte hurriedly wiped herself and stood up. The toilet tissue, where it had glanced across her swollen bud, had set off a tremor of lust which she felt peculiarly anxious to assuage. Her fingertips drifted there again, brushing across her pubis, stroking tantalisingly over her swollen flesh.

'No!' Yolande said quickly, sharply. Reaching out, she yanked Charlotte's hand away, grabbing her by the wrist. Her gaze once more fell to the apex of Charlotte's thighs and she let out a low groan. 'Oh, God, I'd love to . . .' she muttered, looking anguished.

Charlotte realised she was shaking. There seemed, incredibly, a distinct tension in the air, of the kind she had only experienced with Cadell before. Moisture trickled from her, tantalising her sensitive vaginal lips. Sighing, she sank back against the wall. Her legs were splayed, almost too weak to support her; her entire body trembled and burned with desire. If only Cadell were here now. He would be able to quench her lustful yearnings.

Yolande moved closer. A strange light shone in her eyes and she bit down on her bottom lip as she slid a questing hand between Charlotte's thighs.

Immediately, Charlotte recoiled, but her embarrassment was heavily outweighed by curiosity. The girl's touch was light but knowing, her fingers sliding easily into the cleft between Charlotte's sex-lips and gently parting the swollen leaves of flesh. With each tentative caress, Charlotte's clitoris throbbed more urgently, contracting with a dart of pleasure and then expanding each time Yolande's fingertips glanced across it.

The urge to reach that pinnacle of desire was overwhelming, more urgent than Charlotte's previous need to pee, or her desire to escape Bad Alpendorf and to walk up the aisle with Cadell. She could taste her need. It dried her mouth and lingered on her lips. It rushed through her like a torrent of stormy water, obliterating everything else.

'Please,' she gasped, sinking further back against the wall, pressing her naked buttocks against the cold tiling and tilting

47

her pelvis to make a more accessible offering of her body.

In answer to her plea, Yolande's fingers moved faster, tantalising in tiny circles, stoking the burning lust inside her. Both girls were so intent on their pleasure that they didn't hear the soft swoosh of the bathroom door swinging open.

'Well – what have we here?' Madame's voice, sharp and unexpected, was like a gunshot.

Yolande leapt back immediately, guilt flooding her face. 'I'm sorry, Madame, I was just –'

Madame's glower cut her short. 'Go to bed, Yolande,' the woman said thinly. 'I'll deal with you in the morning.'

Fearful of what might happen next, Charlotte shrank back, as though attempting to blend in with the tiling. She felt a knot of dread clutch at her throat as the forbidding woman turned her attention to her.

'Have you not been made aware of the rules?' Madame asked.

'I . . . I . . .' Charlotte could hardly get a word out, her trepidation was so great, choking her, constricting her windpipe like a noose.

To her horror, the woman squatted down in front of her. She peered intently at the lewd display of sex flesh between her thighs, so swollen and flushed with shame. And, as if that were not humiliation enough, Madame then reached out and parted the flesh still further, with fingers that felt cold and cruel, until Charlotte's clitoris was fully exposed.

'This is good,' Madame observed, with just the merest glance at Charlotte's face, which burned with mortification. 'But Yolande was naughty to try to take advantage of you.'

'She wasn't – she just . . .' Charlotte began to protest feebly.

Despite her humiliation and the overwhelming urge to escape from the woman's clutches and her close scrutiny, she felt a resurgence of desire.

I must be sick, she thought, a desperate passion swimming in the pit of her belly.

Madame pinched her swollen clitoris crudely between thumb and forefinger. 'Do not attempt to make excuses for Yolande,' she warned Charlotte, pinching harder until tears sprang to the young woman's eyes. 'She knows she has disobeyed my instructions and she will be punished.'

'H-how?' Charlotte gasped. Her clitoris felt as though it were on fire yet, to her surprise, her desire had not diminished one iota.

A cruel smile tainted Madame's vermilion lips. 'Publicly, I think,' she said. 'And very harshly.' All at once she released her pincer-hold on Charlotte's throbbing bud and slid her hand between Charlotte's legs instead, stroking, probing, investigating. 'Very wet,' the woman observed, as though she were talking about the weather.

Charlotte's cheeks flamed as Madame continued to inspect her body, both visually and with keenly inquisitive fingers. She had never been touched by another woman before today, and yet it seemed pointless to try to rail against the ignominy of the situation. Cadell had warned her to behave and to obey the instructions she was given at all times. And, although Madame hadn't actually said anything by way of instruction to her, Charlotte felt her compliance was expected.

'May I be allowed to return to bed?' she dared to ask after a moment.

To her relief, Madame nodded and stood up. She wiped her fingers, glistening with Charlotte's juices, on a hand towel which hung on a nearby rail.

'Of course you may. I think you will be a good student, Charlotte. You have got off to an uncertain start but I am sure we will grow to understand each other, *n'est-ce pas?*'

Charlotte was surprised by Madame's lapse into French but nodded enthusiastically, believing correctly that this was what was expected of her.

'Good,' Madame responded, leading the way to the door and turning down the light, 'then I shall look forward to instructing you. Sleep well, *ma petite.*' Her tone was surprisingly gentle. 'You have a very full day ahead of you tomorrow.'

The sound of cow-bells greeted Charlotte as she gradually slipped into wakefulness the following morning, adding to the sudden surge of excitement that assailed her. Within moments of waking, she realised she was in a very different place to normal and the events of the previous night had left her with a voluptuous sense of anticipation: as though she had been given a glimpse of the mysterious world of sensual delight and erotic depravity available to her.

Without doubt, it left her wanting more, craving a knowledge that she sensed was within her grasp. It excited her, yet scared her in equal measure. During the past few weeks, she had been increasingly shocked by the discovery of her own sensuality and the powerful feelings it invoked. It made her realise that there was a lot more excitement for her to discover and, after last night, she had begun to realise that Bad Alpendorf held the key to those secret pleasures.

She realised now what Cadell had been alluding to when he'd said that it would take him a lifetime to teach her all there was to learn, and that he was only capable of revealing to her a small portion of her sensuality. There were things a mere individual like himself could not possibly emulate, he'd said. And it was only now, as Charlotte recalled with mounting excitement, the wondrous feel of Yolande's fingers between her thighs – or even Madame's – that she truly understood what he had meant. No matter how hard he might try, or wish it, Cadell could never reproduce the unique touch of another woman. Nor of two men, or several men and women together, Charlotte mused with a tingle of anticipation.

The depravity of her thoughts surprised but no longer shocked her. It was as though the closed book of her sensuality had now been opened and was being revealed to her, page by tantalising page. The inscriptions on each curious leaf were the hieroglyphs of pure pleasure and, she was certain, were sure to become easier to decipher as time went on.

'Hello; I see you are awake at long last.' Adèle walked over to Charlotte's bed and stared down at her. She was already dressed and, when Charlotte sat up, she noticed Sanchia and Yolande were similarly attired, in plain white pleated skirts and short-sleeved blouses.

'Did you sleep all right? Did Madame give you a hard time last night?' Yolande asked. She appeared only mildly concerned as she swept a silver-backed brush over the sleek cap of her chestnut hair.

'She was very angry,' Charlotte told her with a frown. 'I – I

50

hate to tell you this, Yolande, but she told me you will be punished for what – what happened.' She broke off when she noticed how curiously the other girls were looking at her and Yolande.

'Why, what happened?' Sanchia sounded intrigued. She came over to Charlotte's bed and sat down, everything about her appearing to bounce with exuberance.

Despite her consternation about Yolande's fate, Charlotte couldn't help smiling.

'We were caught indulging in a purely innocent moment,' Yolande supplied, before Charlotte had a chance to answer the young Spanish girl. 'I daresay Madame will make my punishment a vile and public one.'

'She did mention something about it being in public,' Charlotte murmured, hardly understanding what Yolande was alluding to. She naively assumed the punishment would be some kind of verbal dressing-down in front of all the other students.

'You must get dressed, Chattie,' Adèle cut in, with a hasty glance at her platinum and black onyx watch. 'Would you like me to show you where the medical room is?'

Charlotte, who had been hoping for some breakfast before the next ordeal, flashed an enquiring look at Yolande. The young woman had already offered to show her the way and she didn't want to risk offending her new 'friend'. However, Yolande appeared not in the least perturbed by Adèle's attempt to usurp her.

'Oh, yes, your medical,' she murmured, raising her eyebrows ever so slightly and glancing at the other girls in a way which made Charlotte feel even more nervous. 'Yes, Adèle, you show her how to find our esteemed Herr Doktor. Chattie, I'll see you later on. I daresay Madame will take me aside as soon as she possibly can. I don't know how long I will be delayed.' She spoke in an ironic tone.

After this exchange, Adèle's manner became brisk. Urging Charlotte to hurry up and finish dressing, she hustled her toward the door and out along the corridor. This time, they went in the opposite direction to the bathroom and down another couple of wood-floored passageways before reaching

51

a door bearing a mahogany plaque with the word '*Doktor*' inscribed upon it in gold.

'Here we are,' she said, giving Charlotte a little shove toward the door. 'Try not to be too embarrassed. The doctor is a little impersonal, but kind.'

'Thank you for the advice,' Charlotte murmured. She put her hand on the door handle and raised her other hand to rap smartly on the wood with her knuckles. As a deep voice coming from within bade her to enter, she flashed a nervous smile at Adèle.

'I'll see you later, darling,' Adèle promised her, before bestowing a peck on her cheek.

As the voice once again repeated the instruction to enter, Charlotte depressed the handle and pushed the door open. Stepping over the threshold, she was surprised to find the room in almost total darkness. As she squinted in the gloom, she could just about make out the indistinct figure of the doctor, seated behind a small wooden desk.

'Come in, child, come in,' the doctor said.

His voice was deep and heavily accented and, as Charlotte drew closer to him, she noticed that he was squat, quite ugly and almost bald, with only a fringe of silvery hair skimming the tops of his ears. She shuddered inwardly, hating the thought of this man examining her and having to remind herself that, to him, she was probably of no more interest than a lab specimen: a collection of cells and blood vessels and organs, all held together by muscle and sinew.

However, the look he gave her as she approached the desk dispelled such notions immediately. His beady eyes, black like lumps of coal in his fleshy face, roamed over her wilfully, making her feel as though she hardly had need to take off a stitch of clothing.

'Very nice,' he murmured, rubbing his pudgy hands together, as though in anticipation. 'Very nice indeed. The girls who come to this school just get better and better.' Relaxing back in his chair, he let out a sigh of satisfaction. 'What a job I have! How many other men would gladly pay for the privilege?'

Feeling distinctly uncomfortable, Charlotte hovered by his desk, unsure of what she should do; every fibre of her being screamed at her to flee. However, she felt a resurgence of her old spirit and, as such, refused to feel intimidated. She stood her ground, waiting patiently for the doctor to give his instructions.

All at once the door to the medical room opened again and this time a very different man entered. Tall and imposing, with white hair cropped very close to his head, he was dressed in a black pinstriped suit, of the kind Cadell habitually wore. A gold fob linked the front of his high-buttoned waistcoat to a shallow pocket. He was clearly in his middle years, Charlotte noticed, but not in the least portly. If anything, he appeared rather too thin, though the suave way his suit hung on his frame indicated that perhaps his physique was more muscular than one might imagine at first glance.

The doctor greeted him in an indistinct form of German, which Charlotte assumed was *SwitzerDeutsch*, though the newcomer answered in perfect, if a little stilted, English.

'Hello, my good friend. How are you today? All the better for having this young lady to examine, I would say.'

With his hands thrust deep in his trouser pockets, in a relaxed and casual manner, he flashed an approving glance at Charlotte, who instantly blushed. Now she felt as though she were a specimen on a laboratory slide. The gaze of each man was keen and assessing, casting up and down her trembling body, perusing her as though they were intent on registering every minute aspect of her physique.

'Now, young lady,' the doctor said at last, 'undress if you please, behind the screen over there.' He waved a hand to the far side of the room. Charlotte peered hard but couldn't see anything. 'Ah, I am so sorry,' the doctor added, appearing to realise her confusion.

With a surprisingly brisk movement for one so portly, he got up from his chair and hastened to the window, where he drew back a pair of heavy gold chintz drapes. Immediately, sunlight flooded in, forming a yellow pool on the hardwood floor and highlighting the general shabbiness of the surgery.

Charlotte's gaze instantly alighted on the screen the doctor had mentioned. No wonder she hadn't been able to see it before. It was made of black lacquered wood and depicted faded woodland scenes of cavorting nymphs and fauns.

'Please,' the doctor said, waving his hand once again in the direction of the screen.

Feeling extremely nervous, Charlotte went behind the screen and began to undress. As far as she could tell, though she glanced around, there was no robe or gown of any kind for her to put on. When she had finished undressing, she put her head around the screen and asked tentatively what she should wear.

To her consternation, the two men laughed.

'Wear?' the doctor said, 'What is the point of you wearing anything?'

'But a gown . . .' Charlotte protested, feeling her hateful blushes rising again.

'Please, do not be such a baby,' the other man cut in. 'How can you expect the doctor to examine you properly, if you are wearing clothes?'

'And where is the nurse?' Charlotte added, refusing to be ridiculed by either of them. 'Am I not entitled to have a nurse present?'

'You are not in England now,' the doctor cut in. 'We are not so strait-laced here.' He smiled at the other man, who shrugged and gave a nod. 'But, if you wish it,' the doctor continued, 'I will arrange for a female to be present.'

'I do wish it,' Charlotte said. 'I wish it most strongly.'

After staring at her for a long moment with pursed lips, he let out a vexed sigh. 'Very well,' he said, reaching for the black telephone on his desk. 'I will attend to it immediately.' He spoke a few curt words of his curious dialect into the mouthpiece, then replaced the receiver with a look of satisfaction. 'Someone will be here momentarily,' he told her.

Standing naked behind the screen, Charlotte waited, her nervousness growing by the second. Presently, she decided to risk another demand.

'There is one other thing,' she said, poking her head around the side of the screen again. The two men immediately glanced up. 'I hope *he* is not planning to remain here.' She nodded in the direction of the imposing white-haired man, who was now seated upon the visitors' chair beside the doctor's desk.

She shrank back instinctively as the man in question rose

from his chair and started to make his way across the room toward her. At the screen he halted, then stooped forward so that his face was directly level with hers. For the first time Charlotte noticed that his eyes were a profound blue, almost like those of Cadell, and for a minute she found herself warming to him. Then he spoke, shattering all her illusions.

'My dear child,' he said, enunciating each word carefully. 'Do you not realise who I am?'

As she shook her head dumbly, Charlotte shielded her breasts and pubis with her hands. If he should venture beyond the screen . . .

'Then someone has been very remiss,' he went on. 'You should, at the very least, have been informed of my existence. You see, Charlotte, I am the owner of this school. Max Spieler.'

'But I thought Madame . . .' Charlotte protested.

'Madame is my sister. She has full authority here. But on my say-so. Is that understood? I am the one to whom she reports. So you see, my dear, you cannot – will not – have leave to evict me from my own premises. If I choose to remain in this room for the entire day, remain I will.'

Charlotte felt the heat of indignation rise quickly. 'I cannot have you here. It is insupportable!' she exclaimed hotly. After her impulsive outburst, she fell silent, biting her lip, wondering what might happen next. To her surprise, Herr Spieler smiled. But there was no humour in it, she noticed, glancing at his eyes.

'You have no choice in the matter,' he said simply. 'I choose to remain and witness your examination. And your duty is to obey.'

'I will not have it!' Charlotte stamped her foot, anger overtaking all sense of reason.

In a flash, Herr Spieler was around the screen, grasping her by the shoulders and shaking her until her teeth chattered in her head. Her breasts bobbed uncomfortably, but she had no way of shielding them; Herr Spieler's vice-like grip kept her arms pinned to her sides.

'You will have exactly what I decide you have,' Herr Spieler said, his tone harsh. All at once, his angry expression tempered to one of wry amusement. His eyes mocked her as they swept insolently over her naked breasts, which rose and fell rapidly on her heaving ribcage. 'So this is what all the fuss was about. These two little peaches. Do you think I have not seen a pair of breasts before? Do you believe yours are so special?'

Releasing his grip on her shoulders, he slid his palms inwards, following the protruding line of her collarbone until his fingertips met.

'So, you are still angry, child,' he said as he pressed his fingertips against the pulse which thrummed wildly at the base of her throat. 'Or perhaps you are nervous now – frightened . . . ?'

'Angry, very angry,' Charlotte insisted, tossing her head disdainfully. 'When my fiancé hears of this –'

'He will congratulate me for reprimanding you,' Herr Spieler finished for her. 'Your fiancé, Mr Fox-Talbot, is a sophisticated man. He knows the way we conduct ourselves here. That is the reason why he chose Bad Alpendorf for the completion of your education.'

Charlotte had to concede, if only to herself, that Herr Spieler spoke the truth. Cadell had left her under no illusion that he knew all about the school and wanted her to apply herself to its teachings, no matter how bizarre the methods employed.

As her temper calmed, so her breathing slowed a fraction. All at once, she was reminded that she was standing stark naked in front of this stranger. Yet there was something oddly compelling about his demeanour and the way he looked at her. Like Cadell, Herr Spieler managed to hold her in his thrall simply by the expression in his eyes and by the powerful, charismatic aura that surrounded him.

Consequently, she hardly made a murmur when his hands slid down from her throat to envelop her breasts. The touch of his skin upon hers was warm and beguiling. Slowly and with precision, he began to caress every part of her breasts, moving his fingertips lightly over her silken flesh, tracing the curve of their outline, cupping their fullness.

Without intending it, Charlotte sighed. Once again she felt consumed by a familiar, desirous languor. It was as though the doctor's surgery, and even the building that surrounded them, had melted away, leaving herself and Herr Spieler cast adrift in a place without form or time. They might have been in a woodland glade, or on a distant planet, Charlotte was so mesmerised by his seductive caresses.

And while he touched her, he murmured words of approval: for her shape and smell, and for the texture of her skin. In a lower tone, he expressed his appreciation of her nipples, pointing out the way the buds of blush-pink puckered flesh blossomed forth as soon as his fingertips glanced across them.

'These are very responsive,' he murmured darkly, his fingertips enclosing her hardened nipples, pinching lightly.

He rolled the excited flesh between his fingertips and tugged at her nipples, drawing them out further until the tips of her breasts formed little cones. Then, to Charlotte's anguish, he suddenly pinched each nipple hard, squeezing the swollen flesh very tightly between thumb and forefinger. He tugged more determinedly, the fingers of each hand forming a vice that gripped more and more painfully until Charlotte cried out.

'You are a bad girl, Charlotte,' he said, still increasing the pressure and ignoring her whispered pleas for mercy. 'And bad girls must be punished. Did you think I was about to reward you for your insolence?'

She couldn't look at him and, with tears of pain and humiliation smarting behind her closed eyelids, Charlotte shook her head. 'No,' she whispered. 'But . . . You're hurting me.'

At this, Herr Spieler laughed thinly. 'Hurting you? Of course I'm hurting you. Punishment is all about pain. But tell me, child, can you not feel a little pleasure inside, too?'

'No, it just hurts. Oh, please stop!' The tears were rolling freely down her cheeks by this time. Her nipples felt as though they were on fire. And yet . . .

To Charlotte's surprise, she suddenly felt a flicker of interest deep in the pit of her belly. Like a wicked viper that had just awoken, it thrashed from side to side for a moment, then coiled upwards to her navel. At the same time, she felt her feminine parts swelling, becoming moist.

'I – I feel – something,' she murmured, sounding amazed. She opened her eyes and gazed right at him, confusion filling her eyes along with the remainder of her tears.

'Good.' Herr Spieler nodded approvingly, though his stern

expression didn't waver. 'Now, how does this make you feel?' As he delivered the words, so he released her aching nipples and delivered a stinging slap to each breast.

Immediately, Charlotte felt a strong surge of lust. It sparked wildly, then consumed her totally, making her want to beg for more. When she dared to glance up at Herr Spieler's face again, she noticed that his eyes were no longer flat or inscrutable. Now, they glittered like sapphires. They glowed with an intensity that left Charlotte gasping for breath.

'Don't – look at me like that,' she whispered.

She was rewarded by a second slap to each breast. This time, she closed her eyes momentarily and rocked on her heels as the third slap came. In self-imposed darkness, she savoured the piquant sensation of pain overlaid by pleasure.

'You will not tell me what I can and cannot do,' Herr Spieler told her, tweaking her nipples painfully again before releasing them and taking a step back. 'I give the orders and expect to be obeyed without question. Understand this, child. I punish if I am displeased, yet punish more severely and more satisfyingly when you please me.' He paused, his voice softening slightly as a smile curved his lips and touched the corners of his eyes into light creases. 'And there is one thing I can promise you, my dear young Charlotte. You will come to crave the second form of punishment far more readily than the first.'

His threat held a beguiling sense of promise, which Charlotte found difficult to ignore. Instinctively she put her own hands to her stinging breasts, in an effort to soothe them. She felt only the slightest twinge of embarrassment when she noticed that he was watching her caress herself. If anything, it excited her to realise that, for the first time, she had captured his interest. Licking her fingertips, she circled them around her burning nipples, her gaze never leaving his face.

'There will be more to you and me,' he said thickly as he watched her fingers soothe her aching buds. 'Much, much more . . .'

His speech was interrupted by the sound of a knock at the outer door and then the familiar stern tone of Madame's voice. 'Is the girl still here?'

'Yes.' The doctor's voice came from the other side of the

screen. 'She is just preparing herself. Your brother is with her.'

'Ah – I see.'

Charlotte thought Madame sounded cross and gave a guilty start when the woman walked around the screen and stood, hands on narrow hips, staring at her and Herr Spieler. Her eyes were narrowed, her expression black and forbidding. To Charlotte, whose heart had begun to thud again, it seemed as though a storm were about to erupt in that tiny room.

Then Herr Spieler said something to his sister in *SwitzerDeutsch* and the tension evaporated. Madame almost smiled and put a tender hand briefly to her brother's cheek. While this exchange took place, all Charlotte could do was remain as motionless and inconspicuous as possible. She felt as though she were intruding on something private and enviably intimate, such was the rapport between her two guardians.

All at once, Madame turned to her. 'Child, you have put me to a great deal of inconvenience this morning. Now I trust you will behave yourself during the examination. We haven't the time to waste on girls who are prone to hysterics.'

'Oh, yes, Madame,' Charlotte responded emphatically. 'I didn't mean to make a fuss; it's just that, in England –'

'Yes, yes,' Madame interrupted, appearing impatient, 'I have no interest in your excuses. Now come with me; let us make you comfortable for your examination.'

The woman led Charlotte, naked and quaking with trepidation, around the screen. Now Charlotte could see that a chair, similar to that of a dentist, had been set up in the middle of the room. At one side of the chair a tall anglepoise lamp was positioned to provide a pool of harsh uncompromising light over whoever reclined in it. Which will be me, Charlotte thought nervously, her stomach tightening uncomfortably at the prospect.

The doctor was instantly by her side, rubbing his pudgy hands once again, beads of sweat already forming on his brow as he cast an assessing glance over Charlotte's naked body.

'Excellent,' he murmured. 'Would you like to take a seat my dear?'

He indicated the chair and Charlotte slipped nervously onto it, sitting bolt upright, her arms wrapped around her torso, her legs clenched tightly together.

'Don't be silly, child,' Madame admonished. 'How can the doctor possibly examine you like that? Are you going to cooperate, or shall we be forced to strap you down?'

Charlotte was horrified. 'Strap me down? No, oh, please; I don't want to do this.' Even as she protested, she allowed Madame to move her arms so that her hands rested lightly on the padded arms of the chair.

'What about her legs?' Madame asked, glancing over her shoulder at the doctor.

'Just leave the rest of her to me,' he replied.

As he spoke, he moved to the side of the chair and began to crank a handle located there. With each turn of the handle, the bottom half of the chair parted and raised, separating and lifting Charlotte's legs until she reclined in the most undignified position she had ever been in.

'Now,' the doctor said, glancing between her widespread thighs with a gleam of satisfaction in his eye and drawing a chair close to the foot of the table, 'at last I can begin my examination.'

Chapter Five

Charlotte's head seemed to be filled with a muted hum. She felt unreal, detached from herself, as though it were not her own body that lay open to inspection. She realised the humming sound came from the blood rushing like a torrent through her veins to cause enormous pressure at her temples. And it was with the greatest difficulty that she forced herself to resist the urge to leap up from the chair, in order to escape the humiliating situation.

When she felt her trepidation ease just a little, Charlotte glanced sideways, to her right. Herr Spieler and Madame stood beside the chair, she noticed; Madame was positioned by her shoulder, Herr Spieler at the point where her right knee was bent back toward her chest. Between her legs sat the doctor, now clad in a white coat, which looked sufficiently medical but hardly disguised the fact that his corpulent body overflowed the edges of the low wooden chair.

Charlotte tried hard not to let her gaze linger on the doctor. To witness his face, peering so intently between her legs, would be an abomination. Just knowing that he was doing so filled her with a terrible sense of shame. And to understand that at any moment he would touch her was even more appalling: something she tried desperately not to think about, as she let her head roll back and concentrated on staring up at the magnolia-painted ceiling instead.

'I think we need a little light,' the doctor said, throwing a switch on the lamp. Although the rest of the chalet was only equipped with old-fashioned gas-lighting, here apparently, in the doctor's surgery, electricity was allowed to prevail. 'Ah, that is much better,' he pronounced as Charlotte's naked torso was thrown into sharp relief.

Unable to help herself, Charlotte glanced down at herself. Her body, she noticed, was bathed in a harsh white light, which seemed to make an obscene feature of those parts of her which were roseate. Her nipples, still stiff and swollen from the treatment Herr Spieler had given them, jutted out obscenely. Yet it was her sex-flesh which seemed the most wanton. In her current undignified position, Charlotte could see that every intimate part of her was on display. Her outer lips were drawn back, revealing the soft inner folds of her feminine flesh. And her vagina gaped, like a tiny mouth forming a surprised 'O'. It was some consolation, she thought, that her clitoris somehow remained dormant.

She shuddered inwardly as the doctor moved closer, pronouncing that his examination would start with her breasts. And it took every ounce of willpower for Charlotte to resist recoiling from his touch. As he began to fondle her, as if trying to gauge the weight and fullness of her breasts, she bit down on the tender flesh on the insides of her cheeks to stop herself crying out in protest.

'These are most pleasing,' the doctor said, with a glance at Herr Spieler and Madame. 'Firm yet delightfully malleable. Would either of you like to sample them for yourselves?' He sat back a little, allowing the man and woman free access to Charlotte's breasts.

Herr Spieler gave a half-smile as he declined, saying that he had already had the opportunity to examine them. However, Madame nodded her assent and moved closer, her hands enclosing Charlotte's breasts with uncharacteristic eagerness.

Bending forward over Charlotte, she cupped them in her hands and squeezed, as though testing for ripeness. Then, to Charlotte's increased humiliation, she proceeded to examine the nipples closely. With her hard cold fingers, she tugged at them, rolling the stiff buds around between thumb and forefinger as her brother had done earlier.

When she appeared satisfied, she gave the sensitive buds a disdainful flick, which made Charlotte gasp.

At last, she straightened up. 'I am finished with the breasts. Please continue, Herr Doktor,' she said. Her cold glance swept down Charlotte's helpless body, to linger with a lascivious expression at the apex of her spread thighs.

Charlotte swallowed deeply and could not help but shudder as the doctor touched her sex-flesh with inquisitive fingers. He spread the delicate folds of her intimate flesh wider open, exposing her clitoris fully.

'Ah, such a delicate morsel,' Herr Spieler commented, sounding as pleased as a connoisseur of fine wine might if handed a glass of vintage Châteauneuf du Pape.

Charlotte cringed inwardly as he and Madame stooped forward for a closer inspection, both murmuring words of appreciation.

'Pull back the flesh hood,' Herr Spieler instructed the doctor, after a moment. 'I would very much like to see her little pearl.'

Charlotte had no idea what he was talking about, but she felt her clitoris quiver as the doctor did something to it. His fingertips glanced over her exposed bud, touching a part of it that made her recoil with the piquancy of the pleasure she received. The sensation was so exquisite, it was almost too much to bear.

'She is very sensitive, yes?' the doctor said, touching Charlotte lightly there again.

Charlotte's legs stiffened, her hips immediately jolting upward in response.

'It appears so,' Herr Spieler agreed. He, too, reached out and touched her there, his fingertips acting on Charlotte's desperately eager flesh like tiny, painfully exquisite bolts of lightning.

As though from somewhere in the distance Charlotte heard a low harsh panting of breath. She assumed the sound came from either the doctor or Herr Spieler. It was only when she stopped biting the insides of her cheeks to let out an anguished whimper that she realised it came from deep inside herself.

There was no mistaking the pleasurable signals her body gave her, no matter that it was often the doctor who induced them. All she was aware of was her mounting desire and the full arousal of her sex-flesh, which pulsed and swelled and tingled to an intolerable degree.

She felt close to explosion when, all at once, the touching of her clitoris ceased.

'There, she is fully aroused now,' the doctor pronounced. 'It is too soon to let her reach her crisis. We must save that moment until the very last.'

No! Charlotte wanted to cry out. No, I don't want to wait! Though the thought of losing all control in front of this group of strangers horrified her, she craved the release her body sought even more.

'Continue with the rest of the examination,' Madame ordered, ignoring the wild pleading look in Charlotte's eyes. 'I am interested to see how much she can take inside her.'

Charlotte quaked as the doctor nodded his agreement. She felt her cheeks and throat flame with mortification as he spread her vaginal lips far apart. He held her body open, peering inside her for a moment, before indicating that Madame and Herr Spieler should do the same.

'Finger her,' Herr Spieler said to the doctor. 'Start her off gently. I want to see how she responds.'

The doctor nodded. 'Very well.'

Charlotte watched with mounting trepidation as the doctor flexed his fat fingers, preparing to insert them inside her.

'Oh, no, please . . .' she moaned, her fingers clutching wildly at the padded leather arms of the chair.

'Hush. Silence, child,' Madame warned, flashing her a stern glance. 'The doctor must prepare you adequately for the insertion of certain instruments.'

Before Charlotte could protest further, or demand to know what instruments Madame was referring to, the doctor reached down with his free hand and produced a thick tubular metal object.

'Do you think the vagina can take it yet?' Herr Spieler enquired, eyeing the instrument. 'Please, allow me to feel her for myself.'

A low groan escaped Charlotte's lips as the doctor's fingers slid out of her, to be replaced by those of Herr Spieler.

'Only three fingers,' Herr Spieler said, sounding displeased. He glanced at his sister. 'Birgitte, please stimulate the clitoris again. We need to have her much wider than this.'

'Ah – oh, no . . .' Charlotte let out an anguished cry as Madame's fingertips touched her swollen bud again and began to rub gently back and forth. At the same time, she felt her vagina being filled by another of Herr Spieler's fingers.

'That is much better,' he commented, sliding his fingers in and out of her rhythmically. 'See how wet and open she is now. I fancy I could get my whole fist inside her.'

'Then do it, brother dear,' Madame urged, her own caresses relentlessly pleasurable. 'Let us see if she can take it.'

Charlotte groaned loudly and clutched at the arms of the chair as she felt his knuckles pressing against her opening. A moment later, a huge hardness filled her, stretching her more widely open than she could have dreamt.

Madame was still stroking her clitoris, which Charlotte felt was hugely swollen. Then, as if she weren't already receiving stimulation enough, the doctor began to pluck insolently at her nipples, drawing them out into stiff, fiery cones.

The pleasure was relentless. The arousal Charlotte felt was so acute that, when her crisis finally came, she screamed out and tossed her head from side to side as her lower body jolted upward from the leather seat and began to spasm.

She felt the muscles in her belly tightening and relaxing as the waves of pleasure just seemed to go on and on. And when Herr Spieler withdrew his fist from her, he immediately filled the clutching void of her vagina with the metal cylinder.

Charlotte felt herself begin to ride the instrument instinctively, her strong muscles trying desperately to draw the cold inanimate object deeper inside her.

'This is very impressive,' Herr Spieler and Madame murmured at the same time.

Through heavy-lidded eyes Charlotte saw the way they exchanged approving glances and heard the approbation in their tone.

'Her vaginal muscles are indeed excellent,' the doctor concurred, feeling inside her once again, his pudgy fingers probing and scissoring. 'They are still gripping, even now.' As he fingered her, so he held the instrument he had removed above Charlotte's face. To her mortification, she saw how her own creamy juices now streaked the once-shiny metal. 'Should I try her with some of the others?' he asked Madame and Herr Spieler. 'Though I think perhaps it is not necessary.'

'Quite right,' Madame agreed as she took a step back from the chair. 'I think the girl has proved how adequately she can accommodate a large object. My brother's fist is quite a size, would you not agree?'

As Herr Spieler held his fist up and regarded it with a wry expression, so the doctor laughed and Madame made a sound which Charlotte supposed could pass for laughter. Hearing the way they talked about her, of her body and its capabilities, made her cheeks burn with shame. Yet, at the same time, she also felt a curious pride, as though she had unwittingly passed some sort of test.

If she was left in any doubt at all, the way Madame spoke to her next and stroked away the damp tendrils of hair that clung to her face, begged no question.

'You have borne the examination well, my child,' she said, in a voice that hinted at tenderness, though her expression remained stern as always. 'Get up now and get dressed. I suppose you must be hungry, after all that exertion?'

Too weak to offer any verbal reply, Charlotte merely nodded. But she did as she had been told and found herself walking very gingerly across the room to the screen. Her whole body felt as though it had been put through a wringer. Particularly down below, where her pelvis ached and her vagina still maintained the vaguest sensation of being filled.

'I expect you will be feeling a little sore,' Madame called out to her as she dressed. 'I will ask one of the girls to prepare a soothing bath for you. When you are ready, go to your room. You may have your breakfast there while your bath is being drawn.'

Feeling too weak to argue, Charlotte walked around the screen on shaky legs. Somehow, she had managed to achieve some outward semblance of normality. Yet inside, she no longer felt like her old self at all. Now, it seemed, she had been reduced to a mere object of sexuality. Like a toy.

Madame and Herr Spieler had not been interested in her mind: only in the size and shape of her breasts, the wetness and openness of her vagina and the responsiveness of her clitoris. They had laid her open and bared every intimate portion of her to their view. With their eyes and hands, they had devoured her with a licentiousness that she had never encountered before.

And though at the time she had felt shamed by it, and of allowing herself to lose control in front of them, she now felt a certain sense of power. If she could capture the interest of a daunting couple like Herr Spieler and his sister, merely by displaying her body to them, then how much more easily could she manipulate a lesser human being?

As she walked slowly back to her room, she pondered on the young men who had courted her during her débutante year. They had all been eager then to get to know her, and that was while she had been ridiculously naive. If she were to meet them now, just a mere six months later, they would find her a very changed woman . . .

'Ah, Charlotte, you did not hear me calling you?' Sanchia touched her lightly on the arm.

Still deep in thought, Charlotte gave a start of surprise. 'Oh, you startled me!'

Sanchia smiled broadly, showing two rows of perfectly even white teeth. 'Madame sent me to find you,' she said. 'One of the housemaids will be along in a moment with some food for you. You had quite an ordeal this morning, no?'

'How did you guess?' Charlotte's expression was rueful.

They had reached the door to their dormitory by this time and, as Sanchia opened the door to let Charlotte pass, she gave her a cheeky wink. 'I went through it too, remember,' she said. 'I can recall how awful it was.' She paused and gave a throaty laugh. 'Ah, *Dios mio*, to think I was so naive.'

'Do you mean you wouldn't mind it so much, now?' Charlotte asked, flopping onto her bed. All at once she felt exhausted.

Sanchia pursed her lips, then smiled again. 'Maybe, maybe not. I am not the shy young girl from Madrid that I was when I came here.'

'But you haven't been at Bad Alpendorf very long,' Charlotte commented in amazement. 'You make it sound as though you have been here for a lifetime.'

'Ah, in some ways it seems as though I have,' Sanchia said, sitting down next to Charlotte and idly stroking her hair. 'Do you know something? I always wanted to have blonde hair like yours.'

At this Charlotte laughed. 'And I always yearned for long raven tresses. Perhaps we should swap.'

'Ah, I wish,' Sanchia responded wistfully. 'But no, I am happy now with the way I look. Here, at least, I am different. There are many blonde women in Switzerland.'

Their conversation was interrupted by the sound of the door opening. A maid entered, carrying a tray.

'Ah, Lisette,' Sanchia said, 'Mademoiselle will have her tray here, please.'

The maid nodded and scuttled toward them, her demeanour anxious and submissive. With a friendly smile, Sanchia took the tray from her and thanked her. When Charlotte sat up, Sanchia placed the tray across her lap.

'Eat up,' she said, sliding from the bed. 'And do not be too long. I am going to run you a bath.'

After Sanchia had gone, Charlotte tried to eat something of the tasty array of food set before her. But, though she felt ravenous, she found she could only manage a few bites. Presently, she set the tray down and stood up, stretching hugely. She was surprised to find that her body ached and she looked forward to the bath Sanchia was preparing for her. With a sigh of near-contentment, she crossed the room, exited it and made her way down the corridor to the bathroom.

The first thing Charlotte noticed when she entered the bathroom was the pungent aroma of the steam rising from the bath. It smelt of sandalwood and jasmine and another spicy, exotic fragrance she couldn't discern.

'Madame's special elixir,' Sanchia said. 'At least, that is what she calls it. It is supposed to soothe the mind and invigorate the body. Or is it the other way round?' As she pondered this, she cocked her head to one side, making Charlotte laugh.

'It hardly matters either way,' Charlotte assured her, giving her a friendly pat on the shoulder. 'All I need right now is to immerse myself in warm water and relax.' Reaching for the button at the waistband of her skirt, she hesitated and gave a pointed glance at the door. To her consternation, the young Spanish girl made no effort to leave.

'Do you mind if I . . .' She waved her hand at the bath, her eyebrows raised in a questioning manner. Surely the girl could take a hint?

'No, please, go right ahead.' Taking pity on Charlotte, Sanchia wandered over to the window and pretended to gaze in rapture at the breathtakingly beautiful view of the valley and the mountains beyond. To be truthful, after only a couple of weeks, she was beginning to tire of such unremitting greenness and longed to return to the vibrancy and colour of Madrid.

'Madame instructed me to bathe you,' she said without turning round.

'That's very thoughtful, but I prefer to attend to my own toilette,' Charlotte argued gently.

She felt her heart sink when Sanchia gave her a rueful smile. 'Madame's instructions,' the Spanish girl responded evenly, using the very words that, as both young women knew only too well, left no room for argument.

Deciding that perhaps she was being a bit silly, considering all that had happened to her already since her arrival at Bad Alpendorf, Charlotte gave a sigh of acquiescence, shrugged, then began to disrobe.

Sanchia tried her hardest not to glance over her shoulder at the new girl as she was undressing. *Dios mío*, but it was a temptation! From the moment she had arrived at Bad Alpendorf, the English girl had held such a fascination for her.

It was not just her fair English rose colouring, or her bearing. Adèle was of the same type physically, yet was nowhere near as alluring as this girl.

No, the new girl had something else, something *oscuro*; an indefinable thing. The French would say Charlotte had a certain *je ne sais quoi*, Sanchia thought. Her allure was purely sensual, but in a way that was natural and not flaunted. Which made the discovery of her sensuality all the more desirable to someone as passionate as Sanchia.

There were depths to this girl that Sanchia ached to plumb. She was certain Charlotte had no experience of other girls, and yet she was sure she had not mistaken the curiosity in the

English girl's eyes the night before. The way Charlotte's gaze had lingered on her bare breasts and sex had sent a frisson of desire through Sanchia, inducing a raw aching need to feel those slender and oh-so-refined fingers stroking her nipples and the furrow between her legs.

There was no denying that Sanchia was always hungry for sexual fulfilment. Day after day she walked around in a state of permanent arousal, her whole body thrumming to its own erotic beat. Her nerves were constantly strung taut, the endings charged, every sensual part of her alive to the merest possibility of gratification.

And whenever someone new came on the scene, particularly someone as beautiful and wholly desirable as the English girl, all her senses went on red alert. Sanchia had no illusions about herself. She was a greedy and passionate young woman, with a lust for life and the varied experiences it had to offer her. And when she saw something she wanted, she had to have her desires assuaged – preferably immediately. Patience was not a word that existed in her vocabulary.

It was with a pang of regret that she turned around and saw that Charlotte was already fully immersed in the steaming water. A shaft of desire sliced through Sanchia as she noticed the way the English girl had somehow managed to pin her hair up, exposing the length of her alabaster neck. Sanchia's lips tingled. She ached to press her mouth against that smooth white skin and to inhale the girl's own sweet perfume. She wanted to run her lips across those silken shoulders, to kiss her armpits and allow her tongue to trail a lazy path down to those beautiful raspberry-tipped breasts . . .

'Oh, I forgot to bring my soap and flannel,' Charlotte said, her rueful observation breaking through Sanchia's desirous thoughts.

She glanced curiously at the Spanish girl, wondering what it was that absorbed her so and appeared to send her mind on a journey that was miles away from this austere bathroom. Back to Madrid, I dare say, Charlotte thought, sinking lower into the water. She stretched blissfully and luxuriated in the fragrant clouds of steam that enveloped her. The water was so soothing, the ache in her muscles and the soreness between her thighs was receding already. Indeed, it seemed the shameful episode that morning had already become little more than an extraordinary memory.

Only half-aware of Sanchia's movements in the steamy bathroom, Charlotte sensed rather than watched her move around until, all at once, she felt a cool hand on her shoulder.

'There are always spare bars of soap and wash-cloths in the cupboard,' Sanchia said. She held out a square of white towelling and an oblong bar of pink soap. 'You can use these.'

'Thank you; you are most kind,' Charlotte murmured as she reached for the soap and flannel.

Acting in a teasing manner, Sanchia snatched the items away. As she did so, she shook her head. 'No, please, Chattie, allow me to bathe you. Madame's instructions,' she added again, now fully aware that the newcomer would hardly dare argue with such a statement.

And Charlotte could hardly be aware that this last part was more her own interpretation, Sanchia mused, feeling a little wicked for deceiving her. Madame had only charged her with the drawing and supervising of Charlotte's bath, not actually bathing her. However, Sanchia felt this was an opportunity not to be missed. How often in the future might she have good reason to touch and explore the young Englishwoman's naked body? This situation seemed heaven-sent.

With a feeling of trepidation, Charlotte tried to demur. But the fiery Spanish girl was nothing if not persistent. She simply would not accept any of Charlotte's arguments.

And little wonder, Charlotte thought privately, when they are so feeble and naive.

Much to Charlotte's surprise, it took relatively little time for her to relax and start to enjoy Sanchia's ministrations. Sanchia's touch was light and soothing, the soapy flannel a sensuous caress as it swept a film of creamy lather over Charlotte's shoulders and down her arms. Sanchia worked assiduously, taking great care to soap the back of Charlotte's neck, behind her ears, under her arms and in the crooks of her elbows.

She was so engrossed and Charlotte so relaxed, eyes closed, a dreamy expression on her face as she reclined in the bath, that neither girl heard the door open and close softly behind an unexpected visitor.

They smelt him before they heard him; Charlotte's eyes opened and Sanchia's head whipped round simultaneously as the enticing tang of citrus toilet water touched their nostrils.

'So sorry to disturb you ladies,' Max Spieler said, looking anything but contrite. 'I saw all the steam through the glass panels in the door and wondered if someone had left a tap running by mistake.'

'Well, as you can see, there really is no need for concern,' Charlotte countered, trying to sound bold as she attempted to sink further under the water. The clouds of steam were starting to dissipate now, and she was only too aware how clearly her naked body would be visible through the water.

'There is no need to feel embarrassed, *meine kleine Kirsche*,' Max Spieler said, unable to hide his amusement. 'Remember, you have nothing I haven't already seen and touched this morning.'

Charlotte burned with shame as she recalled the events Herr Spieler alluded to. It hardly took any concentration at all to conjure the sensation of his hands slapping her breasts, or his uncompromising fist insolently filling her wet open body.

As if the recollections themselves were an aphrodisiac, Charlotte felt her body begin to respond. Her nipples tightened under the scant covering of filmy water, her sex burgeoning automatically between her tightly clenched thighs as she recalled the twin delights of pleasure and humiliation. She squeezed her buttocks and inner thigh muscles more tightly and delighted at the immediate stimulation this gave her clitoris. Her outer labia compressed the tingling little bud like a mouth; the surrounding water added to the illusion of wet lips sucking at her sensitive flesh.

A single glance at Herr Spieler's face was all it took for her to understand that he knew she was feeling aroused. In response, his eyes glittered, their vibrant colour darkening to navy.

'Undress please, Sanchia,' Herr Spieler said, as if it were the most natural request in the world. 'I want you to climb into the bath with Charlotte; that way, you can bathe her properly.'

'Of course, Max,' Sanchia responded, causing Charlotte to glance at them both in surprise.

Sanchia's blithe use of Herr Spieler's Christian name gave Charlotte immediate cause to think that the young Spanish woman and their uncompromising host shared a degree of intimacy that she would never have suspected otherwise.

But of course, it made perfect sense, Charlotte told herself in the next instant, hardly able to help her gaze straying to Sanchia as she proceeded to undress. How stupid must she be to think that she was in any way special to this man? To imagine that he might have singled her, Charlotte Hetherington, out for unusual treatment. No doubt he treated all the young women at Bad Alpendorf in the same intimately seductive manner.

To her amazement, Charlotte found that the shattering of her illusion in no way had a marked effect on her. The probability that Herr Spieler and Sanchia were more than merely tutor and student – that they were, in all likelihood, lovers – did not bother her in the slightest. If anything, it excited her to imagine his hands caressing the Spanish girl's naked breasts and bottom and to conjure the image of their hot desperate bodies cleaving to each other.

She pictured Sanchia, her full breasts jutting out eagerly, her long dark hair cascading over a mound of white pillows as she arched her back in supplication to Herr Spieler. In her mind's eye, Charlotte could easily imagine those lithe olive-toned limbs – which were revealed to her now as Sanchia dispensed with her skirt and blouse – wrapping tightly around Herr Spieler's slim athletic body and her pelvis thrusting wantonly against his, urging him deeper and deeper inside her.

Charlotte trembled with longing as she allowed the images to play out in her mind and watched the Spanish girl slip eagerly out of a rose-pink silk camisole and knickers.

For a moment Sanchia paused, her uncharacteristic stillness attracting the attention of both members of her audience. Her full brown-tipped breasts lifted enticingly as she arched her back. Like a cat, she stretched luxuriously, then scooped up

73

her long curly hair and held it on top of her head.

She was making a display of herself, Charlotte realised, amazed and envious of the young girl's wanton pride. Clearly, she was enjoying the effect she was having on Charlotte and Herr Spieler.

No matter how hard she tried, Charlotte could not quell the rush of desire that overtook her as she gazed, transfixed, at the naked goddess posing with such abandon beside her. Nor could she deny the expression of lustful approval on Herr Spieler's face.

When he spoke, Herr Spieler's voice sounded oddly thick. 'Very lovely, my child. What a picture you make.' He paused to clap his hands together briskly. 'Now, into the water with you, you little minx, before it cools. Charlotte, sit forward a little, would you? Let Sanchia slide in behind you.'

There was a brief moment when Charlotte's first instinct was to demur. It was difficult for her not to cling to her old morality, she realised, as she hesitated for just a fraction before scooting her bottom forward obediently. Thankfully, the bath was long and wide, providing plenty of room for two people. And Charlotte only had to bend her knees a little to accommodate the young Spanish girl.

As Sanchia slipped into the water behind her, Charlotte felt first the brush of her inner thighs on her hips and then the soft sensuous touch of Sanchia's bare breasts pressing against her back. A slight gasp escaped both young women as this happened. And Charlotte risked a tentative glance over her shoulder at the young girl, in return for which she received another of Sanchia's cheeky winks. Clearly, Charlotte thought, this is not such an unusual scenario for her as it is for me.

At Herr Spieler's instruction, Sanchia immediately resumed her duties. Picking up the flannel and smearing it liberally with soap, she proceeded to wash Charlotte's back and shoulders. With great care, she smoothed the lather over Charlotte's bare skin, then rinsed it, holding the flannel aloft and squeezing it hard so that the water cascaded freely over Charlotte, rinsing the soap away.

When she was done, she leaned forward, squashing her breasts against Charlotte's back, her lips pressed against

Charlotte's left ear. 'I am going to bathe your breasts now, darling,' she breathed, in a way that sent tingles of excitement through Charlotte.

Charlotte's first instinct was to protest but she knew she couldn't. And in the back of her mind she was aware that she didn't really want to. The more she thought about it, the more she realised that she actually yearned to feel the young woman's hands caressing her breasts. In truth, she realised she had been craving the chance to become intimate with the Spanish girl since she had first set eyes on her.

How quickly we lose our morality, Charlotte thought, amazed at herself but poised with lustful anticipation all the same.

Charlotte was only vaguely aware of Sanchia's movements behind her as the Spanish girl lathered up the flannel yet again. And, as she waited in breathless anticipation of that first caress, she felt her heart begin to pick up speed. At the same time, Charlotte became aware of a distinct unravelling of desire. It started in the pit of her belly and spiralled upwards, before exploding into a warmth that encompassed her entire pelvis.

Though the water was cooling rapidly, her body felt hot and heavy. And the moment she felt the slick caress of the wash-cloth sweeping across her jutting breasts, she groaned freely. This was not a time to grasp at the last vestige of her old coyness, she realised, arching her spine so that her breasts were thrust further forward. She had to seize the moment.

'Leave the wash-cloth, Sanchia,' Herr Spieler ordered, his voice appearing heavy and muted as the blood thrumming in Charlotte's ears served to obscure it. 'Use your hands. I want to see you caressing those breasts properly.'

'Ah, oh, no! Oh, that's so wonderful . . .' Charlotte couldn't disguise her pleasure as the young Spanish girl slid her hands around her torso and slicked a thick film of creamy lather up over her breasts.

Charlotte's nipples sprang to attention immediately and she let her head drop back to rest upon Sanchia's shoulder. She felt completely submissive to the young girl's delicate ministrations. It was a new experience to abandon herself totally to someone her own age and sex, but she felt no shame in it.

To take her pleasure in this way seemed entirely natural.
It was . . . almost innocent . . .

Chapter Six

There was not one moment during the hours she spent that afternoon with Sanchia and Max Spieler that Charlotte did not feel totally at ease. Going with the flow seemed to her the most appropriate usage of words, as she watched more steamy water cascade into the bath from the heavy taps and felt Sanchia's small but infinitely seductive hands slide down her torso and between her parted thighs.

She let the upper half of her body relax against Sanchia, her head lolling back on the young woman's shoulder as she bent her knees and flexed her hips, so that her sex-flesh was made more accessible to Sanchia. It was as though she were submerged, not just physically but mentally too, in beauty and in warmth. The steamy fragrant water relaxed her to the same degree that the sensation of Sanchia's body pressed against hers beguiled her.

There was nothing she wanted to hide from these two people, she mused dreamily, as she felt Sanchia's fingers stroking her outer labia apart. And there was nothing she felt she couldn't achieve. No level of pleasure too high. No pinnacle of discovery too remote and inaccessible. Everything she desired was there for the taking. She only had to go with the flow.

Max knelt on the bathroom floor, mindless of the damp seeping into the knees of his trousers, the whole measure of his concentration filled to capacity by the entrancing sight of the two young women in the bath.

They made such a beautiful picture. Water-nymphs, cavorting naked. Sirens, glorious as nature intended, steam rising from their shoulders. Breasts damp with moisture, flushed with warmth, their silken skin glistening as they slumbered upon gently heaving chests.

And their hair. Oh, how he loved the way it hung in wet clumps down their backs, while a few damp tendrils clung to their lovely faces. They seemed so relaxed, the pair of them. So totally at ease as they rested against each other, Charlotte's fingers idly trailing in the water, Sanchia's knowingly caressing the curly thatch between Charlotte's thighs.

Max could not take his eyes off the two young women; yet his vision could hardly encompass the whole scene at once. To do so, he would have to remove himself a little, put distance between himself and the bath in which they reclined. This he did not want to do. He wanted to be as close to them as possible. As close as they would allow. He felt privileged to be there. To be a witness to their private, wholly feminine pleasure.

The way Sanchia took such delight in the new girl's body was to be expected, he supposed, suppressing a smile. In the short space of time that she had been at Bad Alpendorf, Max had come to know and to understand the young Spanish girl well. She was lovely to look at and naturally gregarious. Without doubt, she was also the most freely expressive and sensually abandoned young woman who had ever stepped through the portals of the chalet school.

And yet, in her own way, this new one was a singular delight. She appeared fresh and innocent, ignorant of the capacity contained within her for the pursuit of pleasure. Yet he could already tell that she harboured the willingness to learn.

She had endured the doctor's examination well that morning. Much better than most. How was she to know that the vast majority of new entrants to the school at Bad Alpendorf failed that first hurdle? That they packed their bags and fled afterward? Those were the young women who would, at best, only ever enjoy a mediocre sex life with their husbands and were unlikely to ever take a lover.

Charlotte, on the other hand, he recalled, had passed the initial test with flying colours. Though she had visibly burned with shame throughout her morning's ordeal, she had not professed disgust, nor leapt from the doctor's examination couch and cowered in a corner. No, not this one. Like the others who remained at the school, she had not only endured but, by the end, had clearly enjoyed the experience.

No doubt she would be the last to admit that she had enjoyed it though, Max thought with a wry smile; the girls who got over that first hurdle and stayed hardly ever did.

Sanchia was one of the exceptions.

Max flicked a fond glance in the direction of the Spanish girl as he recalled the way she had, from the very first moment, wholeheartedly embraced the unusual formula of humilation and pleasure that made the chalet school so successful. He wished in a way that she would never leave there. She was an asset to the school.

Unwittingly, through the pursuit of her own hedonistic pleasure, Sanchia helped to ease girls like Charlotte into new and sensual experiences. There was a beguiling innocence behind her advances toward the other girls that made the whole process of self-discovery far more appealing to them. But alas, there had been a few like Sanchia before her, and eventually they had all left Bad Alpendorf as planned, in order to seek new and far wider horizons.

'The water is getting cool, Max,' Sanchia murmured, breaking through his thoughts. 'Please pass me a towel.'

With a nod, Max got up reluctantly and held the towel for Sanchia to step into.

'No, Charlotte first,' Sanchia insisted. As she deposited a kiss on the young woman's shoulder, Sanchia murmured to Charlotte to get out of the bath.

One glance at Max holding the towel made Charlotte hesitate. She felt relatively safe in the bath, half-submerged in the rapidly cooling water. And yet she knew she would have to get out sometime. She glanced at her hands. The skin on the pads of her fingers had turned pink and wrinkled.

'You do not want your whole body to follow suit, surely?' Max said, sounding amused as he realised what she was thinking.

Charlotte flushed. 'Not really,' she murmured. 'Please hand me the towel.'

Not wishing to push the young woman too far and too fast, Max did as she asked: though he was forced to smother a chuckle as she struggled to wrap the towel around herself before stepping properly from the bath.

When she had both her feet on the mat, her toes curling into the deep pile, she glanced at him. And it was this one single glance that made Max's stomach lurch in a way that was so rare, he had almost forgotten he was capable of such strong emotion.

Unable to help himself, he stared at her. She looked about sixteen years old as she stood there. Her blonde hair was curled into damp tendrils around her face, which bore the expression of a startled fawn. Perfect ivory teeth clamped the pink fullness of her bottom lip as she nervously clutched the towel around her. And her bare shoulders, still glistening with water droplets, twitched occasionally as she shivered.

In that pose, she looked at once innocent and yet more desirable than he could ever have thought possible. Her appeal was undeniable and was made all the more beguiling because it lay not in the artifice of skilful makeup, nor a wardrobe of fashionable clothes, but in the air of vulnerability and sensuality that cloaked her.

She was a woman with a child's eagerness to learn, to experience new things. Her mind was there to be opened to the possibilities of erotic pleasure. Her body was, as he recalled, clearly capable of being tuned to the many and varied scales of sensual gratification.

At that moment Max felt like offering up his thanks to whichever god had created her and ruled the planet. She was there to be taught and he, through divine intervention, was the man lucky enough to have been chosen to lead her along the path to sensual fulfilment.

'Max, you look a little odd. Are you feeling all right?' Sanchia touched Max on the arm, disturbing his reverie yet again.

He smiled down into her earnest nut-brown face, loving the liquid sensuality of her dark eyes. 'I am fine,' he said. 'I was just thinking what a lucky man I am, to be in the company of two such beautiful women.'

Sanchia immediately gave a husky laugh and Charlotte, who had been feeling nervous up to then, smiled. Max Spieler really was quite the gentleman, she thought, feeling warm all over when he glanced at her and returned her smile.

'Chattie, you must be feeling the cold,' Sanchia said a moment later, hurrying over to her. Though clad only in a small towel herself, the young Spanish woman seemed hardly conscious of her own needs as she took up another towel and began to pat Charlotte's legs dry.

Charlotte looked down at the top of Sanchia's dark head and wondered why she didn't feel more awkward. Here she was, having shared a bath with this girl, and with a man who was a virtual stranger as an onlooker, yet she felt extraordinarily calm.

To be truthful, Max Spieler's comment had gone a long way to assuage her anxiety. Somehow, it was difficult to believe that there was anything wrong in what they were doing. And yet why should she feel that way in the first place? she asked herself in the next instant. They were all adults. And Cadell had been the one who insisted she come here, his instructions to her leaving her in no doubt that he wanted her to participate in everything that went on at the school.

Added to that, both Max Spieler and Sanchia were very desirable people. There was no getting away from the reality, Charlotte thought, as she flicked her gaze from one to the other. Sanchia was busy blotting the moisture from her body now, the palms of her hands transmitting an unmistakable warmth as she pressed them against the towelling which covered Charlotte's torso. In the meantime, Max looked calm and relaxed as he leant against the wall, hands deep in pockets, his impossibly long legs crossed casually at the ankles.

He was watching them with a calm detachment that made Charlotte burn with the desire to do something that would put a spark in those enigmatic blue eyes.

With a burst of devilment, she 'accidentally' let her towel slip to the floor.

'Whoops!' she said, staring straight at Max.

Instantly, her heart took a leap of delight. There it was, the spark of interest she had been craving. It lit up his whole face and, when she glanced a little lower, she couldn't help wondering if the bulge at the front of his trousers had been quite that noticeable before.

81

He desires me, she thought, all at once aware of the effect she was capable of having on him. And she could no longer deny it, she desired him.

In an instant, the atmosphere around the three of them changed. From innocent playfulness, they each became charged with an erotic tension that linked them inextricably and drew them closer together.

Charlotte was the first to act. She took a bold step toward Max and felt a surge of desperate longing as he straightened up and grasped her by the waist, pulling her hard against him. Her instantaneous arousal was so powerful, it drove the breath from her body.

The touch of his broad masculine hands around her naked midriff sent tingles of desire through her. Charlotte felt her knees sag a little under the weight of her desire, and was grateful for the reassuring solidity of Max's body as she cleaved to him. She could feel his body heat emanating through his clothing, the rhythmic beat of his heart and the hard bulge at the front of his trousers pressing into her belly, as he wrapped his arms around her and smothered her face and neck with kisses.

She let her head drop back as Max continued to lay a trail of kisses down her throat and across the upper swell of her breasts. Her nipples hardened, the sensitive buds chafing against the rough tweed of his waistcoat. Behind her, she could sense Sanchia moving about and was not surprised to feel, a moment later, the tantalising caress of slender and unmistakably feminine fingertips stroking the length of her spine.

Sanchia's breath was warm and sweet on the side of her neck, as the young woman swept the soft pads of her fingers over Charlotte's naked back. Her fingers traced meandering paths, circling, moving across from one side to the other in zig-zag fashion, then describing intricate whorls and figures of eight.

If it had not been for the pleasure of Max's wet mouth suckling at her breasts, Charlotte might have become completely entranced by the Spanish girl's hypnotic caresses. As it was, she arched her back, letting out a low moan as she thrust her breasts more wantonly into Max's cupped hands.

Her nipples tingled between his lips, hardening all the more as he nipped teasingly at them. The sensation was mildly painful yet pleasurable, and Charlotte found herself moving her feet apart quite willingly as Sanchia's stroking fingertips skimmed over her buttocks and began to tantalise her inner thighs.

It was not the first time she had ever experienced the sensuality of another woman's caresses. But she had never been with both a man and a woman at the same time before. And the contrast between hard and soft – Max's muscular solidity and Sanchia's velvety feminine warmth – felt indescribably wonderful.

After a short while, the three of them slipped into a natural rhythm, hands and lips never leaving each other for an instant as they caressed and ground their bodies against each other.

Eventually, eager for more pleasure, Charlotte started to grope mindlessly at Max's buttons. With an awkwardness born of desire, she somehow managed to unfasten them and drew his waistcoat over his shoulders and down his arms. She tossed it away, to a far corner of the bathroom, and then made sure his shirt followed it.

With enormous delight, she pressed her palms flat against the hard plain of Max's naked back and then, with increasing daring and using only her fingertips, began a sightless exploration of his musculature and the defined knobs and ridges of his spine. To her delight, at the base of his spine, she encountered two small dimples either side. Into these she pressed the pads of her index fingers, a gesture which inadvertently urged his lower body closer to hers.

Max groaned and slipped a hand between his body and Charlotte's when she did this. While his fingers encountered the coarse fabric of his tweed trousers, which encased the hard bulge of his stiffened penis, so the back of his hand delighted to the warmth and silky texture of Charlotte's skin.

'Here Max, let me help you with those buttons,' Sanchia murmured.

Like an angel of mercy, the young Spanish girl moved gracefully around Charlotte and sank to her haunches beside the English girl and Max. She reached up and gently moved Max's hand out of the way before deftly unfastening the buttons at his fly.

She finished undressing him with a skill that many courtesans would have been pleased to acquire, Max thought, as he allowed Sanchia to slip the shoes and socks off his feet and finally remove his trousers and underpants.

In the meantime, Charlotte seemed quite oblivious to what Sanchia was doing. She appeared lost in another realm and did not make the slightest protest as Max slipped his liberated hand between her thighs.

His other hand still cupped her breast and he tweaked gently at the nipple as he slid a finger along the moist cleft between Charlotte's outer labia. The young woman whose body was, of her own volition, flattened against him, began to whimper as he stroked her flesh expertly. Her hips jolted and her whole body trembled as he sought out and began to caress the hard little bud that was the core of her desire.

Without disturbing the rhythm of their lovemaking, all three, seemingly of one accord, sank to the bathroom floor. Thankfully, the varnished wooden floor was strewn with thick rugs and it was upon one of these that they happened to lie.

Max hovered above Charlotte's supine body, one arm bearing his upper body weight as his other hand continued to stimulate her intimate flesh. In the meantime, Sanchia knelt beside them both and moved to take Max's stiff penis in her mouth.

'I want to see you pleasure her with that clever mouth of yours,' Max murmured to Sanchia a few minutes later, when he could bear her ministrations no longer.

Her dark eyes danced wickedly as she met his gaze. 'I do not mind,' she said, sharing a conspiratorial look with him.

They both knew that, far from minding, the young Spanish girl was eager to taste the new girl and to discover the delicate folds of her sex-flesh properly, with her fingertips and tongue.

Lost in a haze of bliss, Charlotte hardly noticed Max and Sanchia exchanging places. The teasing fingers left her sex only for the briefest moment before returning, and then she couldn't help but let out a cry of sheer joy at the first moment she felt the soft caress of a tongue there.

Raising her head a little off the mat, she opened her eyes to see Sanchia's head buried between her thighs. It gave her quite a jolt to realise that it was the other woman who pleasured her so seductively, and not Max. But after a moment, it hardly seemed to matter. There was too much pleasure, too much glorious sensation for her to demur.

'Wet and juicy, eh?' Max enquired. He flashed a wicked glance between Charlotte's thighs before transferring this look to her face.

Charlotte burned with shame and desire. She was behaving in such a wanton fashion, she could hardly believe it of herself. How often before had she lain on a bathroom floor, naked, with her legs spread wide apart and two complete strangers making love to her? Never.

Yet a more pressing question was, she thought a moment later, as she felt Sanchia's tongue do delicious things to her straining clitoris, how many more times might this happen in the future, now that she had agreed to liberate herself?

'And did Max fuck you while you were licking Charlotte's clit?' Yolande asked Sanchia later. She spoke in a matter-of-fact way that made Charlotte gasp with surprise.

Both Charlotte and Sanchia were back in their room. With hardly time to recoup their energy after such a wonderful but tiring episode, that afternoon, they had been joined by their other two room-mates.

Immediately, Yolande had sensed that something had happened between Charlotte and Sanchia, and had insisted on being given details. To Charlotte's mortification, the Spanish girl displayed no reticence about revealing every last salacious detail. And, furthermore, she described every aspect of their afternoon encounter with undeniable relish.

Faced with Sanchia's candour, all Charlotte could do was throw herself face down on her bed and bury her flaming face as deeply as possible into the soft down of her pillow. Try as she might, though she was able to disguise her shame, she was unable to block out the sound of Sanchia's voice. To Charlotte's increasing shame, the Spanish girl continued with her blithe description, leaving nothing out. And it shocked Charlotte even more that Yolande should appear to take such base pleasure in encouraging Sanchia to describe the minutiae of their encounter and, indeed, that she should use such coarse language in the process.

'Please, do you have to?' she begged uselessly, her plea somewhat muffled by the pillow.

'Oh, Chattie, don't be such a spoilsport,' Yolande teased her, nudging her lightly on the shoulder. 'I would tell you about my escapades – if I had any,' she added, sounding a mite wistful.

Even Charlotte couldn't help smiling at this, though the others couldn't see her amusement, with her face pressed into the pillow.

'If you were leading such a sheltered life, how is it that Madame has seen fit to add another reason for punishment to your rapidly growing list of misdemeanours?' Adèle asked, her acid voice cutting through their lighthearted banter like cheesewire.

At this, Charlotte forgot her own embarrassment and raised her head. She rolled over and stared enquiringly at Charlotte. 'Punishment, by Madame? Why?' she asked.

Now, it seemed, it was Yolande's turn to blush. 'I did something else that Madame has seen fit to disapprove of,' she admitted, looking sheepish.

'What? What?' Charlotte was agog. She sat up on the bed and hugged her knees to her chest.

'Well, you wouldn't know it yet, but the others would,' Yolande began, glancing briefly at Sanchia and Adèle. 'Some of the classes held here concern the development of physical control.' She sounded as though she were aping Madame in the way she spoke, and by the expression on her face.

Charlotte giggled. 'What do you mean, physical control? Is it something to do with sport?'

At this, even Adèle managed a thin laugh, though Sanchia and Yolande both threw back their heads and roared.

'Oh, Chattie, you are so sweet and innocent, sometimes,' Sanchia purred, coming to sit on the bed beside her and stroking her calf. 'I cannot believe you are the same person who –'

'Yes, quite. But that is of no consequence,' Charlotte cut in quickly, afraid of what Sanchia was about to say. She felt she had suffered enough humiliation for one day.

However, she couldn't ignore the lustful warmth she felt at the young woman's proximity. That afternoon, they had become lovers, and she had experienced the hitherto unknown pleasure of watching two other people make love. Though Max had not attempted to have intercourse with her, he had shown no such reticence about plunging his hardness into Sanchia's willing body.

With a rapid blink of her eyes, Charlotte forced herself to dispel the imagery from her mind. There would be time enough for reflection and graphic examination of her recollections later, she told herself firmly.

Thankfully, Yolande seemed far too keen on explaining herself, to bother about Charlotte's own misdemeanours.

'I daresay you will find out all about it for yourself, soon enough,' Yolande said, piquing Charlotte's curiosity still further. 'But I will try to explain. You see, Chattie, as you must have realised by now, the curriculum at this school is all about self-discovery. And, as Madame explained when I first came here, before you can expect to give and receive pleasure, you need to know your own body intimately.'

At this, Charlotte shuddered and pursed her lips. 'Are you talking about . . . masturbation?' she whispered, unable to stop herself from sounding shocked and at the same time hardly able to get the word out.

'Yes, exactly.' Yolande appeared delighted that Charlotte had understood her straightaway. 'Madame encourages us, in a group, to explore our own bodies and to bring ourselves to the brink of orgasm.'

Trying hard to dismiss the notion of having to touch one's self at all, let alone as part of a group, Charlotte said, 'Why only the brink? Surely if you reach your – er – crisis –' she still found it difficult talking about such intimate things '– that is proof enough of your success.'

'Of course it is,' Sanchia said, taking over from Yolande, who seemed to be having difficulty smothering a grin. 'But while it is relatively easy to achieve one's *little death*, it is much harder to delay it. To master such self-control is a feat in itself.'

'And one which this young madam still hasn't quite got to

grips with,' Adèle cut in wryly, throwing a sagacious glance at Yolande – who smirked.

'So, you – you lost control, somehow?' Charlotte queried, feeling not quite sure what they were all talking about.

'Very definitely,' Adèle said. 'I was there. Yolande had hardly started when she suddenly started coming like an express train. Madame was not best pleased, I can tell you. We had strict instructions to wait until the hour was up.'

'An hour!' Charlotte gasped.

'I failed,' Yolande cut in, looking far less miserable than she might, Charlotte mused, if she had failed, say, a history test.

'And failure deserves punishment,' Adèle said. 'God, I don't mind telling you, Yolande, I envy you.'

Charlotte flashed the other English girl a glance of surprise. There was nothing in her tone that hinted at sarcasm, which she might have expected from Adèle. Nor was her expression anything other than envious.

'Well, you would, Adèle,' Yolande responded. Without bothering to explain her remark – which, Charlotte couldn't help noticing, both Adèle and Sanchia seemed to understand immediately – she got up and walked over to the wardrobe that housed her clothes. 'Anyway, if we've all stopped chatting, I think we should hurry up and get ready for dinner. Woe betide us all if we give Madame another reason for doling out punishments,' she added with a broad wink.

Chapter Seven

It took Charlotte the best part of a week to understand fully the concept of Madame's punishments. She found it incredible that anyone should enjoy even a modicum of pain and humiliation. And when she attended her first class in self-pleasure, she found it even more inconceivable that any one of the young women gathered in that small candle-lit room should willingly caress their own bodies, in full view of the rest.

She had been at the chalet school at Bad Alpendorf for five days, by which time – apart from the initial medical examination and her impromptu encounter with Sanchia and Max Spieler – the classes at the school had so far centred around nothing more extraordinary than any she might expect from a normal finishing school.

So far, she had improved her knowledge of fine wine and gourmet food; had arranged various selections of flowers to visual perfection; and had become completely cognisant with such diverse subjects as high-fashion, interior design, how to distinguish the best in coffee, port and Havana cigars – not to mention the correct way to knot a bow-tie.

These, she understood, and deemed acceptable, were all things which would make her passage into high-society as Cadell's wife that much smoother.

Having got off to such an unusual start, this innocuous interlude at the chalet school had the effect of delusion. It encouraged Charlotte to take a relaxed approach to each day's syllabus. Gradually, she dropped her guard. She stopped expecting to find an erotic encounter waiting for her around every corner. And she even learnt to take with a pinch of salt the interested glances she received from her fellow students. Surely, she told herself on these occasions, there is no harm in someone appreciating another of her own sex? Beauty was, after all, in the eye of the beholder.

Such was the gradual renewal of Charlotte's inherent naivety that, on that fifth day, when she made her way briskly to the room Madame had instructed her to go to for her next lesson, she had no reason whatsoever to assume that this tutorial would involve anything at all out of the ordinary.

The first inkling she had that something different was afoot was when she entered the room and noticed that it was furnished not with traditional seating but with large velvet-covered cushions and bolsters.

Even more strange a sight were the mirrors, which had been placed in front of each cushion. And the fact that the curtains were drawn – presumably to provide privacy for some reason or another – gave Charlotte a strange feeling of premonition. Her stomach knotted instantly and her brow furrowed with consternation as she glanced about her.

She found it strange that the room was cloaked not in sunlight but in shadow. The dark atmosphere was brightened by groupings of thick creamy candles, which flickered brightly and dripped their wax on to filigree silver trays. Some of the candies were scented; musk mingled with jasmine and rose.

Their flickering light and captivating perfume, coupled with the contrived intimacy of the surroundings, all served to lend Charlotte the impression that she had inadvertently stepped into another woman's boudoir.

At any other time and in any other place, Charlotte might have found the setting intriguing, even seductive. But this was the middle of the day and she was in a place of learning. Exotic scents and a deliberately sensually provocative atmosphere did not a classroom make, she mused, wondering if she had time enough to leave.

It was already too late, she realised with a sinking heart as a tall girl with long straight mid-brown hair entered the room.

'Am I in the right place for the self-expression class?' Charlotte asked the young woman.

'I guess,' the girl responded with a shrug. Her accent clearly revealed her to be of American origin. 'How long have you been at the school?' She flicked her long hair over her shoulder.

Without waiting for Charlotte to answer, she began to prowl around the room with a loping gait. Eventually, she appeared to tire of this activity and stopped dead. As though her bones had suddenly melted, she crumpled down upon the nearest cushion – a bolster covered in velvet, which was a deep purple in colour. After a moment, she moved so that she was seated astride the bolster. Then she flopped forward from the waist and rested the side of her face on the cushion and proceeded to stare off into space.

Used to clear speech, brisk movement and impeccable manners, Charlotte regarded the American girl with avid curiosity. Her mode of speech was a lazy southern drawl, and every movement she made was executed with a casual, almost careless, air. Everything about her unusual demeanour made Charlotte think that the girl was either supremely confident, or not entirely all there, mentally.

Either that, or she couldn't care less about the impression she made on other people, Charlotte mused, her interest in the young woman very definitely aroused.

'This is my fifth day,' Charlotte said, wandering over to where the girl lay. She gazed down at her, though the girl didn't look up. 'Madame directed me here, but I think she must have made a mistake.' She laughed lightly and, in the next instant, almost jumped out of her skin when she heard Madame's voice ring out behind her.

'I never make mistakes, young lady,' Madame said. Her voice was stentorian as it resonated around the room.

Charlotte shook visibly, and even the flames on the candles appeared to tremble in sympathy. Only the American girl seemed unperturbed.

'Oh, you startled me, Madame,' Charlotte managed to gasp out. She automatically clapped a hand to her chest and straightaway felt her heart hammering behind her ribs.

She felt guilty, though she had no idea why: other than that perhaps her observation had been a little indiscreet. What was more, she couldn't help wondering why it was that this woman should inspire such trepidation in her. She was not usually prone to feeling in awe of people: save the King, the Prime Minister or the Pope, maybe.

91

'You might well feel startled, Charlotte,' Madame said, interrupting Charlotte's thoughts. She raised her eyebrows and looked down her nose at Charlotte in the disdainful fashion that Charlotte had come to recognise as characteristic of the woman. 'Do you believe I am in the habit of making errors?'

'Oh, no, Madame. I did not mean . . .' Charlotte tried to explain herself, but broke off abruptly.

All at once she felt ridiculous. Frustratingly, her cheeks flamed, which instantly prompted her to curse her lack of sophistication. Heavens, the woman had a way of making her feel as though she were no more than three years old!

'Good. I am glad to hear it,' Madame responded evenly. As she spoke she threw a glance over her shoulder. Clearly Charlotte was no longer of interest to her. 'Hurry up, girls,' she called to the four young women who now hovered with uncertainty in the open doorway. 'Adèle, close the door behind you, please, and lock it.'

'Yes, Madame.'

Charlotte was surprised to see Adèle there, and even more amazed to witness the change in her demeanour. The Adèle she had already come to know quite well (and learnt to dislike), having shared a room with her for five nights, was far more self-assured than the young woman who bowed her head and hastened to do Madame's bidding.

Having closed the door and locked it, Adèle walked swiftly up to Madame and handed her the key. As Madame's bony fingers curled around the key, Adèle amazed Charlotte still further by bending her head to kiss the back of the woman's hand.

'That will be all, Adèle,' Madame responded, seeming not in the least surprised by the young woman's action. She neither frowned nor smiled, but remained as enigmatic as ever as she shooed Adèle over to a cushion with a dismissive wave of her hand.

Quick to do as Madame bade her, Adèle sat, as did all the other young women present.

Only Charlotte remained standing.

'Why are you not seated, girl?' Madame asked, when she noticed the way Charlotte hovered with uncertainty.

'I . . . I . . .' As was customary when in the dour woman's presence, Charlotte found herself lost for words.

'Sit, girl. Sit,' Madame ordered. 'And slip off your underpants. Adèle, did you bring the chart from my desk?'

Charlotte hesitated still. She glanced up at Madame. Had the woman really just asked her to take off her knickers, or were her nerves so fraught that it was possible for her to imagine such a thing?

She felt so confused that she failed to hear Adèle's reply to Madame's question. Nor did she notice that the older woman had walked over to an easel positioned at the far end of the room.

'We have only one new girl here today,' Madame began as she picked up a wooden pointer. 'She is called Charlotte and she is from England.' As she spoke, she directed the end of the pointer at Charlotte, who quaked under her scrutiny.

All the other girls, apart from Adèle, craned their necks to look at her.

Realising she had become the centre of attention, Charlotte blushed again. 'Er, hello everybody,' she whispered, not knowing quite how else to respond to their inquisitive looks.

The other girls chorused back their greetings, until Madame rapped the pointer sharply on the top of the easel to silence them.

'Quiet, girls,' she ordered sternly. 'There is much to be achieved here today. Adèle, you will start us off. Please explain, for Charlotte's benefit in particular, the philosophy behind this class.'

With the utmost grace, Adèle rose from her seated position and cleared her throat. Everyone turned their heads to look at her. Even Charlotte, who didn't much care for Adèle, was intrigued to learn from her what this lesson was all about.

'The reason we are all here, as most of you already know,' began Adèle, in a clear, articulate voice, 'is to get to know ourselves. Our bodies are more than just a convenient way of housing our brains, moving us from place to place and one day, hopefully, a means to producing future generations. They are an instrument of extreme pleasure.'

Charlotte sighed inwardly, wishing the infuriating girl would

93

tell her something she didn't already know.

'Now, that is something of which you are no doubt already aware,' Adèle went on, as if she could read Charlotte's mind. 'But what a lot of us do not realise is how easy it can be for us to attain different levels of physical gratification. The simplest way is to get to know our own bodies intimately first. That way we are equipped to direct others – be they our husbands or lovers – how best to pleasure us.'

'It is quite like learning to play a musical instrument,' Madame interjected, flashing a brief smile at Adèle who, with a glance of gratitude at Madame, sat down immediately. 'Once one has an instrument in one's possession, it is only natural that one should learn how to create beautiful music with it. Each one of us moves to a different rhythm. And it is up to us, as individuals, to learn that rhythm and to teach it to others. Particularly to those who wish to play you as well as you do yourself,' she added, her tone and expression lightening a fraction.

All at once Charlotte realised what this lesson was all about. Masturbation.

The word rang in her head like a giant bell, echoing over and over until she felt the urge to clap her hands over her ears to block out its resonance. She opened her mouth to protest. She wanted more than anything to tell Madame that she couldn't possibly take part in this particular class.

'Charlotte, if you please, I would like you seated,' Madame said, before Charlotte could say anything. 'That bolster over there is free. Please remove your underpants and sit astride it like Buffy.'

Almost in a daze, Charlotte followed Madame's glance. Clearly Buffy was the name of the young American woman. To Charlotte's surprise, she saw that the American was sitting upright astride the bolster and looked surprisingly alert. When she looked down, Charlotte saw clearly the thick chestnut thatch of hair at the apex of Buffy's thighs.

'Don as the woman says, take your knickers off and get your bare ass down there on the cushion,' Buffy drawled, earning herself a disapproving glance from Madame.

'Thank you, Buffy,' Madame said reprovingly. 'I would prefer

it if you referred to me by name rather than as "the woman".
And kindly do not interfere.'

'Gee, sorry,' Buffy responded, looking as though she couldn't
care less.

There was no doubt, Charlotte decided, as she hastily pulled
off her knickers and sat gingerly astride the red velvet bolster
allocated to her, that the American girl had complete disregard
for authority.

Under normal circumstances, Charlotte would have found
this an admirable trait, but she didn't much care for the way
Buffy had spoken to her. Her terminology was so uncouth.

'Now, I want you to hitch up your skirts, open your legs
wide and position the mirror in front of you, so that you can
visually examine your own body,' Madame said, as though her
instruction were the most natural thing in the world.

Stiff-backed as usual, she began a circuit of the room, making
sure that everyone did exactly as she asked.

When Madame approached her, Charlotte couldn't prevent
the warm flush that suffused her throat and face. When she
looked straight ahead of her she could see, as clearly as anything,
the pink split-plum vision of her sex. The outer lips of her
vulva were slightly parted, revealing the edges of her soft inner
folds; just below her clitoris, her vagina pouted beguilingly, its
rim smeared with a little creamy fluid.

'Already halfway there, I see,' Madame commented,
stopping beside her.

Charlotte blushed harder. She wasn't so naive that she didn't
understand exactly what Madame meant. Nor could she deny
the surge of arousal she felt, each time she glanced at the
reflection of her body in the mirror. The velvet under her bare
bottom felt warm and sensual, while the occasional draught of
cool air whipping across her exposed flesh made that part of
her tingle with exhilaration.

To Charlotte's surprise, and not a little consternation,
Madame sat down beside her. The woman picked up
Charlotte's hands, which hung limply by her sides, and placed
them upon the silky-haired triangle that covered her mound.

'Use your fingers to open yourself out,' Madame encouraged
her, working Charlotte's rigid fingers for her. 'That is correct;

spread those lips wider. Wider still . . . Expose yourself to your own eyes. Now, tell me, what do you see?'

When Charlotte tried to reply, she was surprised to discover a lump blocked her throat. She coughed gently. 'I – I see . . . myself,' she murmured, knowing her response was lame.

'Can you see your vagina?' Madame asked.

Charlotte nodded dumbly.

'Then touch it,' Madame said. 'Stroke your fingers around the outer rim. Ah, now does that not feel good?'

Feeling the pleasurable tingles that her own fingertips transmitted, Charlotte managed to whisper that yes, it did feel good.

'Now slick some of that moisture up that lovely pink slit of yours,' Madame urged her, her voice sounding oddly thick. 'Take your fingertip higher, over your clitoris.'

As soon as Charlotte felt her moist fingertip slide over the sensitive bud of her clitoris, she let out a low moan.

'Ah, yes,' Madame murmured, looking vaguely amused. 'I can tell that you have found it.'

'I can't keep doing this, Madame,' Charlotte said pleadingly, when she had been stroking her clitoris for a few excruciating moments. 'The sensation is too intense.' Her cheeks still flamed with mortification as she gasped out the words.

'Then you must be particularly sensitive there,' Madame said. 'Try moving your fingertips around the edge of your clit. Or up and down in the way Buffy is doing.'

Charlotte followed Madame's glance across the room.

'Come with me,' Madame said in the next instant, surprising Charlotte and shocking her even more by holding out her hand to her. 'I want you to observe Buffy at close quarters as she pleasures herself. I think perhaps you two are more similar than you might think. You can learn from her.'

Eaten up by curiosity but burning with embarrassment, Charlotte allowed the dour woman to lead her across the room and complied with her instruction to sit astride the bolster, facing Buffy.

'I want you to take the place of Buffy's mirror,' Madame said, moving away slightly. 'Use your fingers upon yourself to copy her caresses exactly.'

Feeling more full of shame than she had ever felt before, Charlotte moved her hands between her thighs. She hardly dared to meet Buffy's eyes and instead concentrated on the exposed portion of flesh between the American girl's legs.

With her outer lips held wide apart with the fingers of one hand, Buffy exposed her clitoris to Charlotte's gaze. It was already hugely swollen, Charlotte noticed, curiosity outweighing her embarrassment somewhat.

In her mind, Charlotte told herself that this situation was not all that different to the exciting time she had spent with Sanchia. Then she had not minded the young woman viewing her naked body at close quarters, nor even touching her with hands and mouth. In view of that, surely this was far more innocuous?

'Stroke your clit like this,' Buffy said, startling Charlotte from her reverie. 'Make an upside-down vee with your fingers and rub up and down.' As she spoke, so she demonstrated. Using her fingers just as she described, she trapped the hard bud of her clitoris between them and began to move them rhythmically up and down.

With only a moment's hesitation, Charlotte followed suit. Straight away she felt little tremors of sublime pleasure radiate from that most sensitive part of her. Her arousal mounted quickly, but she couldn't quite reach the pinnacle for which she yearned.

Buffy was already there, she noticed, feeling a sharp pang of envy. The American girl, whose face had at one moment been screwed up as though in fierce concentration, now let out a huge groan and dropped her head back. Her mouth opened and closed, emitting tiny gasps of pleasure as her fingers kept up their relentless rhythm. With a huge shudder that rocked the bolster from side to side, she came.

After a moment had passed the American girl raised her head and gazed blearily at Charlotte. 'Can't you get there, honey?' she asked, sounding sympathetic.

Despising herself for envying Buffy's radiant expression, Charlotte shook her head in despair. 'It is no good,' she said. 'Every time I get close, something seems to block my way.'

'Then what you need, honey, is a good fantasy,' Buffy replied, sounding matter-of-fact. 'Works for me every time.' When Charlotte didn't respond, she added, 'If you haven't got a fantasy, think of something you've done in the past. Or something you've seen. A picture maybe, or a scene in a film . . .' Her words trailed off.

Or at least, in Charlotte's mind, they appeared to. The truth was Charlotte felt incapable of hearing what the girl was saying to her. She had found a new distraction. All at once her mind had become filled with the memory of that afternoon with Max and Sanchia . . .

Two bodies, that was what she saw when she closed her eyes. Heads, one dark, one impossibly fair, bobbing up and down in unison, responding to the rhythm of their bodies. Further down . . . bodies joined. Hips butting hips. Dark-toned thighs, their muscles quivering. Paler thighs, working like pumps, driving the powerful weapon at their apex deeper inside wet, open, willing flesh. The slap-slap sound of flesh meeting flesh. The unmistakable scent of sex . . .

'Aaahh . . . !' Charlotte let out a strangled cry as the image, combined with the assiduous working of her fingers, produced wave after wave of pleasure, its intensity sublime.

Afterward, she felt only triumph. She had done it. She had made herself come.

The dinner party held two days later at the chalet school had all the hallmarks of a very grand affair. There was definite excitement in the air as silver and plateware were sorted and polished, fresh flowers cut and arranged in huge crystal vases, and delivery vans came from far and wide to drop off their wares at the tradesman's entrance.

Among the temporary staff hired by Madame for the occasion were two more cooks and a very elderly looking butler, who looked like a vulture in his black suit, his shoulders stooped and scrawny neck emerging from the loose white, heavily starched collar of his shirt.

Best of all, as far as Charlotte and her three room-mates were concerned, was that afternoon classes were cancelled. This was so that they could spend a few hours resting and then the remainder of the time paying special attention to their toilette. In addition, they were allowed to choose an evening dress from their own clothing, instead of having what they should wear dictated to them.

Charlotte chose a pale eau-de-nil sheath of shantung silk, with deeply scooped decolleté front and back, which showed off the smooth silky-skinned swell of her bosom and the proud flawless sweep of her shoulders.

Yolande whistled when she saw her.

Charlotte, who was just fastening a silver filigree chain around her neck, smiled at her friend as she glanced around.

'This is so exciting,' Charlotte said, grinning happily as she began to wind her hair around her fingers and pin it deftly into a chignon. She allowed a few loose tendrils of hair to hang down. The pale blonde tendrils graced her delicate face and neck and softened the otherwise severe hairstyle in a way that she knew became her very well. She took one last look in the mirror, gave a smile of satisfaction, then turned to look at Yolande.

The young Swiss woman was dressed, very simply, in a pale mauve shift with a drop waist. Around her neck, she wore a single strand of pearls.

'Is that what you are going to wear? I thought you would want to dress up more,' Charlotte commented, without thinking. She clapped a hand over her mouth immediately, her eyes widening with shock when she realised how derogatory her comment must have sounded. 'Oh, gosh, I'm sorry, Yolande. I didn't mean . . . That is, you look lovely. As always . . .'

To Charlotte's relief, the young woman didn't look in the least perturbed. Her straight white teeth glinted in the light from the gas lamp as she grinned. 'My choice of clothing for tonight is quite academic,' she said. An unexpected blush touched her rounded, apple cheeks, causing Charlotte to flash her a quizzical look. 'You'll see why, later,' Yolande added, when she caught the way Charlotte was looking at her, 'bearing in mind that this is to be my punishment night.'

All at once Charlotte was contrite. 'Oh, no: not tonight, of all nights,' she exclaimed, looking horrified. 'I cannot believe even Madame could be *that* cruel.'

'Oh, but she could, believe me,' Yolande responded, looking extraordinarily happy for one who was about to be punished,

Charlotte thought. Yolande's eyes glowed with excitement. 'Believe me, Chattie, there is no need to feel sorry for me. I can't wait.'

Yolande disappeared some time before the appointed hour, telling the other three girls that she would see them at dinner. Surprisingly, Charlotte thought, glancing at Sanchia and Adèle, none of her room-mates seemed at all perturbed by this. But she was. She felt an unaccountable gnawing at her stomach. Something unusual was afoot and it was clear to her that the rest of her fellow students shared a secret that she was not party to.

When the three remaining girls all trooped into the dining room, some three-quarters of an hour later, Charlotte was the last to notice that Yolande was already there, waiting for them. A handful of guests had already arrived and were milling about the room, chattering and sipping drinks.

As she glanced around, Charlotte noticed that clusters of candles were set in silver candelabra about the room. Slender and pale ivory in colour, the candles glowed and sent out darts of pale yellow light that glanced off gleaming silver and ice-perfect crystal glassware, lending a very luxurious, almost decadent atmosphere to the surroundings.

With a sigh of pleasure, Charlotte accepted a tall flute of champagne from the tray of a passing waitress, then glanced around. After a moment her contented gaze alighted on the seated figure of Yolande. Immediately, her expression froze.

With wrists and ankles bound with purple ribbon, Yolande was seated, stark naked, on a high-backed wooden chair.

Frozen to the spot in disbelief, Charlotte stared and stared.

It was clear to her now that this public display was Yolande's punishment. And no matter how horrified Charlotte felt – especially when she allowed her curious gaze to travel down the length of Yolande's torso to alight on the pouch of pink feminine flesh, clearly visible between her parted thighs – it was clear that her young friend didn't share her consternation.

There was no denying that the radiant smile on Yolande's face, though totally at variance with her shaming position, told its own story.

Just as Charlotte was about to make a move toward Yolande, to offer some kind of consolation, Madame's voice rang out. The sound of it was clear and true as she invited everyone to take their places at the table.

'Apart from Yolande, of course,' Madame said, flashing a glance at the young Swiss woman who sat red-faced but radiant. 'There will be time enough after dinner to enjoy our evening's entertainment,' she added, her gaze travelling across the faces of her guests back to the seated figure of Yolande, who glowed with anticipation. One or two men and women who hovered close to Yolande pulled wry faces. 'Please, my friends,' Madame said to them, smiling broadly for once, 'do not let eagerness rule you. Remember, the more drawn-out the anticipation of an event, the more rewarding the final pleasure.'

Murmurs of agreement and approval ran around the room and one by one, or in small groups, the guests began to drift away from the seated figure of Yolande and toward the heavily-laden dining table.

With a final glance over her shoulder at her friend, Charlotte reluctantly joined the others at the table and took her seat. It was no little consolation when she discovered that she had been placed next to Max Spieler. With a grateful sigh, she picked up the heavy damask napkin which lay next to her place-setting and laid it carefully across her lap. Then she turned her head and caught Max smiling down at her.

Inside, she glowed with pleasure. Thanks to Max's easy-going charm, the evening ahead seemed just a fraction less of an ordeal.

Chapter Eight

As the evening progressed, Charlotte might have been forgiven for thinking that this dinner party was no different to the many others she had attended with her parents. The food, wine and conversation that circulated the table were excellent. And the warmth from the flickering fire, combined with the rush of lustful heat she felt whenever Max Spieler's arm or thigh happened to brush hers, served to urge her toward a state of heightened awareness.

All in all, she couldn't help wondering when she had last felt quite this relaxed and happy.

After her dessert plate had been cleared away and a cup of rich mocha coffee placed in front of her, she reclined back in her chair and let out a sigh of contentment.

'Happy, my sweet?' Max asked. He glanced sideways at her, treating her to one of his rare smiles. The smile touched his eyes, making them sparkle invitingly like the ocean and forming endearing crinkles at the outer edges.

'Very,' Charlotte murmured, linking her fingers together and stretching her hands out in front of her, palms outwards. 'The food was superb. Especially the truffles in aspic. I feel I ought to go to the kitchen and offer my compliments to the chef.'

She dimpled as she smiled back at Max. Then she stretched a little, arching then straightening her spine before making herself even more comfortable on the dining chair. Her very actions made it obvious that, despite what she'd said about speaking to Bad Alpendorf's cook, she had no real intention of moving. Though her legs were crossed, she appeared very relaxed as she lounged carelessly in the chair. And, as she reclined against the padded leather back of the dining chair and shuffled her bottom further forward on the seat, the hem of her dress became rucked up.

Just as she put a hand to her skirt to smooth it down to her knees, Max Spieler stopped her by placing his hand on top of her own. A tingle of excitement ran up Charlotte's arm when he touched her. It started at the tips of her fingers and seemed to end at the roots of her hair.

'Please do not cover up those pretty thighs,' he murmured, squeezing her hand. 'It gives me such pleasure to look at them.'

Charlotte gave him a pert smile in return but, just as she was about to offer him a cheeky retort, an unfamiliar voice came from her right-hand side. 'I should think not; I have been admiring those legs all evening.'

At the sound of the voice, Charlotte whipped her head around. The person who complimented her was a dark-haired young man. He appeared to be only a few years older than she, Charlotte estimated. And now she recalled that he had spent the entire meal conversing with the woman seated at the other side of him. Consequently, Charlotte had hardly bothered to acknowledge his existence. Now though, as she turned to look properly at him, she felt a faint flicker of interest.

He was as dark and swarthy as Max Spieler was fair. His eyes, which were framed by long, thick lashes, were the colour of acorns and were set in a face that seemed to have been carved by a master sculptor. His brow was high, his cheekbones equally so, the hollows beneath deep and shadowy. As Charlotte gazed in dumb admiration at him, she realised the only thing which prevented his countenance from appearing quite girlish was a strong jaw and chin, both of which bore the obvious blue-black hue of five o'clock shadow.

The effect made him look rather like a gangster, she mused with girlish delight. She recalled seeing photographs recently of an Italian-American, Al Capone. They had started appearing in newspapers and magazines with increasing regularity and were accompanied by lurid stories of his exploits. By all accounts, the man was a ruthless gangland racketeer, who had so far managed to elude capture by the New York authorities.

'You remind me of Al Capone,' she said to the stranger,

voicing her wayward thoughts. She was immediately embarrassed by her lack of sophistication. And equally so by her overactive imagination.

To her relief, the young man responded with a burst of laughter that was rich and throaty. Like Beaujolais running down a drain, she mused in delight, her creativity heightened by several glasses of wine and one of cognac.

'I promise you, I am no gangster,' he said when he had finished laughing. 'You can consider me a friend.' He held out a hand to her. His fingers were long and artistic, with perfectly shaped nails and half-moons that appeared very pale in contrast to the swarthiness of his skin. Equally, when he followed his words with a smile, Charlotte noticed how white and even his teeth were.

It occurred to her, right at that moment, that there were a number of visual similarities between this man and Sanchia, which were no doubt the cause of her immediate attraction to him, she reasoned. The comparison she made prompted her to ask him if he was Spanish.

'No, oh, dear me, no!' he exclaimed with a look of mock-horror. Then he smiled again. 'Do not worry, little bird, I am not really offended by your assumption. But my parentage is Italian, not Spanish. My name is Eduardo, by the way.'

Charlotte couldn't help grinning at him as she shook his hand. In a short space of time and with only a few words, he had managed to totally disarm her.

'I am Charlotte,' she told him. 'Or you can call me –'

'I shall continue to call you "little bird", if you don't mind,' Eduardo interrupted. 'I think it suits you.'

Intrigued, Charlotte felt compelled to ask him what sort of bird she reminded him of. She knew she was flirting shamelessly now, but felt unaccountably carefree. Even the knowledge that Max was seated at the other side of her, eavesdropping on her conversation with the young Italian, did nothing to dampen her enthusiasm.

'A dove, I think,' he said, with barely a moment's hesitation. His eyes dropped to a point somewhere below her chin. 'With breasts like those, I could hardly compare you to any other bird. The dove has a magnificent chest, you know, and is extremely delicate and beautiful.'

Charlotte blushed as she tried her hardest to acknowledge his compliment gracefully. To her relief, their conversation was interrupted by the sound of Madame clapping her hands together briskly.

'Ladies and gentlemen,' Madame said, her voice sounding uncharacteristically high-pitched and tinged with excitement, 'I hope you have all enjoyed your meal.' She paused as there came a general rumbling of approbation from around the table. 'In that case,' she went on, when the rumble died down, 'it is my further pleasure to invite you to sample this evening's entertainment.' She pushed back her chair and rose majestically to her feet. 'My friends,' she announced, waving a careless hand toward the opposite end of the room, 'I give you – Yolande!'

Having forgotten all about her young friend for the duration of the meal, Charlotte now experienced a lurching sensation inside.

A hushed silence followed Madame's pronouncement. Then, all at once, the sound of chair-legs scraping on the floor was echoed all around the table as everyone appeared to get up at the same time. Feeling mortified on Yolande's behalf, Charlotte deliberately hung back. She had no desire to witness the spectacle of her friend being ogled by a dozen strangers.

'Will you not join me?' a softly accented voice asked. It belonged to Eduardo.

As Charlotte glanced up at him, she noticed that he was once again holding out his hand to her.

'Come along, child,' Max Spieler prompted, sounding quite stern. 'It is not good to keep one of our guests waiting.'

Under the duress of the two men's urging, Charlotte accepted Eduardo's hand and allowed him to pull her from her seat. She felt a little unsteady, she realised, cursing herself for drinking so much. As she teetered slightly on her heels, so she felt Eduardo's arm slide around her waist to steady her.

He was wearing a loose dark suit, tailored in a rich fabric. And as he continued to hold her steady, Charlotte noticed how hard and muscular his body felt beneath the loose clothing. Now they were both standing, she also realised that Eduardo was not nearly as tall as Max. Even so, he was still an inch or so taller than her, despite the fact that she was wearing heels.

Hardly able to take her eyes off Eduardo's face, Charlotte managed to flash a glance toward the opposite end of the room. To her dismay, she noticed that Yolande was currently being pawed by a couple of the older men and one of the women – a plump, dark, matronly type in an emerald-green gown that appeared far too tight for her ample figure.

'Oh, poor Yolande. Max, can't you do something to stop them?' Charlotte implored.

'Stop them?' Max raised his eyebrows a fraction. 'Why should I try to stop them?'

'Because this treatment of her is inhumane, that's why,' Charlotte said. With a fierce wrench, she pulled herself away from Eduardo's grasp. 'If you won't do something to stop it, then I will!'

She felt her heart pounding as she raced to the other end of the room. Just as she came within a foot or so of Yolande, firm hands grasped her round the waist and lifted her from the floor.

'No you don't, young lady,' Max growled in her ear. 'Your friend has consented to provide this evening's entertainment. Would you deny her and our guests their fun?' He put her down carefully but kept a tight hold on her.

'She consented?' Charlotte breathed in amazement. 'Are you telling me that Yolande wanted to do this? Yolande!' She turned her head and looked back at her friend. Her steady gaze implored Yolande to glance up.

'Yes, Chattie?' Yolande responded calmly. She had one man's hand on her breast and the other man's hands between her legs. The woman, meanwhile, was caressing her bared stomach. Allowing her head to drop back, Yolande arched her spine voluptuously and sighed with pleasure. 'More,' she breathed encouragingly, as though she had already forgotten about Charlotte. 'More . . .'

All Charlotte could do was stare in amazement at her friend. It was obvious, even to the most naive of people, that Yolande was actually enjoying the attention given to her. Her face bore a blissful smile and her nipples were hard and distended. It was clearly not the reaction of someone who felt distressed.

'Oh – I – er – nothing,' Charlotte mumbled lamely, while doubting that Yolande was even listening to her any more. With an overwhelming sense of defeat, she sank into the nearest empty place, which happened to be at the end of one of the long sofas.

A smiling Eduardo made himself comfortable on the arm of the sofa, while Max squatted in front of her.

'You just do not understand yet, do you, child?' Max said. He was smiling gently at her.

'Understand what – that you're all barbarians?' Charlotte retorted. She felt that her response could have been more ardent but, in all honesty, Yolande's wanton behaviour had rather taken the wind out of her sails. 'I do not . . . cannot . . . understand the point of this place,' she added after a moment, when Max simply continued to gaze in silence at her. 'I mean, the rules at Bad Alpendorf are so strange and the morals of you people . . .' She finished on an incredulous note.

'Morals, eh?' Max's gentle laughter was echoed by that of Eduardo. 'Do you hear that, my friend? This young lady talks of morals, and yet they hardly seemed to matter a couple of days ago when she let me watch her behaving in a very intimate fashion with her friend over there.' Max shot a fleeting glance at Sanchia who, Charlotte noticed with a sinking feeling, appeared to be enjoying the attentions of two of the male guests immensely.

Max's mocking retort set Charlotte aflame with mortification. 'That was . . . different,' she stuttered, remembering the incident he referred to only too well. 'That was . . .'

'It was you acting on your desires instead of your morals,' Max pointed out in an ironic tone.

'No.' Charlotte shook her head defiantly.

'Yes,' Max insisted. 'Now, to prove my point, my sweet. If I were to run my hand up your thigh, like so. And slide my fingers beneath the leg of your panties, like so. And caress your rude little clit, like so . . .'

'No. Oh, stop, stop!' Charlotte was horrified by his actions and tried to push his hand away, but to no avail.

With her fingers clamped firmly around his wrist, she tried not to squirm as his fingers stroked insolently at the swollen flesh between her thighs. Yet all she succeeded in doing by protesting so vehemently, it seemed, was to attract the attention of some of the other guests. While she tried to deny the way Max aroused her so easily, she burned with fury and indignation as one or two of the guests ogled her and made lewd comments.

Despite the way she pushed at his hand, Max refused to stop caressing her. 'Do not try to play the innocent maiden with me,' he said thickly, his fingers rubbing mercilessly up and down her cleft. He nodded at the young man seated on the arm of the sofa beside her. 'Eduardo, would you be so good as to pull up Charlotte's dress? I would like you to see for yourself the effect I am having on her.'

Eduardo smiled. 'It would be my pleasure.'

Helpless against the erotic whims of the two men, Charlotte whimpered with shame as the young Italian began to draw her skirt up over her thighs. Her attempts at pushing his hands away were hopelessly ineffectual, particularly when, with a growl of annoyance, Max caught both her wrists with his free hand and clamped them firmly together.

'Stop this ridiculous behaviour at once, Charlotte!' he warned her in a low voice. 'Or I shall be forced to find even more ways to humiliate you.'

'More ways?' Charlotte gasped in amazement. 'Do you not think this is bad enough?'

As she spoke she glanced down to her lap, where the pale flesh of her thighs above her garters seemed to gleam like alabaster. Under the insubstantial crotch of her white silk cami-knickers she could clearly see the outline of Max's knuckles as his fingers stroked her sex. And to her shame, she couldn't help noticing how the silken fabric between her open thighs appeared to absorb the moisture her body produced, resulting in a damp stain that was clearly visible.

A rush of warm breath touched the side of her neck. 'Please, let me see you,' Eduardo urged, his fingertips drifting to the tops of her inner thighs. 'I want so much to touch . . . to explore . . .' His husky voice became more ardent, his accent thickening, giving away the extent of his desire.

As he spoke, lust flickered suddenly in Charlotte's belly, the heat of it licking at her womb. Yet, with a surge of defiance, she tried to quell her arousal.

'No, I will not let you do this to me!' she cried, squirming again. Her wrists chafed where Max held them tightly and her clitoris pulsed remorselessly, despite the humiliation she felt.

To her surprise, Max's grip around her wrist slackened. 'If that is how you feel, then go,' he said, releasing her abruptly. In the same instant, he withdrew his hand from between her thighs. 'Go on. Get up,' he insisted, tugging down the hem of her dress. 'Pack your bags and say goodbye to your friends. I will ask one of the groundsmen to drive you to the station.' He spoke flatly, with no hint of emotion.

In stunned silence, Charlotte stared at him. Max's words were as shocking as his expression. He appeared so cold and uncompromising that her eyes immediately filled with tears. All at once, she realised that the last thing she wanted to do was leave Bad Alpendorf. For many reasons. Not least that Cadell would be so angry with her that he would probably call off their engagement and because . . .

. . . *I don't feel ready to leave Max yet*, she admitted to herself, the realisation taking her by surprise.

It seemed inconceivable to her that this strange, enigmatic man should have somehow managed to capture something deep and passionate within her. Yet he had, she realised, as she gazed back at him. And it was with a sinking heart that she understood she had been thwarted: not by Max's intransigence, but by her own wanton desires.

She wanted to stay. If she did nothing at all with the rest of her life she knew that, right now, she had to discover all about herself and to learn everything Max had to teach her. Frustrating though it seemed to her, it was as though she were starving and only Max held the key to the larder.

'I don't want to leave,' she admitted wearily. 'I am not ready yet.' With a deep sigh, she shrugged her shoulders.

Immediately, Max's expression softened. 'I agree, you are not ready yet, my sweet girl,' he said. 'You still have a lot to learn.'

'I know.' Charlotte hung her head in shame. She felt

ridiculous. And, for once, she was the cause of her own humiliation.

'Will you allow me to teach you?' Max asked. 'No matter what that teaching might entail?' He raised his eyebrows inquiringly.

For a moment Charlotte held her breath. He was asking a lot of her. But what real choice did she have? If she wanted to stay at Bad Alpendorf – if she wanted to learn about herself and about true sensuality – then what good could possibly come of denying whatever Max asked of her?

Slowly, she nodded. 'Yes,' she whispered, her gaze still downcast.

There followed a moment of silence, while she continued to battle with herself, then all at once she felt a surge of her old indomitable spirit. Lifting her chin defiantly, she looked him straight in the eye. 'Yes, Max,' she repeated, sounding more resolute this time. 'I want you to teach me everything you feel I should know. I agree to put myself in your hands. But please,' she said quickly, feeling compelled to add a footnote to her uncharacteristic compliance, 'do not abuse my faith in you. I place my trust in you, Max. And I will do whatever you say. But, I beg of you, do not ask more of me than you feel I could cope with. Can you promise me that?'

For a moment, Max regarded her levelly, his blue-eyed gaze holding hers as he tapped his lips with his forefinger in a contemplative manner.

'So,' he responded at last, 'you think you are in a position to extract promises from me, do you?' His expression remained stern for a moment; then it crumbled, allowing a twinkle to appear in his eyes. 'Of course you can be assured of me, my sweet child,' he continued, his tone and expression softening considerably. Leaning forward, he placed a light kiss on Charlotte's lips. 'I would never abuse your trust. That I can promise wholeheartedly.'

The relief Charlotte felt was almost tangible. It had worried her greatly to think she had made Max angry with her. His disappointment seemed more than she could bear. And, after a short while, when Max suggested that the three of them – himself, Charlotte and Eduardo – might be more comfortable

111

in his study, away from prying eyes, Charlotte agreed straightaway.

After sharing a brief word with his sister, Max led the way to his private domain.

It was the first time Charlotte had been there and, as she glanced around the small but hospitable room, she realised that the shelves groaning with books were the only things that bore any similarity to the décor of her father's study. Everything else, from the comfortable modern furnishings to the contemporary cream and eau-de-nil paint-scheme, spoke of stylish informality.

As soon as they entered the room, Max switched off the main light and crossed the darkened room to turn on a couple of wall lamps instead. The lamps were concealed by upside-down triangles of white glass, decorated with a pale green geometric pattern. He kept the lighting low so that just one portion of the room was bathed in a pale glow. Beneath the lamps sat a long divan-style sofa, covered in a pistachio velveteen fabric. And in front of the sofa stood an equally long low table, made of light-coloured natural wood.

'Please sit,' Max said, gesturing invitingly toward the sofa. 'Make yourselves comfortable, while I pour us all a drink.'

Charlotte felt she should refuse any more alcohol, but she didn't want to argue with Max again so soon after they had called a truce. And besides, she thought, as she made herself comfortable on the sofa next to Eduardo, perhaps a little more Dutch courage wouldn't go amiss. She was certain that Max hadn't invited her and Eduardo here simply to talk.

It didn't take her long to discover that her assumption was absolutely correct.

'My dear Charlotte,' Max said, placing a brandy balloon on the table in front of her, 'do you not feel a little uncomfortable in such a restrictive garment? Would you not prefer to slip it off, so that you can relax properly?'

Realising that this must be some sort of cue, Charlotte felt a rush of nervousness. Even though her heart was hammering, she acquiesced to Max's suggestion. Then she stood up, turning her back to Max so that he could lower her zip. The sequined dress slithered to the floor to pool around her feet, leaving her clad only in her white cami-knickers, pale grey stockings and silver shoes. As a breath of cool night air glanced across her almost-bare shoulders, Charlotte shivered.

'I shall light the fire,' Max said, leaving her where she stood – awkward and unsure – and striding over to the large brick fireplace at the far end of the room.

Like everything else, Max's skill at lighting a fire proved admirable. Within minutes, the pile of logs in the grate was alight, sending long tongues of yellow and orange flame and a faint plume of purplish-grey smoke flickering up the chimney. Straightaway, the room was filled with the strong fragrance of pine, which reminded Charlotte of childhood games of hide and seek in the forest her parents had sometimes taken her to.

While Max had been concentrating on lighting the fire, Charlotte hadn't moved a muscle. Now, if she gazed in one direction she could see Max straightening up and smoothing the creases from his trousers as he uncoiled his long lithe body. And if she looked a little to her left, her vision was filled with the sharply contrasting image of Eduardo, who looked as sleek and handsome as a panther, reclining with ease on the divan.

Instinctively, Charlotte knew that both men intended to have her that evening. And, though she felt nervous at the prospect, she also felt excited and incredibly aroused. There was no denying, she mused, feeling a desirous warmth flood her lower belly, that being the object of desire of two very different but equally attractive men had a certain and highly erotic appeal.

All at once, she felt very grown-up. Possibly even sophisticated, she thought, as she considered how she must look to them. As a direct contradiction to her unsure state, her stance was proud: shoulders thrown back, ample breasts jutting forward, stomach pulled in until it was almost flat. And there was nothing about her underthings to shame her. Her cami-knickers were of the finest quality: hand-sewn and edged with the purest rose-patterned Chantilly lace. Even her silk stockings had a matching lace trim and were secured at mid-thigh by grey velvet garters.

When one looks this good, there is nothing to be afraid of, Charlotte told herself firmly. Consequently, as Max approached her with his customary loping stride, she found herself returning his appreciative gaze with an enigmatic half-smile.

'Warm enough for you now, my sweet?' Max asked her. As he spoke, he ran his hands over her shoulders and down her arms; he took her hands lightly in his. 'Come,' he added, as she nodded, 'sit between myself and Eduardo. The poor boy must be feeling quite neglected, by now.' As he spoke, he walked backwards, moving closer to the sofa and drawing her with him.

Max sat down, leaving a space between himself and Eduardo. Only when he nodded meaningfully at the space between them did Charlotte hesitate for a moment. She remained standing, her trembling knees barely brushing the soft velveteen edge of the sofa as she gazed down at the two men.

All at once, her nervousness was dispelled as a powerful feeling of self-confidence assailed her. Only now did she truly realise that she wanted to enjoy whatever it was the two men had to teach her and, equally, that she had the ability to give pleasure in return.

'Sit,' Max urged her again, patting the space beside him.

With a slight incline of her head, Charlotte turned and sat, executing each movement as gracefully as possible. She had yet to learn how to act in a more seductive manner, she realised. Although that would no doubt come with time. For now, it suited her to appear as composed and relaxed about the situation as she possibly could.

Moving to cross her legs, as she habitually did when she sat, she was surprised when Eduardo stilled her movement with his hand.

'Please don't,' he implored her gently.

'I agree with Eduardo,' Max said. 'I think we would all derive a lot more pleasure if you were to sit with your legs slightly apart.'

'But that's so indecorous,' Charlotte protested half-heartedly. Amusement twinkled in her eyes, along with excitement, as she allowed her thighs to slip apart slightly. 'I don't know what my mother would say.'

114

'Perhaps thinking of your mother is not a good idea, right at this moment, my dear,' Max countered, sounding equally amused. 'In fact, it might be more acceptable if we were to continue your education along a literary vein, for now.'

To Charlotte's surprise, Max sprang from his seat and crossed the room to one of the bookshelves. After a moment's deliberation, he selected a weighty-looking tome and returned to sit beside her again.

'Here,' he said, placing the book on her lap, 'you might enjoy leafing through this. And you too, Eduardo,' he added with a pointed glance at the young man seated to her left.

The book felt heavy on Charlotte's thighs. It was large but quite thin and covered by cracked brown tooled leather. On the front, in gold leaf, the book bore an intriguing title: *Answers To A Maiden's Prayer*.

Overcome by curiosity, Charlotte opened the book and flicked over the flyleaf. She had no idea what to expect from the contents, but her gaze became immediately transfixed by the photograph on the first page. It depicted a young slender woman with long fair hair, together with a representation of the pagan god, Pan. The location was a clearing in a wood, or a forest of some kind, in which the young woman was kneeling, naked, on a bed of leaves in front of Pan.

Though the picture appeared at first glance entirely innocent, apart from the girl's nakedness, it gradually dawned on Charlotte that all was not what it seemed. And, as she studied the picture more closely and realised that her first impression had been correct, she felt a gathering of nervous excitement inside her.

'What do you feel when you look at that picture, my sweet?' Max prompted her gently.

Charlotte was quick to reply. 'I see a young girl, kneeling naked in a forest in front of Pan.' She glanced hastily at Max as he made a disparaging sound. 'What is the matter?'

'I didn't ask you what you could see,' he said to her, frowning slightly, 'I asked you what you *felt*.'

There was something in the way he spoke, and the dark, intense way he looked at her that turned Charlotte's insides to water.

'I – I feel quite disturbed by it,' she replied at last, after studying the picture again for a few minutes.

'In what way disturbed?' This time it was Eduardo who prompted her.

'Well,' she murmured, glancing briefly at the young Italian before returning her attention to the book, 'there is something strangely atmospheric about this scene. I can't quite put my finger on it but . . . Oh, just a minute, look at the expression in Pan's eyes.'

'Yes?' The two men spoke in unison.

Charlotte took a deep breath, considering her choice of words carefully before replying. 'He looks sort of . . . I don't know . . . lascivious, I suppose. As though he intends to do something . . . um . . . sexual to the girl.' She stumbled over her words, feeling a blush steal over her. It had just dawned on her that the atmosphere that linked the three of them, though they were seated beside each other quite innocently, seemed charged with erotic tension.

'That's very good, my dear,' Max said encouragingly. 'Carry on.'

'Well,' Charlotte continued, returning her attention to the photograph, 'I can't help thinking that perhaps Pan is intending to do something to the girl. To ravish her, perhaps?' She ended on an inquiring note and, when she glanced at Max, she couldn't help noticing that he looked amused. 'Was it something I said?' she muttered, surprised at how irritated she felt. It was like being back at school again; forced to feel hopelessly out of her depth, when all she ever strove to do was achieve the right answer.

'No, please, Charlotte, do not be so sensitive,' Max chided her gently. 'There is no right or wrong answer when one is describing one's feelings.'

'But, Max,' Eduardo interrupted, 'I must ask Charlotte why she feels that the most obvious solution is that Pan intends to ravish the girl. Tell me, my little bird,' he added, turning his attention to her, 'do you believe that sensuality is all about sexual intercourse?'

'Isn't it?' Charlotte shot back, unable to disguise her amazement, nor her embarrassment that a complete stranger

116

should talk to her of such intimate matters.

'Not at all.' Eduardo and Max spoke in unison again. It was as though the two men were actually one person, Charlotte thought, wondering if perhaps all the alcohol she had consumed that night had addled her brain.

'Then what is it about, might I ask?' she demanded. Feeling very much out of her depth, she pouted and stuck out her chin in an obstinate manner.

To her annoyance, the two men laughed, though their laughter bore no trace of malice, only genuine amusement.

'I fail to see what is so funny about . . . about sex,' she responded crossly.

Putting a restraining hand on hers, Max urged her to turn the page.

When Charlotte did as he asked, her eyes widened with shock. The sight that met her eyes was so appalling, so degrading, that she slammed the book shut hastily.

'I take it you feel revolted by that particular scenario,' Max said calmly, taking the book from her. 'Might I ask why?'

All Charlotte could do was shudder. 'I can't imagine why any woman would want to do such a vile thing,' she said, after a moment.

'Vile? You call giving pleasure vile?' Max pursed his lips.

'Pleasure for him perhaps,' Charlotte responded, trying desperately to banish the image of Pan's stiff member from her mind's eye. In the picture, the beast's thick penis was thrust deep into the mouth of the young girl, who continued to kneel at his cloven-hoofed feet.

'And why not for her, too?' Eduardo asked. 'Do you not believe a woman could enjoy touching and tasting such an intimate part of a man?'

'No, I do not,' Charlotte said firmly. 'There is only one place for a man's penis.' There followed a collective sigh from the men either side of her. 'I wouldn't expect either of you two to agree,' Charlotte went on, crossing her arms and legs defiantly, 'considering that you are both men. But try asking another woman if I am not right.'

'Just supposing,' Eduardo said after a moment, apparently

117

ignoring her argument, 'that I was to put my head between your thighs and lick your intimate flesh. Would you consider that appalling?'

Charlotte's response to his suggestion was instantaneous and vehement. 'I most certainly would,' she declared. However, it shamed her when a fiercely passionate heat engulfed her pelvis, proving to her that her body had other ideas.

'You look as though you are having second thoughts,' Max said. 'Now, let us just suppose – in the interests of your continuing education, you understand – that we were to allow our young friend here to try what he suggested?'

'No!' Charlotte shot back quickly, sounding horrified. Reacting automatically, she crossed her legs and arms in a resolute and protective manner.

'Are you sure?' Eduardo murmured. As he spoke, he stroked his fingertips delicately along her thigh. 'I promise to stop if you really do not like it.'

'Really, I couldn't allow it,' Charlotte insisted; though her protests sounded feeble, even to her own ears.

'Not even as an experiment? And bearing in mind that you showed no such reticence when Sanchia did exactly the same thing to you,' Max continued. 'As I mentioned before, it would be in the interests of your education. Or was it your intention that you should only take those classes you find wholly acceptable and deny those you do not? Perhaps you can enlighten me, my sweet.'

The hint of irony in Max's voice caused Charlotte to frown. There was no doubt he was challenging her.

The damned man has me backed into a corner and he knows it, she thought, feeling an undeniable ripple of excitement. Well, if he intends to force his will upon me, not physically but perhaps by threatening me with expulsion again if I refuse, perhaps I should not be so hasty as to deny him outright.

Though she didn't realise it, this was all the excuse she needed for abandoning herself to her hidden desires.

'Very well,' she said, giving a deep sigh; it raised her full breasts in such a way that both men were instantly distracted from gazing at her face. 'If you really think I must go along with this appalling practice, in order to improve my education, then I suppose I have no choice . . .'

Chapter Nine

With a hasty sip of her brandy, Charlotte reclined on the divan between Max and Eduardo. She feigned nonchalance as she stretched her arms out either side of her across the back of the sofa, her fingertips delicately entwining in the hair at the nape of each man's neck. She had no idea what to expect, nor if she could handle the consequences of her decision.

So much had happened to her in such a short space of time. Yet sensuality, it seemed to her, was like a never-ending road, one that was full of unexpected twists, steep inclines and deep pot-holes. There was so much she had learnt already, and yet so much that still remained to be discovered. And although she often doubted her capacity to complete the journey without falling by the wayside, looking upon her sexual education as an expedition into the unknown excited her and made her tremble with anticipation.

Her thoughts were arrested by the electric touch of Eduardo's hand on her knee. 'Slide lower in the seat, little bird,' he murmured suggestively, smiling at the way she jumped at his touch. 'Spread your legs. Yes, like that. Perfect.'

Charlotte felt her stomach fluttering as she complied. She held her breath as the young Italian slid his hand up the inside of her thigh. His touch was nothing more sinister than a light caress. It was soothing yet tantalising, causing the downy hairs on her legs to prickle in response to the thrilling sensations it provoked.

Despite her trepidation, Charlotte felt her body respond in a sensual way. Her nipples tightened into hard little buds that peaked insolently through the delicate silk of her camisole, while between her thighs she felt her sex-flesh moistening and becoming engorged.

'Oh!' she gasped as Max lowered one of the straps of her camisole and allowed her nipple to leap out. It was instantly captured by his searching mouth. Her head dropped back and she sighed as he drew the nipple deep into his mouth and began to swirl his tongue temptingly around it.

As he suckled her, Max felt for her other strap, dragging it down her upper arm to bare both her breasts. With a groan of desire, he squashed the full globes together then began to tongue both nipples simultaneously.

Charlotte gave herself up eagerly to the caresses of the two men. Her breasts felt full and heavy in Max's hands, and she whimpered with pleasure as he kneaded and suckled at them. Meanwhile, further down her body, she felt her clitoris tingling and her vagina moistening as Eduardo continued to describe tiny circles on her inner thighs with his fingertips. His caresses felt so close to *that* part of her that she couldn't help shivering with pent-up arousal.

Though part of her dreaded the anticipated intimacy, she ached for him to touch her. And it was only with the greatest restraint that she managed to prevent herself from grabbing Eduardo's hand and thrusting it obscenely between her legs. Instead of behaving in such a wanton manner, she chose to raise her hips slightly from the sofa, to make a silent yet obvious offering of herself to him.

Eduardo was quick to catch on. And eager to oblige her, it seemed. With deft fingers, he unfastened each of the three seed-pearl buttons that kept the crotch of her camiknickers joined. As he slid the last one through its loop, Charlotte let out a jagged breath. Her arousal was complete. Her desire for physical gratification seemed the only thing that mattered to her any more.

'Ah, such a delectable fruit: like a ripe fig,' Eduardo exclaimed *sotto voce*, the low growling tone of his accented voice almost causing Charlotte to swoon with lust. 'I ache to taste it.'

She felt her inner thigh muscles quivering as he spread her legs further apart; she sensed him moving from her side to kneel on the floor between her feet. A moment later, his hands slid up under her hips, cupped her buttocks and dragged her lower body to the edge of the sofa. Feeling as helpless as a rag-doll, Charlotte allowed him to position her with the soles of her feet resting on his thighs and her knees splayed wide apart. The wantonness of her pose made her want to cry out with shame, and yet she felt her arousal soar to even greater heights as she watched him gaze with adoration upon her wilfully displayed body.

'First I will sample the juicy outer parts,' Eduardo mumbled, pressing his lips to the plump folds of her sex and moving his lips tantalisingly over her desirous flesh. 'I will lick and nibble them, like so.'

The touch of his mouth on such an intimate part of her and his lascivious comments sent a keen jolt of arousal through Charlotte, making her jerk her hips.

'Keep still, my pet,' Max urged her soothingly. His hand stroked across her naked breasts as he spoke. 'You will enjoy this, I promise you.'

'Oh, yes, I'm sure of it, too,' Charlotte managed to gasp out as she felt Eduardo's tongue sliding wetly down the cleft between her outer labia. All of a sudden, he spread her vaginal lips apart and drove his tongue deep inside her. 'I . . . Oh . . . Oh . . . Yesss . . . !' His indecent action took her totally by surprise, causing her words to be expelled on a long hiss of desire.

Speared by Eduardo's tongue, Charlotte squirmed. Flames of passion were licking at her insides, their ardent nature not dampened one iota by Eduardo's tongue as he began to swirl it tantalisingly around the outer rim of her vagina. She felt herself straining toward his mouth, her sensitive flesh tingling, her inner muscles contracting rhythmically, almost as though they were trying to seize onto his tongue and hold it fast.

Through eyes glazed with lust, Charlotte concentrated on gazing at Max. The deep blue pools of his eyes beguiled her, held her, prevented her from giving into the desire to let her eyelids droop under the weight of her arousal. She was in a trance, a state of such fierce and unrestrained ardour that she could no longer protest against anything the two men might care to do to her.

She spread her legs as far apart as she could, then arched

her back. Keeping her gaze locked with Max's, she cupped her breasts in her hands and offered them up to his lips.

'Tell us what you want,' Max murmured beguilingly to her. 'Voice your needs, my sweet, and everything you desire shall be yours.'

Charlotte hesitated for the merest fraction. 'I want – I want you to pleasure me with your mouth,' she stammered, her voice harsh and jagged with lust. 'I want you both to lick me. Lick all of me. Oh, I want so much to feel the passion inside me explode.'

'You want to come, is that it?' Max asked. He sounded slightly amused, though his eyes were not smiling. They were dark with the desire he so obviously felt for her. 'Tell me, my little one, would you like to reach your crisis?'

'Yes, oh, yes, please,' Charlotte cried, almost beside herself with arousal.

'Then say it,' Max insisted, his tone gentle but uncompromising. 'Tell me *exactly* what you want. There is no need for false modesty here. This is just between the three of us.'

'Oh, damn you, Max!' Just for a moment Charlotte felt like hitting him, such was the frustrating way he toyed with her. 'I want to come. I want to . . . jolly well . . . come!'

Not for the first time, she rued her own strict moral code. She wished she wasn't so strait-laced. She wanted so much to be able to scream and curse and put a voice to the myriad salacious thoughts that filled her mind.

Max couldn't help laughing at the frustration which so obviously lay behind her response. 'Ah, my poor little Charlotte,' he teased as he stroked her breasts and began to tug at her nipples, drawing them out and pinching them lightly until they were fully distended. 'You really must learn to control that temper of yours.'

He glanced away from her to the young man kneeling between her splayed thighs. 'I think, under the circumstances, we should let her have her way this time, Eduardo,' Max said. 'Perhaps it would not be wise to provoke her too much.'

There was a twinkle in Max's eyes as he spoke and, in the next instant, he slid his hands down her torso and over her silk-covered belly, to cup her bared pubic mound. Then, to Charlotte's mortification, his fingertips spread outwards, splaying her outer lips apart in an insolent and degrading fashion, revealing the full extent of her arousal.

'Lick her clitoris, my good man,' he said to Eduardo. 'Can you not see how eagerly that rude little nub of flesh yearns for your tongue?'

Charlotte had hardly a moment to offer up any kind of protest. Not that she was at all sure she was capable of protesting any more. So what if her most intimate flesh was spread wide open for both men to see and to touch? At this moment she felt past caring. She just wanted . . . needed . . .

'Ah, oh, my God!' She screamed aloud as Eduardo bent his head and she felt the first flickering touch of his tongue on the distended bud of her clitoris. She jerked her hips wildly as he continued to lick her but, in a flash, his hands came up and held her hips fast, forcing her to yield to the demanding caresses of his lips and tongue.

Her response was instantaneous: a wildfire rush of all-encompassing pleasure that obliterated every thought, every other sensation.

Such was her enjoyment of the moment that she did not hear the door to Max's study open, nor the whispered comments of the people who had entered the room just in time to witness her display of wild and shameless abandon.

The first sensation of which Charlotte became aware, as she continued to ride the high-rolling wave of pleasure, was something slick and hard nudging at her tongue. Her mouth was already open in a silent scream, and several inches of the object had slid between her lips before she realised something strange was happening to her. With eyelids fluttering open, she gazed blearily for a moment at something she did not recognise.

A split second later, her eyes widened when she realised that she was staring directly at a man's groin. The pubic hair was dark and wiry, very profuse. At the same time, a strong musky odour assailed her nostrils. But what horrified her the most was the realisation that she had his penis in her mouth.

All at once, the man thrust his pelvis forward, his stiff

member nudging at the back of Charlotte's throat, making her gag.

'Ugh – glugh!'

Charlotte couldn't believe what was happening to her. With all her might, she pushed hard at the torso in front of her and, at the same time, wrenched her head away. When she glanced up, her hand automatically coming up to rub her throat, she found herself staring into the face of a portly middle-aged man.

'How – how dare you?' she spat at him, thoroughly revolted. Swiping the back of her hand across her mouth, she narrowed her eyes and tried to inject as much venom and loathing as possible into her response.

To her annoyance, the man merely gave a mirthless chuckle. As his lips curved into a sardonic smile, he wrapped his fingers around the stiff shaft of his penis and stroked his swollen glans across her cheek, leaving a sticky trail of viscous fluid on her soft skin.

Hardly able to believe the man's contemptible behaviour, Charlotte recoiled and treated him to a baleful glower. She rubbed hard at the patch on her cheek; the skin felt tight where his fluid had dried onto it. The sight of the bulging plum-like head of his penis revolted her, as did his obvious delight at being able to humiliate her so easily.

'Shame on you, Max,' the man said as he continued to rub himself in an unselfconscious fashion. 'You haven't got this one properly trained.'

His accent revealed English middle-class origins. And, purely from his over-indulged appearance and pompous manner, Charlotte leapt to the assumption that he was a banker. She had met many men of the same ilk at her father's house and was quick to spot them, even in a crowd.

Though she still felt revolted by him, the thought brought a sardonic smile to her lips.

'Be fair, Samuel,' Max responded evenly. 'Charlotte is our latest acquisition. There is a lot she has yet to learn.'

'I should say so,' the man countered. 'I tell you what, Max, leave her alone with me for an hour or so. I could give her a few lessons.' He laughed crudely.

As Charlotte cringed and deliberately averted her gaze from

the obscene sight of the stranger's stiff member and supercilious expression, she couldn't help noticing how Max's previously genial demeanour now took on a hard edge.

'That is enough,' Max said sharply. 'I do not remember inviting you to my private quarters. Please go.' There was no hint of friendliness in his voice. With a sigh of displeasure, he turned and pulled up the straps of Charlotte's camisole, covering her breasts.

'Ah-ha, do I detect a hint of possessiveness?' the man countered. Far from appearing affronted, he seemed amused by Max's hostility toward him. With a twisted smile, he turned to the two other men standing beside him. 'What do you think, chaps – could it be that good old Max has finally fallen victim to his own success? A little too big for his boots, tonight, wouldn't you say?'

Charlotte's anxious glance flashed from one faceless and colourless man to the other. As a pair, the crude Englishman's companions were quite unremarkable; it riled her greatly that they should deem themselves judge and jury, nodding their agreement and muttering derogatory comments about Max. How dare they try to ridicule a wonderful man like Max, when they themselves were obviously nothing special?

For a moment, her indignation on Max's behalf made her forget all about her own embarrassing predicament.

Clearly furious, Max rose up to his full height. His action caused all three interlopers to take a couple of steps back. A look of alarm crossed their faces. Obviously, Charlotte thought, they assumed Max was close to striking them.

However, he made no move toward them. Instead, he spoke calmly, but with such authority that Charlotte quivered with admiration.

'Get out,' Max said sternly to the three men. 'Make your excuses to my sister and leave this house immediately. I don't ever want to see you here again. Go back to Zurich, all of you. You are no longer welcome in Bad Alpendorf.'

Though Max sounded calm and in control, Charlotte couldn't help noticing how a vein in his temple had begun to throb. Nor could she miss the way he clenched his hands into angry fists at his sides.

'Max, it is all right, really.' Fearful that he might explode with rage, Charlotte leant forward and placed a placatory hand on his arm. To her dismay he shrugged her off.

'Sh, do not try to interfere, little bird,' Eduardo whispered to her. Whipping off his jacket, he draped it across her lap to spare her blushes further. 'Stay calm,' he added, taking her hands in his and squeezing them reassuringly.

One of the men made a disparaging sound. Then their leader, Samuel, appeared to reach a decision. Tucking his penis back inside his trousers, he fastened the buttons on his fly.

'This does not bode well for you, Max Spieler,' he said, without glancing up from his task. 'You know I could report you to the authorities and have this place closed down.' His gaze flickered up to meet Max's stony glare head on. Like a couple of stags with antlers locked, neither man seemed prepared to back down.

'There is no need for that, surely?' Charlotte intervened hastily, deliberately ignoring the warning glances both Max and Eduardo flashed at her. With difficulty, she steeled herself to come out with what she planned to say next. 'Max, you told me yourself that I need to learn certain things. Perhaps now would be the right time . . .'

'It is the right time. Or it was,' Max interrupted her, still sounding angry. 'But they shall have no part in your education. I won't allow it. My friend here offers up only empty threats.' Max paused to glance witheringly at the pompous Englishman who stood directly in front of him. 'He knows as well as I do that he could land himself equally in hot water, were he to try to blackmail me. Believe me, any attempt at intimidation will be at his own peril.' Max flashed another glance at the man, who immediately narrowed his eyes.

'You think you have the upper hand here, Max,' he said tersely, 'but, rest assured, you haven't heard the last of this.' With a final glare at Max and Eduardo, the Englishman turned and glanced at his two friends. 'Come on, chaps, let us leave these people. There is plenty more sport to be had away from this place.'

It galled Charlotte that all three men laughed in a derisory fashion. However, they offered up no further argument and, as soon as they'd left, slamming the door to the study behind them, she let out a sigh of relief.

'What a shame,' Eduardo said eventually, breaking the uncomfortable silence that linked the three of them. 'Our little bird was so enjoying herself. To have her pleasure wrecked by such –'

'They are nothing,' Max cut in, sounding disparaging. He shook his head crossly. 'Ah, but those types are just the sort I have no wish to encourage. The men who come here must have a proper appreciation and respect for our young students.' To Charlotte's surprise and relief, he winked at her. 'You girls are too lovely to suffer at the hands of oafs,' he said.

Glowing with elation at his compliment and reassurance, Charlotte smiled at him. 'My pleasure has not been spoilt,' she told Max. 'Not really. I hope that unfortunate scene was a mere interruption, nothing more.'

At such a bold pronouncement, Max and Eduardo both laughed. 'Ah, such a trooper, as the English would say,' Eduardo teased her. As he spoke he slid his jacket off Charlotte's lap and allowed his gaze to dwell on the damp pink flesh that now slumbered between her thighs. 'Do you wish to carry on, my little bird?' he asked.

With only a moment's hesitation, Charlotte nodded. 'I do wish it,' she said.

'Then we shall have another cognac to revive us,' Max announced, picking up the bottle and replenishing their glasses. 'After which, Charlotte may return to the classroom, so to speak.'

'And then what happened?' Charlotte's three room-mates were all agog as she related the story of what had transpired in Max's study, after her unfortunate encounter with the loathsome Samuel and his friends. It was well past midnight and all four were clearly exhausted, yet none of them could sleep for the excitement of that evening's events.

Yolande had already described, in great and salacious detail, all that had happened to her that night. She made it clear she had enjoyed every minute of her punishment and hoped that future transgressions would lead to a repeat performance.

'Well,' Charlotte began, thinking back and feeling a tingle of excitement as she did so, 'we drank our brandy and then I learnt how one should properly appreciate the male form.' Her smile was more in the form of a smirk.

'Oh for goodness sake, stop being so childishly obtuse, Charlotte,' Adèle cut in tersely. 'Haven't you ever seen or tasted a man's prick before?'

'Adèle!' Yolande and Sanchia responded in unison.

'No, that's all right,' Charlotte reassured them. She would be damned if she was going to allow the frosty Englishwoman to blight her evening. 'Adèle's question is a valid one and the answer is no, I had never tasted a penis before tonight. Obviously, I had seen one or two before, but I had never had the opportunity to study them in quite so much detail.' She made it sound as though she were talking about a species of rare flower or insect.

Sanchia laughed. 'But now you have satisfied your curiosity – eh, *querida*?' she said, with a devilish twinkle in her eye.

'Quite,' Charlotte responded with a nod. For a moment she shared a conspiratorial look with both the young Spanish woman and Yolande. Then she turned her attention back to Adèle. 'You know, Adèle,' she said, trying to sound nonchalant, 'I should watch yourself, if I were you.'

Adèle's ice-blue eyes narrowed. 'What do you mean?'

'I mean,' Charlotte said, clearly enjoying herself, 'that Max is not all that enamoured of you. It appears that, were it not for Madame, you would have been expelled from Bad Alpendorf well before now.'

'That is utter rubbish!' Adèle retorted, for once appearing to lose some of her usual sang froid. 'Madame adores me.' Tilting her chin in a haughty manner, she began to rake her fingers through her bobbed blonde hair. Her action showed how agitated she really felt.

'Uh-oh, it seems you have struck a nerve there,' Yolande commented sagely, flashing a cheeky grin at Sanchia and Charlotte. She inclined her head in Adèle's direction. 'Some of us need to learn that pride comes before a fall.'

'Quite right, Yolande,' Sanchia interrupted. 'Adèle, you know as well as any of us that Madame adores no one. Rather, it is other people who adore Madame.'

'Then I am the exception,' Adèle insisted. With a disparaging sigh, she pulled back the covers on her bed and climbed onto it. Then she drew the sheet and blankets up to her chin. 'If you are not all in bed before Madame makes her rounds, you will be the ones in trouble,' she commented rudely. 'I, of course, will once again be the only one in her good books.'

'You are a bitch, Adèle,' Sanchia countered, with a glower. Despite her obvious annoyance, she climbed into her own bed. 'Be sure of one thing, *putanita mia*, one of these days you will get your – how do you English say? – just desserts.'

'Especially if I have anything to do with it,' Charlotte murmured under her breath as she, too, conceded to the rules at Bad Alpendorf and settled herself down for the night.

Silence reigned in the small dormitory and was broken only by the sound of irregular breathing, which presently slowed and transformed into gentle snores. Yet Charlotte found it impossible to sleep.

If it were not bad enough that she still felt elated by all that had transpired between herself, Max and Eduardo, she mused, making herself as comfortable as she could upon the fleecy underblanket, Adèle's continual goading was driving her to the point where she felt she had to retaliate.

But how? she wondered, trying hard not to notice how the fine filaments of the lambswool seemed to tantalise the still-swollen flesh between her thighs. And once she'd worked out exactly how to engineer Adèle's downfall, the next question had to be how soon she could expect to accomplish her mission.

Chapter Ten

The days that followed the evening of the dinner party were bright and clear. Summer was now in full bloom, leading Charlotte to appreciate the singular beauty of her surroundings. Bad Alpendorf was hardly more than a tiny Alpine village, yet it was well populated and consequently always seemed alive with vibrant energy.

One aspect of Charlotte's new regime which she particularly enjoyed was her daily walk, which she usually took with her three room-mates and was always accompanied by Madame. Their favourite route was one which took them through the forest that fringed Bad Alpendorf, skirted the lush green fields populated by dairy herds, and led back through the centre of the village.

On this particular day the four girls were surprised when Madame announced that she would not be able to accompany them on their walk.

'I am expecting a visitor,' she said, appearing slightly miffed by the prospect. 'It is unfortunate but unavoidable. Therefore I must place my trust in you girls and ask you to adhere to our usual route. When walking through the forest, it is imperative that you do not deviate from the path. The forest is very dense in places, and it is easy for someone who does not know it as well as I to become lost.'

'Just like Little Red Riding Hood,' Charlotte giggled, without thinking, and thus earning herself a withering glance from both Madame and Adèle. 'I . . . I mean the part about straying off the path into the forest,' she stammered, feeling suitably idiotic.

With a show of sisterhood, Yolande flung her arm around Charlotte's shoulders and gave her a friendly hug. 'I wonder how many big bad wolves are lurking in the undergrowth,' she joked.

'Quite a number, I would think, if the village men are anything to go by,' Sanchia cut in, flashing both Yolande and Charlotte a huge grin.

Their light-hearted banter only served to make Madame look sterner still. She flashed a warning glance at all of them. 'You will not fraternise with the village men,' she said. 'I forbid it.'

Although her sweeping glance took in all three of them, Charlotte couldn't help noticing how Adèle pretended not to notice that Madame included her in the equation.

'Silly bitch,' Charlotte muttered under her breath, feeling more strongly than ever that the supercilious young Englishwoman should be brought down a peg or two. Adèle really was beginning to rile her to the point where action needed to be taken.

Neither Sanchia nor Yolande seemed irked by Madame's warning and, when the older woman wasn't looking, Sanchia winked at Charlotte. Then, assuming an innocent expression, she turned to Madame and asked her for an explanation.

'I am surprised you have to ask, Sanchia,' Madame replied tersely. 'The local men are all average. And as you know – or at least you should do, by now, if my brother and I have taught you anything at all – the average man is an uncouth boor.'

'But some of the village men are so handsome,' Yolande protested. 'Surely a dalliance with one of them . . .'

'Pearls before swine!' Madame cut in vehemently. For a moment she glared at Yolande and sucked in her hollow cheeks so hard Charlotte fancied she might implode. After a moment, the older woman let out a protracted sigh, then added in a patient tone, 'What I am trying to impress upon all of you is that you are, without exception, beautiful, cultured, finely tuned young women – in the sensual sense. The local men, on the other hand, are no more than common beasts.' Her thin lips curled into a sneer. 'They would behave with you like rutting animals, given the opportunity.'

Although Adèle shuddered at the description Madame gave, Charlotte couldn't help noticing how Sanchia's and Yolande's eyes seemed to gleam with excitement. And she couldn't help acknowledging that she, too, felt a certain thrill at the thought of being taken sexually by someone not of their class, especially if it were in such a base fashion. It would no doubt be a far cry from the sophisticated attentions she had received from Max and Eduardo.

But exciting all the same, she mused, with more than a flicker of interest. How thrilling it would be to experience how the other half enjoyed their sexuality.

All at once, Charlotte felt a surge of rebellion rise up inside her. It had always been in her nature to strike back at the bounds of conformity and to break rules when they were forced upon her. Particularly if they struck her as being without proper merit. Yet, since her arrival at Bad Alpendorf, she had pretty much applied herself to doing as she was told. Now, though, Charlotte felt an overwhelming urge to rebel. And what better way, she thought, as the plan took shape in her mind, than to broaden her sexual horizons by turning seductress, instead of always allowing herself to be the seduced?

Although Charlotte trusted Sanchia and Yolande, she kept her thoughts to herself. They were both adventurous young women, but she had no doubt that one, if not both of them, would try to dissuade her from acting rashly and insist that it was in her best interests to conform.

To avoid any chance of this happening, Charlotte did her best to behave quite normally during their outing. She chatted to her friends with deliberate ease as all four of them headed off in the direction of the forest and kept to subjects that were entirely innocent, so that no one could possibly believe that her pretty little head contained even one licentious or rebellious thought.

In truth, both were present. Charlotte's eagerness to discover what the outcome of her decision might be was too potent to subdue. And to add to her lust for adventure, her erotic senses appeared to be at an all-time high. Admittedly, most of the time, she felt sexually charged, her whole body alert to the possibility of sensual gratification. But today, everything seemed heightened: from the scent of the pine trees and the wild flowers that carpeted the forest, to the gentle but insistent pulsing between her thighs.

As they neared the village, on the penultimate stretch of their journey, Charlotte felt her heart miss a beat. She could see ahead of her, down the long straight road, that a lot of people were milling about the village centre today. Indeed, the heart of the village was very concentrated, with only two shops – a grocer and a haberdashery, which between them catered to most people's needs, inside and out – in addition to a small café-cum-public-house and a blacksmith's forge.

The forge was one of the girls' favourite places to stop and catch their breath before they started out on the last part of their walk, up the steeply inclined path that led away from the village up to the chalet school. Madame always frowned on their pleas to be allowed to stop at the café, but was quite content to allow them to spend fifteen minutes or so watching the aged, very bent figure of the blacksmith at work.

Today was no exception. As they drew close to the large brick and wood workshop, Charlotte could see that the old man was stooped as usual over his anvil. He was wielding a fearsome-looking hammer in his right hand and holding something steady on the anvil with his left.

Nudging each other, the girls marvelled at the sight. It seemed the old man's decrepit appearance belied his strength. The hammer looked as though it weighed more than he did, yet his skinny arm didn't waver.

As the girls trooped up to the open doors and clustered just inside the entrance to the forge, the old man put down the hammer and turned around. Having attempted to straighten his bent figure, he wiped the palms of his hands on the workman's apron tied around his waist. With a fleeting smile at their little group, he uttered a string of words in Swiss, which Yolande rapidly translated for the rest of the group.

'He welcomes his pretty maids,' she said with a chuckle, flashing a pert smile at the old man. 'He says he hopes all his days will continue to be brightened by such loveliness.' After this brief translation, Yolande spoke a few words back to him, for which all four girls received a wide toothless grin. 'I told him we like watching him at work and admire his skill. I said that we wouldn't miss it for the world,' she said.

The old man said something else, directing his speech this time solely to Yolande. But before she had time to open her mouth to tell the others what he had said, all four girls were distracted by the emergence of a second figure from the shadowy interior of the forge.

As he stepped into the bright pool of light, which was cast through the open doors over the spot where they stood, Charlotte noticed that the figure was that of a young man. Heart-stoppingly good-looking, he was tall, fair-haired, broad of shoulder and stripped to the waist, revealing an incredibly muscular physique. His skin was tanned a golden brown and glistened under a thin film of perspiration.

Like the others, Charlotte felt her breath catch. He was quite the most arresting sight, his fair hair appearing as a nimbus of light around his well-sculpted face. On further inspection, she noticed his features were at once handsome yet childishly endearing, with a broad high brow, straight nose, full-lipped mouth and the most exquisite pair of cornflower-blue eyes.

It must be the eyes, Charlotte thought to herself, as she felt her senses reel and something indefinable inside her quicken. I cannot resist a pair of eyes so blue . . .

When she realised she was staring blatantly at the young man, she tried to avert her gaze. But, before she could look away, she heard him speak and felt compelled to meet his gaze head-on.

'Hello. You must be the young women Herr Drichter has told me so much about,' he said in heavily accented but perfect English.

All any of the four girls could do, it seemed, was nod dumbly. Herr Drichter was the old blacksmith. Surprisingly, Charlotte was the first to recover her composure. She held out her hand to the young man and introduced herself, before effecting introductions on behalf of her three companions.

'I am surprised we have never seen you here before,' she added, thinking the young man must be a new recruit of the old blacksmith.

'I usually come here in the evenings,' the young man said, 'after my studies.' His smile turned into a sheepish grin. 'My greatest wish is to continue the blacksmith tradition, but my parents have other – let us say, more academic – aspirations for me.' With a shrug of his muscular shoulders, he turned to the old man and uttered a few words in Swiss. 'I told him that he should have a rest now. He has been working hard all day,' he told them. He said a few more words to the old blacksmith, who gave the young man another of his toothy grins and nodded.

As it transpired, the old man invited the four young women to join him for coffee and pastis at the café. For a moment, they hesitated; then Charlotte said, 'I can't imagine Madame would have any objection to us accepting such a kind invitation. After all, it would be very bad manners not to.'

'I agree,' Yolande declared instantly. Without further hesitation, she spoke to the old man, her smiles and nods indicating to the others that she was accepting his invitation on behalf of them all.

As the old man began to remove his apron, Charlotte glanced back at the young bronzed Adonis, as she had started to think of him. 'I – er – that is, we don't know *your* name,' she said, smiling coyly.

'Ah, such bad manners,' the young man replied, shaking his blond head. 'I am Jan.'

Charlotte's smile broadened, 'Hello, Jan,' she said. 'It is a real pleasure to meet you.'

They stood gazing at each other in utter silence for a moment, Charlotte feeling that his unexpected appearance was heaven-sent and trying desperately to transmit her interest in him with her eyes.

All too soon, their private wordless communion was interrupted by the other girls, who announced that they were ready to leave.

'Are you staying here to mind the shop?' Charlotte asked Jan, wishing with all her might that she could find a plausible reason to stay behind with him.

He nodded. 'Alas yes; I have much work to do.' He gestured toward the brazier, which blazed just a short distance away from them. 'There are many horses here that need new shoes.' His words were accompanied by a deep throaty chuckle, which turned Charlotte's insides to water.

'Then perhaps we'll meet again, some other time?' she said hopefully.

He smiled at her. 'I hope, yes. You are by far the prettiest girl in Bad Alpendorf.'

Inside, Charlotte glowed as brightly as the brazier, but she resisted the temptation to flutter her eyelashes and instead smiled coolly at him.

'Thank you,' she said, accepting his compliment with a graceful nod. 'I am most flattered.'

As she left the workshop with the other girls and Herr Drichter, Charlotte risked a backward glance over her shoulder. Jan had not moved. And her last impression was of a muscular young god, his body gleaming and dappled with sunlight; she felt that he desired her as much as she desired him.

Although she had been longing for the opportunity to go into the café, Charlotte was surprised to find herself feeling frustrated at the prospect now. Sanchia and Yolande were clearly enjoying themselves, laughing and chattering and teasing the poor old blacksmith unmercifully. Even Adèle seemed more relaxed than usual, all of which boded well for a jolly end to an enjoyable afternoon.

However, Charlotte was no longer in the mood for jollity. All she could think about was Jan, and how much she yearned to feel his strong arms crushing her, his hard body pressed up against hers. In her mind's eye, she stripped away his trousers, surprising herself by trying to conjure the mental image of his lower body naked. She guessed his buttocks and thighs would be as well formed and muscular as the rest of him, and imagined that his penis would be thick and hard. Indeed, she was no longer the innocent she had been, and had hardly been able to ignore the sight of the bulge that had grown and strained at the front of his trousers as they had stared at each other.

I must go back there, she thought, unable to rid herself of the image of him, nor of her overwhelming arousal. This is not an opportunity I can let slip.

But how could she engineer such a circumstance that would take her back to the forge?

All at once, inspiration struck. They were just approaching a part of the village road that was bisected by a cattle-grid.

With studied nonchalance, Charlotte deliberately let the heel of her shoe slip into one of the gaps in the grid, then wrenched her foot hard to left and right. With a pleasing crunch, she heard the nails that secured the heel to the rest of her shoe give way.

'Oh, no! Oh, dear, look what I've done to my shoe on that stupid grid!' Hopping about on one foot, she raised her other foot and wobbled the loosened heel to demonstrate her predicament.

The other girls immediately glanced over their shoulders. Yolande pulled a wry frown. 'Oh, Charlotte, how ever did you manage to do that? You can't possibly walk all the way back to the chalet with a broken heel.'

Charlotte's mouth formed a sorrowful moue. 'I know. Oh, dear . . .' Then she pretended to be struck by sudden inspiration. 'I suppose I could always go back to the forge and ask Jan if there's anything he could do. Perhaps he could knock the nails back in . . .' She felt she had never acted so convincingly in her life.

Clearly, the other girls were taken in by her ruse. All three of them, even the suspicious-natured Adèle, immediately agreed that it was worth a try.

'I don't think I have anything to lose by asking Jan if he can help,' Charlotte said, already turning to make her way back to the forge. 'Don't worry, I'll catch up with you as quickly as I can.' As she spoke, she stooped down and removed both her shoes. 'I'll run all the way,' she added, grinning from ear to ear as she held her shoes aloft.

As she sped back down the road in stockinged feet, Charlotte couldn't help reflecting that it was the first time she had ever run after a man. Literally, she thought, stopping just short of the forge to catch her breath and run the palms of her hands over her hair in an attempt to smooth it. It made her chuckle inwardly to realise that she wished she had brought a little lipstick and rouge with her.

This is not a tea-party you are going to, Charlotte Hetherington, she admonished herself with a wry grin. With a shudder of excitement, she realised her sole intention was to seduce the young blacksmith. The situation was perfect, as if

Fate had listened to her and taken a hand in the proceedings.

Taking care to compose herself first she sauntered through the open door of the workshop.

The first thing Charlotte noticed was that Jan was bent over the anvil, in much the same manner as the old blacksmith had been earlier. The hammer was raised in Jan's right hand, the heavy rounded end glowing bright red. Feeling slightly awed, Charlotte stood and watched the way the muscles in Jan's shoulder and upper arm flexed as he brought the hammer down on the horseshoe. He hit the shoe several times and it was only when he picked the shoe up with a pair of tongs and moved to hang it on a nail on the wall that Charlotte gave a discreet cough.

The horseshoe fell to the floor with a clatter as Jan whirled around in surprise.

'Oh, Miss Charlotte, I did not expect to see you back here so soon.'

The look Jan gave her turned quickly from surprise to pleasure. His blue eyes brightened, then seemed to take on a darker hue as Charlotte walked purposefully toward him.

With a deep breath, she reached out and took the pair of tongs from his hand. Then she placed them carefully on the anvil.

'It was so silly of me,' she said, continuing to gaze straight into his eyes, 'but somehow I managed to catch the heel of my shoe in the cattle grid. I was wondering if there was any way you could mend it?' She held the shoe up, her lips curving into a seductive smile. 'I thought perhaps a nail or two . . .'

It appeared to take Jan a few moments to recover his composure.

'Yes – yes, I am sure it can be mended,' he stammered, looking wary as he took the shoe from her.

He turned it over in his hands, giving Charlotte ample opportunity to admire the strength and breadth of them and imagine those hands doing delicious things to her body. Deep in the pit of her belly, she felt a flutter of excitement as he glanced down at her, his eyes making a sweeping appraisal of her figure. Charlotte followed his gaze and noticed that it came to rest on her rapidly heaving breasts, the upper swell of which showed at the neckline of her blouse like twin half-moons.

'I . . . er . . .' Now it was Charlotte's turn to stammer.

Her whole body seemed to flame as Jan continued to stare at her breasts. There was no mistaking his interest in her, nor the lust that darkened his expression and caused his brow to furrow. His eyebrows, so fair that they were almost white, dipped slightly so that the inner edges touched over the bridge of his nose.

With the greatest effort Charlotte resisted the urge to clutch at the neckline of her blouse, to protect her modesty. Her breasts, it seemed, had grown larger in the past few minutes, the nipples swelling and hardening until they peaked insolently through the two layers of fine fabric which covered them.

'I want you,' she whispered hoarsely, surprising herself with the boldness of her admission. She raised her eyes, her gaze deliberately catching his and holding it steady. 'I want you,' she repeated. 'Now.'

Without giving herself time to think, or to back down, Charlotte raised her hands and placed her palms flat against Jan's chest. His chest was so broad that she had to splay her fingers wide apart to cover it. The pads of her little fingers brushed his nipples as she slid her palms lower, her senses delighting to the sensual texture of his skin and the way her hands seemed to glide so easily over the thin film of perspiration that covered his torso.

Just as she'd imagined, his skin felt like silk over the hardness of his muscles. She slid her hands lower still, her fingertips tracing the clearly delineated ridges of his musculature. As her hands reached the flat plain of his stomach, her fingers hovered tantalisingly just above the waistband of his trousers and he let out an anguished groan.

'You want me, too, don't you, Jan?' she whispered seductively. 'I can tell how much.' As she spoke, she deliberately let her hands drift lower down to cover his groin. The hardness there was unmistakable. A knowing glint came into her eyes. 'Just tell me you want me,' she ordered softly, as she massaged his tumescence.

For just the briefest moment, Jan hesitated. As Charlotte continued to gaze at him, her fingers gently kneading the bulge at his groin, he seemed to be waging an inner battle.

It was a battle Charlotte was determined he should lose. Before waiting for him to answer her, she flicked out her tongue and tasted the perspiration that beaded his throat. She slid her tongue across his chest and flicked the tip of it lightly over the hard bullets of his nipples. Then she glanced up and met his gaze again.

His affirmation, his raging desire for her, was clearly visible in the hazy blue depths of his eyes. He seemed to be having difficulty focusing on her and his breath was coming in short sharp gasps.

In that instant, Charlotte realised that she had the advantage. And, without hesitation, she took charge of the situation.

In one swift movement, she pushed Jan back against the wall, her fingers hastily tugging at the buttons on his fly. She let out a gasp of surprise and pleasure as his penis, unencumbered by underclothes of any kind, sprang into her hands. Just as she'd hoped, it was thick and hard.

Pausing only to lick her lips in a deliberately salacious gesture, Charlotte sank to her haunches and clasped Jan's penis between both hands. For a moment, she paused, studying it, noting the roseate glans and the little tear of fluid that emerged from its tip. Then she raised her eyes to meet his glazed expression once again, deliberately formed an 'O' with her lips, then fed his penis centimetre by delicious centimetre into her mouth.

Jan let out an anguished groan. He jerked his hips instinctively and buried his fingers in her hair. He clutched wildly at her hair as she mouthed him – Charlotte was using all the expertise she had gained through Max's and Eduardo's careful tutelage – and emitted tiny whimpers that gave the impression that he was in pain.

Charlotte knew better than to ask him if he was enjoying her attentions or not. The sensations he would be enduring right now, she knew from her own experience, would be exquisitely pleasurable. His arousal was evident and she had to fight hard against the temptation to let him climax in her mouth. That was not the place she wanted him to come.

With a sigh of regret, she took her mouth away from his

penis and rose unsteadily to her feet, her fingers scrabbling hastily at the buttons on her blouse. As soon as she pulled up her satin camisole and revealed her breasts to him, Jan grabbed them with both hands, his strong fingers kneading her pliant flesh eagerly.

Fierce passion galloped through Charlotte as she felt his hands upon her bared breasts. His hard penis nudged at her belly and, with frantic desperation, she unfastened her white pleated skirt and let it fall to the dusty floor. Her desire for Jan was so great, nothing else seemed to matter: not even the fact that her skirt would be ruined and she would have to find a plausible explanation for Madame. Past caring, Charlotte made sure her French knickers quickly joined her skirt on the floor.

She felt no shame in showing off her body to Jan. And his obvious appreciation more than eradicated any lingering doubts she might have had.

'Lie down,' she ordered him hoarsely.

They both glanced around. The floor was hard and dirty, not the best place for fornication, Charlotte thought, feeling a pang of frustration. Then her eyes alighted on the anvil. It was large and flat-topped: not nearly the size of a bed but it would easily accommodate Jan's upper body.

Reaching an instant decision, she gave a deliberate glance at the anvil, telling him with her eyes where she wanted him to lie.

He hesitated for only a fraction before complying, although he winced slightly as his warm skin met the cold metal. He lay on the anvil, his buttocks just reaching the edge, the soles of his feet planted flat on the floor.

'I am sorry,' Charlotte whispered. 'I know this is not ideal, but . . .'

All her doubts flew away as Jan reached out and dragged her down on top of him.

It was the first time Charlotte had taken the initiative, and also the first time she had made love to a man and not the other way around. Straddling Jan's supine body, Charlotte felt between her thighs for his penis and guided it inside the aching channel of her vagina. She fancied her body let out a sigh of relief as Jan's hardness filled her. Then she began to move instinctively, riding him gently at first, then with increasing vigour as her arousal mounted.

'Ah, those breasts. Magnificent,' Jan uttered hoarsely, reaching up to cup them in his hands. 'Come closer,' he urged her, his fingertips tweaking the distended buds of her nipples.

Placing the palms of her hands on Jan's chest, Charlotte leant forward so that her breasts dangled tantalisingly over him. When he took his hands away for a moment, Charlotte felt her hard nipples brushing his chest as she churned her pelvis with greater fervour. Then she gasped with pleasure as he cupped her breasts again and began to knead them in perfect harmony with the movement of her hips.

Straightaway, Charlotte felt her vaginal muscles begin to spasm. She felt swept away by the power of her orgasm, but it receded just time for her to witness the enjoyment that manifested on Jan's face as he reached his own peak of pleasure. Her breasts ached where he clutched at them, but she was too consumed by desire to care.

The heat from the brazier and the warm sunshine flooding in from outside made her feel as flushed on the outside as she did on the inside. And it was only as she felt her ardour ebb slowly away, to be replaced by a feeling of great achievement, that she realised it might have been a good idea to close the doors to the forge before launching into such an erotic frenzy. Glancing warily over her shoulder she noticed, to her horror, that a small group of interested spectators had gathered in the open doorway. Among them was the old blacksmith and her three friends from the chalet school.

Oh, my God! Charlotte groaned inwardly, her mortification hardly helped by the catcalls that immediately followed.

'Bravo!' a couple of the village men clustered at the doorway called out. The rest of their comments, which Charlotte discerned as bawdy by their tone, were in their own tongue.

Jan gained her undying admiration by hardly turning a hair. He reached up and clasped Charlotte by the shoulders, pulling her close to him so that her naked breasts were squashed against the hard wall of his chest. Then he slid his palms down her back to cup her buttocks.

'Thank you,' he whispered in her ear. 'Don't mind about

them. I'll get rid of them.' He glanced at the group of spectators, his blue eyes sparkling as his mouth formed a grin.

His tenderness and casual aplomb went some way to assuaging Charlotte's feelings of embarrassment. After a moment, she slid herself off him as gracefully as she could and raced to the most remote and shadowy corner of the workshop, snatching up her clothes from the floor *en route*.

After a moment, just as Charlotte was trying desperately to make her trembling fingers operate sufficiently to fasten the buttons on her blouse, her three room-mates joined her. Charlotte was glad to see Sanchia and Yolande but much less relieved to note the supercilious expression on Adèle's face.

'Oh, you are going to be in such dreadful trouble when we return to the school,' the frosty young Englishwoman taunted her, with obvious glee. 'Madame is going to hit the roof. I would hate to be in your shoes when she hears of this. And to think you had the temerity to warn me that *I* might be expelled. I guarantee that you will be the one to be ousted. I expect you will be put on the night train to England, this very evening.'

'Oh, shut up, Adèle!' Sanchia and Yolande cried in unison. They sounded exasperated.

Yolande turned to Charlotte, her expression full of consternation. 'Chattie, how could you?' she implored. 'This is the worst thing you could possibly have done.'

Feeling sick with remorse now, Charlotte began to feel tears prickling at the corners of her eyes. Then she felt a strong hand on her shoulder.

'Do not worry, Charlotte,' Jan said, smiling down at her. 'I will go to see your tutors and tell them this was all my doing.'

'No, I won't let you.' Charlotte shook her head forcefully. 'It was I who seduced you!'

'Does it matter who seduced whom?' Sanchia asked, flashing a grin from Charlotte to Jan and back again. 'If he can get you out of trouble, Chattie, surely it is worth it.'

'No, I won't hear of it.' There was a stubborn set to Charlotte's expression. She folded her arms across her chest, her gaze unwavering as she stared at Jan and her friends. 'I will tell Madame exactly what happened. I will not let anyone else take the blame. If she decides to expel me for this, then so be it. I do not regret one moment of it.' Her gaze lingered on Jan and for the first time since their discovery *in flagrante* she smiled. 'It was wonderful,' she said softly, 'it should be I thanking you.' With a huge sigh, she bent down and picked up her discarded shoes. Her oyster silk stockings were already ruined, the feet blackened and torn from running back to the forge. 'I don't suppose I will ever see you again, Jan,' she added, holding out her hand to him. 'But I won't forget what we shared here, this afternoon. Not ever.'

With an expression of extreme regret, Jan clasped her hand warmly in his. 'I will never forget you either, my beautiful Charlotte,' he murmured. 'It is a memory I will treasure always.'

They left shortly afterwards, a worried-looking Charlotte flanked by Yolande and Sanchia, who kept squeezing Charlotte's hands and muttering words of encouragement to her. Only Adèle remained aloof. And her face was a picture of such triumph that, had Charlotte not felt so concerned about the possible repercussions of her encounter with Jan, she might have felt compelled to push Adèle into one of the ditches that edged the road.

Chapter Eleven

The closer Charlotte came to the chalet, the more nervous she started to feel. And as soon as she walked through the front door and glimpsed the forbidding figure of Madame standing in the entrance hall, waiting for them – arms folded tightly across her narrow chest, foot tapping impatiently – she felt all her previous resolve to stand up for her rights as an adult desert her.

It was not only Charlotte who got the unspoken message. Madame's demeanour told all four of the girls, in no uncertain terms, that she had been waiting there for them for some time and growing more irate by the minute.

'In my study now, all of you,' the older woman ordered sternly, leaving no room for argument.

There was none forthcoming.

Adèle was the only one who didn't look as guilty as sin as all four of them trooped into Madame's study. The air was thick with apprehension as Charlotte, Yolande and Sanchia stood shoulder to shoulder in front of Madame's desk. As always, Adèle positioned herself slightly apart from the rest of them, coolly inspecting the already perfect almond shape of her fingernails as they waited for Madame to close the door behind them.

When they were shut inside the room, Madame lowered herself into the cracked black leather chair behind her desk. 'I presume you have an explanation for your behaviour this afternoon?' she said as soon as she was seated.

She leant forward in her chair, placed her hands on the desk and formed a steeple with her long fingers as she coolly appraised the sheepish-looking little group.

Under the older woman's scrutiny, Charlotte became keenly

aware of the state of her appearance. Her hair was dishevelled, as was her blouse. It was creased and buttoned up badly, a testament to the haste she had employed in dressing after the embarrassing discovery of herself seated astride Jan. Not for a long time, she was sure, would she be able to rid herself of the memory of the faces of the people clustered around the entrance to the forge: all watching her, looking at her bare breasts and buttocks bouncing as she extracted every last ounce of pleasure from Jan's virile body.

She blushed involuntarily and attempted to smooth the creases from her skirt with her hands. Her efforts were in vain. The skirt was beyond redemption. The previously pristine white cotton was now streaked with dirt from where it had lain crumpled on the dusty floor of the forge.

'I think you know why I called you in here, girls,' Madame said at last. Her voice was like thin sharp wire, which tightened around the narrow band of tension that linked them all.

'We can explain, Madame . . .' Yolande began hesitantly, her normal exuberance replaced by an air of repentance.

Wariness lingered too in Sanchia's and Charlotte's eyes. Only Adèle's seemed to gleam with a strange kind of terrified excitement.

Charlotte flashed Adèle a quizzical look, but didn't dare to say anything. The impenetrable barrier of Madame's anger precluded it.

'So, explain,' Madame replied, sitting back in her chair yet still maintaining the steeple-pose of her fingers. She tapped her pursed lips with the tips of her fingers. 'I'm waiting,' she added, when they all seemed to hesitate.

'It was all my fault, Madame,' Charlotte ventured, in a voice that sounded far stronger than she felt inside. Her boldness came from goodness knew where, yet she felt that it was her responsibility to take the blame.

'No, it wasn't. Not at all.' Sanchia was quick to jump in. She turned her candid gaze on Madame. 'Please don't be too angry with us, Madame. The old blacksmith invited us to join him for afternoon refreshment at the café. It would have been very bad manners to refuse him.'

Despite Sanchia's earnest plea, Madame's stern expression

didn't waver. 'You know the café is out of bounds,' she said.

'But he invited us, Madame!' Yolande protested. 'Then Charlotte – well, she broke the heel on her shoe . . .'

'That's right,' Charlotte cut in hastily, 'look.' She held up the offending object to show Madame.

The older woman gave a brief nod. 'And then what happened?' she asked.

'And then . . . And then . . .' Charlotte's guilt made her waver in her response.

'And then Charlotte went back to the forge to ask the blacksmith's apprentice if he could mend it,' Sanchia cut in.

Charlotte flashed the Spanish girl a grateful smile. She clasped her hands behind her back and crossed her fingers hard, praying that Madame would not inquire as to anything else that might have transpired that afternoon. Surely she could not possibly have heard of her transgression already? And hopefully never would.

'Your explanation seems very plausible,' Madame said at length, eliciting a sigh of relief from them all. 'And I would be prepared to give you all the benefit of the doubt, were it not for two things . . .' As Madame straightened up in her chair – looking for all the world like a falcon about to swoop on its prey – Charlotte, Yolande and Sanchia shrank back. 'The condition of Charlotte's clothing is not commensurate with a broken shoe,' Madame continued, her voice tinged with scorn. 'Added to which, I received a hand-delivered note not ten minutes before your return. Needless to say, the contents of the note were shocking in the extreme.'

Charlotte felt her heart plummet and shared a despairing glance with the other two girls. It was obvious that Madame had got wind of her dalliance with Jan. But, despite the fact that she felt extremely apprehensive, at the same time she couldn't help feeling irked by Adèle's coolness.

She behaved, it seemed to Charlotte, as though she were not a part of their group at all, and that whatever bone Madame might have to pick with them had nothing whatsoever to do with her.

'It was all my doing, Madame,' Charlotte cut in hastily. 'The others had no part in it.' She wished with all her heart that she could implicate Adèle in some way, but it simply wasn't possible. Frustrating though it was, unlike her, the girl had done nothing wrong.

'I realise that,' Madame said, surprising them all. 'Only one young woman was viewed behaving in an indiscreet and very licentious manner with one of the young men from the village.'

Charlotte felt her cheeks and throat flame. Oh God, she prayed fervently in her head, please strike me down now. Anything, even the wrath of the Almighty, seemed preferable to Madame's disdain. She dreaded to think what her fate might be. Expulsion seemed the most likely option. And if that were the case, what would Cadell say? And her parents? Oh Lord, her parents. The shame would be unimaginable . . .

'Charlotte has assumed the blame, as well she might,' Madame said, cutting through Charlotte's desperate thoughts. 'But you are all at fault, in one way or another. You all broke the rules and disobeyed me.' She paused for a few agonising seconds. 'Therefore you will all be punished,' she concluded.

As she flashed a wary glance at the others, to see how they had taken the news, Charlotte was surprised to notice a certain gleam in each girl's eye. And Adèle's shone the brightest of them all.

Are they all mad? Charlotte wondered of her room-mates. Her amazement at their odd behaviour over-rode the knowledge that they were all going to be punished in some way, the blame for which lay entirely with her.

Charlotte was distracted by the way Madame placed her hands decisively on the arms of her chair and levered herself to her feet. She drew herself up to her full, imposing height, her spine ramrod straight. 'Please, all of you, take off your clothes,' she said, as though it were the most natural thing in the world to request.

Naturally, Charlotte hesitated, though the other three girls complied straightaway and without question.

'Charlotte, did you hear me? I said, take off your clothes,' Madame repeated sternly.

'I . . . Er . . .' Charlotte began to demur, until she was interrupted by an anxious plea from Yolande.

'Please Chattie, just do as you're told. Don't make this any worse for yourself.'

Feeling very reluctant, Charlotte complied. But her knees shook and her fingers trembled as she fumbled with the fastening on her skirt and the buttons on her blouse. When she was stripped down to her oyster satin camisole and knickers, she hesitated again.

'All of it, for God's sake,'Yolande hissed, as she struggled to pull her panties down over her ample hips.

Though she felt frightened and horribly embarrassed, Charlotte couldn't help also feeling a certain *frisson* of excitement as she watched the other girls' bodies come into view. She had seen them all disrobe many times: at night, or when they were dressing in the mornings, or getting changed for dinner. But this time seemed different.

Perhaps it was the fact that they were not undressing in their own room but in Madame's dark and cheerless study, Charlotte mused as she removed her own underclothes. Or could it be because each pair of nipples were revealed as erect with excitement and each girl's mouth appeared wet and slightly slack, as though lust weighed down their bottom lips?

Whatever the reason, Charlotte thought, there was no escaping the erotic tension that seemed to charge the air around them.

When they were all fully undressed, they stood once again in front of Madame's desk, in a row, bare shoulder brushing bare shoulder. None of them, it seemed, could stop themselves from trembling.

'I want you to come to me one by one,' Madame said, after she had spent a few moments appraising them coolly. 'Adèle, you may be the first. Then Sanchia, Yolande and finally you, Charlotte.'Though she merely glanced at the others, she fixed Charlotte with a beady-eyed stare.

Charlotte quaked. With bated breath, she watched as Adèle strode purposefully around the desk and presented herself to Madame. Like the older woman, her stance was proud: back straight, ribcage lifted, shoulders thrown back.

'Excellent,' Madame murmured, eyeing Adèle up and down with approval. 'You have learned to assume the correct posture well. Now,' she added, her voice becoming slightly husky in timbre, 'what do I expect of you?'

'That I clasp my hands behind my head like so, Madame,' Adèle answered, raising her arms and cupping the back of her pale blonde head.

'That is quite so,' Madame murmured approvingly. She flashed a keen glance at the other three, who stood shivering and gawping all at the same time. They had never known Adèle to behave in quite such an obedient and submissive fashion. 'This is how I expect you all to behave, when your turn comes,' Madame added before turning her attention back to Adèle.

Charlotte stared in amazement as Madame raised her right hand and slapped Adèle smartly across each breast. The firm pink mounds quivered, then began to glow brightly as Madame delivered a series of slaps to them. Her palm was slightly cupped and she adopted an upward sweeping motion as she smacked each pert little swelling.

Unable to help herself, Charlotte let out a groan. She wasn't sure what horrified her most, the shaming spectacle of Adèle's punishment, or the fierce surge of desire she felt every time she heard the palm of Madame's hand connect with the vulnerable cones of flesh that sat high upon Adèle's ribcage.

And as for Adèle herself, Charlotte noticed, she seemed transported into another realm. Her lower lip hung down; her open mouth emitted a series of tiny whimpers. Moreover, her nipples jutted out, hard and erect, their length doubled so that they now resembled organ-stops rather than rose-hips.

'That will do,' Madame said at last, taking a step back from Adèle. 'My dear, you took your punishment well. For that, I will allow you the privilege of chastising your three friends.'

Both Madame and Adèle appeared equally pleased, and it took Charlotte a few seconds to assimilate the implications of Madame's pronouncement. When she did, she protested immediately, only to be silenced by Madame.

'You will take your punishment as decreed,' Madame snapped tersely. 'I think you of all people, Charlotte, should be grateful that this is your only punishment. It would be quite understandable if I were to expel you for the behaviour you have exhibited this afternoon. Think yourself lucky. I am letting you and your friends off lightly, under the circumstances,' she added, leaving no room for further argument.

With the greatest effort, Charlotte resisted the urge to hang her head in shame. Instead, she watched Sanchia and Yolande take their punishment meekly from Adèle. When her turn came, however, she felt as though her legs would not carry her around the desk.

'Hurry up, Chattie, for goodness' sake,' Adèle snapped, mimicking Madame's tone almost exactly.

'I'm not going to let her lay a finger on me,' Charlotte retorted immediately, flashing an angry glance at Adèle before turning to Madame. Her expression became pleading. 'I beg of you, Madame. I'll take my punishment gladly, but only if you administer it. I cannot, will not, allow that bitch to touch me!'

A shocked silence followed Charlotte's outburst. All five women in the room seemed frozen in disbelief. When Madame eventually spoke, it was with icy determination.

'You have a grievance against Adèle. That is most interesting,' she said. 'However, I will not enquire as to why that may be. At least, not for the moment. You will take your punishment as I decreed it, Charlotte, or you will leave this establishment immediately . . .'

The threat hung between them for what seemed like an interminable amount of time. Once again, Charlotte realised, she was being called upon to submit to the will of another, or to leave Bad Alpendorf. There was no middle ground. It was an ethic which Max had tried to instil in her and one she was only just beginning to understand.

'Very well,' she conceded, pursing her lips and flashing a venomous glance at Adèle before meeting Madame's eye with an unwavering stare. 'If that is my only option. I have no wish to leave here.' She decided any further attempt to speak would not be wise. A huge lump had formed in her throat, and she felt she would rather die than shed a single tear in front of Adèle.

As she positioned herself in front of Adèle, in the stance that the other three girls had adopted, with hands cupping the back of her head and fingers interlaced, she glared straight

155

into the other girl's eyes. The stare that met hers was icy cold and uncompromising, sending a shiver down Charlotte's spine.

To her amazement she felt a quickening of excitement, which shocked her. How could it be that, while she felt so much hatred for Adèle, she could also feel this strange quivering of sexual excitement?

It was unthinkable. And yet very real.

She watched with bated breath as Adèle raised her hand to strike her. Adèle's lips twitched at one corner, lending a cruel, slightly sardonic slant to her obdurate expression.

I refuse to feel intimidated, Charlotte told herself firmly as she watched Adèle's hand sweep through the air. Her tension was so acute the action seemed to take place in slow motion. And then she felt the first poignant sting of the young woman's palm and she winced. After two slaps each, her breasts burnt, the pale flesh turning a fiery red. But although she felt horribly shamed by the experience, Charlotte refused to make a sound. Adèle would never know how much this treatment was affecting her.

It took Charlotte all her might to resist the urge to cover her stinging breasts with her hands, to shield them from further chastisement. Her nipples throbbed and she felt a similar throbbing between her tightly clenched thighs. Having been stimulated by her session with Jan earlier that afternoon, the sensual little nub of her clitoris now seemed alive once more. Charlotte was eager to be caressed, to have those pleasurable feelings of orgasm flow through her once again. But it seemed like an unattainable fantasy, right at that moment. And her rampant frustration caused her desire to mount all the more.

As Adèle continued to smother Charlotte's breasts with red handprints, Charlotte risked a glance at Madame. To her surprise, the woman seemed enraptured by the sight of her glowing breasts. Her gaze was fixed on them, her eyes narrowed and unblinking. What was more surprising was that Madame had slipped one of her hands inside the neckline of her blouse. She was caressing herself, gently, mindlessly, her whole attention captured by Charlotte's punishment as it took place right in front of her.

What was particularly shocking about this, Charlotte realised, was that it was the first time Madame had ever displayed any kind of emotion. It had always appeared that she was above such things that most people took for granted: love, pleasure, sensual desire . . . And yet here she was, displaying quite openly that she was aroused by the sight of Charlotte being chastised by Adèle.

Or perhaps it is the sight of my breasts she finds arousing, Charlotte mused. Without thinking, she glanced down at herself and noticed straightaway how full and luscious her breasts looked, how red and swollen the nipples. Like raspberries, they looked juicy. Succulent.

Without meaning to, Charlotte let out a little groan of desire and wished with all her might that someone might take pity on her poor throbbing nipples and suckle them. With a further groan, she closed her eyes and visualised a mouth enclosing each nipple. She could almost feel the warm wetness. The flickering, tantalising touch of a tongue upon those aching buds.

And then it happened . . .

The reality . . .

Gentle hands cupped her breasts and held them up. Moments later, a pair of lips slid over each nipple, enclosing them, sucking hard.

'Aah!' Charlotte dropped her head back and let out a low moan of delight. She didn't bother to open her eyes but thrust her breasts forward in a wanton fashion, whimpering with pleasure when each of her aching mounds was covered with kisses and long, sweeping strokes of a tongue.

Full of desire she arched her back, feeling the muscles in her stomach tighten, the stretching of her skin over her ribcage. The tongues slid lower, marking wet half-circle paths around the undersides of her breasts while the hands roamed her torso. Tickling. Stroking. Tantalising. Delicious glancing touches of fingertips upon her taut, sensitised skin.

'After pain comes pleasure,' she heard Madame murmur. 'And one day, I hope, you will learn to take pleasure in the pain itself.'

The older woman's voice sounded oddly thick. It

mesmerised Charlotte, and added to the desire that was already mounting so rapidly inside her, she felt she might explode with passion at any moment.

'Do not move,' Madame admonished her softly, when Charlotte went to stroke the backs of the girls' heads as they caressed her breasts and torso.

That in itself Charlotte found a torment. She was certain that it was Sanchia and Yolande who stroked and mouthed her so deliciously; she couldn't imagine for one moment that Adèle could be that gentle, that sensuous. In return, she wanted to show them her gratitude, her appreciation.

In that instant, she realised she loved the two girls who, in such a short space of time, had become her friends. She loved and desired them in a way that was so different to her feelings for Cadell. It seemed unthinkable that, once she returned to England, she might never see them again, or spend such sensuous times with them.

The poignancy of her thoughts sharpened her desire. She cried out, feeling waves of erotic love for the two girls flow through her. This was true sensuality. True pleasure.

'Yes, oh, yes, my sweet,' she heard one of them croon.

Delicate fingertips began to glide up and down her thighs. First down the outsides and then, as she moved her feet apart, up her inner thighs. Her whole body felt alive to pleasure. It was eager to receive the gentle caresses bestowed on it.

A wet mouth pressed against the back of each knee, exciting the sensitive flesh there, sending tingles of desire up and down her legs. And, at the same time, another mouth deposited soft sucking kisses on her inner thighs, moving gradually higher until it glanced across the vulnerable pouch of flesh at their apex.

Charlotte began to shudder. Her clitoris throbbed madly. She could feel her juices running from her, copious and tantalising. And as they trickled down, a tongue caught them, lapping eagerly at her flesh, the mouth taking her outer lips and sucking . . . nibbling . . . building up the pleasure, until Charlotte began to rock on her heels.

Strong hands caught her by the shoulders, gripping lightly but firmly. Straightaway, Charlotte knew the hands belonged to Madame and, a moment later, her nostrils picked up the scent of jasmine and ylang-ylang, which Madame always wore.

'Good girl, Charlotte,' Madame's voice whispered in her ear. 'You love to take pleasure in your body, do you not? You are truly wanton.'

'I . . . I . . .' Charlotte felt too overcome to speak.

A tongue now flickered over her clitoris, tantalising the straining bud until she felt close to exploding.

And then she came, in a tumult of sensation. Pleasure flashed through her like an express train through a tunnel. The tunnel was dark and long and yet, all too soon, she emerged from the tunnel into light and she felt her pleasure begin to ebb slowly away.

Full of relief, Charlotte sank back against Madame, who stood behind her, still holding her gently but less firmly now. She allowed her eyelids to flicker open as Madame began to stroke her upper arms.

'There, there,' Madame crooned softly in her ear, as though Charlotte were a child. 'Let yourself be calm, child.'

Somehow, afternoon gave way to evening. Shadows lengthened across the room, making it seem a more mysterious, sensual place.

Charlotte lay on her stomach on a thick rug, her hands lightly caressing Sanchia and Yolande who sprawled naked beside her. Madame and Adèle had long since departed, leaving the three girls to continue enjoying themselves in whatever way they chose. It was liberation of the most exquisite kind: the freedom to explore each others' bodies fully and without restraint.

'Madame and Adèle are lovers, you know,' Sanchia said needlessly.

Charlotte nodded, her fingers tracing lazy concentric circles around the girl's left breast. 'I guessed as much, this afternoon,' she said. 'They are too close, and Adèle is far too confident in her position here, for their relationship to be anything else. I would still like to bring that girl down a peg or two, though,' she added, sounding a mite wistful.

To be honest, all thoughts of revenge had left her mind for

a while. When pleasure reigned, it was impossible to feel vengeful.

'Me too,' Yolande murmured. She rolled onto her stomach and trailed a fingertip lightly down Charlotte's spine, making her quiver with delight. 'But what can we do? The girl never puts a foot wrong.'

Sanchia's laughter was a deep rumble. It started at the base of her throat, making her breasts shudder. Charlotte smiled at the beautiful sight and tweaked her nipples gently.

'We must put our heads together and think of something,' the Spanish girl said. 'After all, we are intelligent young women. Surely, between us, we can devise a plan. Nothing too dire, though,' she added quickly. 'Just something to cause her a little humiliation.'

'A lot of humiliation,' Charlotte cut in, her lips forming a wry smile.

The other two girls nodded, their faces wreathed in conspiratorial smiles. 'All right, a lot of humiliation,' they concurred in unison.

Yolande added, 'It shouldn't be too difficult to come up with something.'

As it turned out, the opportunity to achieve their mutual goal came a lot more quickly than expected. And, along with the opportunity, came a huge, very unexpected surprise.

It was a week, almost to the day, after Charlotte's indiscretion that Max sought her out and asked her if she and her three room-mates could come to his study later on that day. He had some exciting news for them all, he told her.

Immediately, Charlotte was eager to learn all the details. 'What is it about, Max? Go on, please tell me something about it.'

With a smile, Max shook his head. 'Not now, little one,' he said firmly, his hand caressing her shoulder lightly as he gazed down into her upturned face. 'I want to tell you when you are all together.'

'Then I'll go and find the others now and . . .'

'Later this afternoon will be fine, Charlotte,' he said, smiling more broadly at her eagerness. 'Shall we say four o'clock?'

With obvious reluctance, Charlotte agreed to wait. But that didn't stop her racing off to find Yolande and Sanchia. Adèle, she decided, could wait.

The afternoon seemed interminable, the frustration alleviated only by the girls' customary walk with Madame. Since the episode with Jan, Charlotte had been dreading the possibility of bumping into him again with Madame in tow, but fortunately that hadn't happened. And, to all the girls' surprise, Madame even relaxed her rule about not stopping at the café and included a brief sojourn there, before completing their round-trip back to the chalet school.

It was while they were seated at one of the tables outside the café, shaded by a large striped awning, that Charlotte remembered she hadn't given Adéle Max's message.

The young woman stared hard at Charlotte for a moment, then sat back in her chair and swept her hair back from her forehead with a gesture of nonchalance.

'I think you might have had the decency to tell me sooner, Charlotte,' she said, sounding a trifle scathing. 'But, in this case, it doesn't really matter. Madame has already told me all about it.' So saying, she flashed an ingratiating look at the older woman, who smiled back, thus infuriating Charlotte and the other girls.

Adèle really was beginning to annoy them all.

'Well, no harm done, in that case,' Charlotte responded coolly. She reached forward and picked up her cup and saucer. The aroma of the rich dark coffee in her cup swirled up in a thin tendril of steam. She blew gently at the surface of her coffee to cool it before taking a couple of modest sips. The coffee was a delightful blend, not at all bitter, and was sweetened by the rich cream which came from the dairy herds that grazed on the lush fields surrounding the village.

At that moment Charlotte felt blissfully happy, as though she hadn't a single care in the world. The sun was warm on the back of her neck and, though she was wary of getting freckles, she couldn't help but enjoy the soft caress of the sun's rays upon her exposed skin.

I think I could get used to the life of a hedonist, she mused. Her lips formed a wry smile as she reflected on the irony of her thoughts. Her life hadn't been particularly exacting, up to now. She knew she was a lot better off than most, and that she had always led what could be described as a charmed life.

The most difficult time of her life had been since Cadell had proposed, and yet even then there had been only moments which she found difficult to handle. The rest had been pure pleasure.

And she was certain that whatever it was Max had to say to them, the end result was going to be as exciting and enjoyable as every other experience she had had at Bad Alpendorf.

Chapter Twelve

Once again, as she entered the room, Charlotte was struck by the marked contrast between Max's study and that of Madame. As soon as she walked through the door, which he held wide open for her and her friends, she felt her spirits lift. It seemed as though the very essence of Max dwelt within that comfortably appointed room.

It was as sensuous as he was: the colours restful, the fabrics used for the soft furnishings opulent and delightful to the touch. And the books, framed sketches and small *objets d'art* which decorated the walls and shelves were purely and unashamedly erotic. Everything about Max's study was carefully chosen and designed to reflect his unique charisma and concupiscent tastes.

'Sit down, girls; make yourselves comfortable,' Max invited them, with a flamboyant wave of his arm. Without pausing, he strode across the room and picked up a tray, which bore a tall frosted-glass jug and five cocktail glasses.

At Max's instruction, each girl helped herself to a glass and smiled up at Max as he filled each one to the brim with Mint Julep.

Charlotte's nose twitched as she inhaled the cocktail's sharp minty aroma. Then she smacked her lips in a most unladylike fashion after she had taken her first sip.

'This is lovely, Max,' she enthused. 'This is my first Julep of the summer.'

'I thought it would make a change from mulled wine or brandy,' he said, dropping down into an empty chair and stretching his long legs out in front of him. 'This is much cooler, and far more stimulating.' He winked at all of them over the frosted rim of his glass.

Adèle was the only one who didn't giggle in response.

'Now then,' Max said after a moment, 'to business. Or should I say pleasure?'

All four young women gazed at him with rapt expressions on their faces.

Charlotte felt her heart pick up a beat. This was going to be good. She just knew it.

'What is it, Max?' she asked softly.

'Good news,' he said, 'as if you had not already guessed.' He paused, obviously drawing out the tension deliberately. Each girl sat forward a little, emitting a collective air of expectation. Max smiled. 'All right,' he said, 'I will not keep you in suspense any longer.' His smile broadened, his blue eyes twinkling. 'I am not *that* cruel.'

Without further ado, he explained to them that they were all to go on a short trip to Paris. The four girls were delighted and started to chatter excitedly among themselves, reminiscing about past visits to the city.

'This is not intended to be a shopping or sight-seeing trip,' Max warned them, sounding amused.

'Then what is this visit to Paris all about?' Adèle asked the question that was on the tip of all their tongues. She raised a supercilious eyebrow and waited for Max to answer.

'We will be exploring the sensual underworld of Paris,' Max said. He clearly expected a gaggle of questions to ensue and showed no surprise when they did. 'I really cannot explain properly how different Paris is to any other city in Europe,' he continued, when their chatter had died down a little. 'All I can say is that the Parisian bohemian sector is unique. Very erotic. Extremely sensual. You will not have experienced anything like it before.'

'I cannot wait,' Charlotte commented, with more than a hint of irony. 'No, I mean it, Max,' she said when he pretended to glare at her. 'I love the city and adore discovering new things. This trip should prove interesting.'

'Oh, I think it is safe to say you will find it very interesting, all of you,' Max responded, raising his glass to them. '*Salut, mes petites!*'

They boarded a sleeper train to Paris, the following afternoon.

A porter hovered by the small group as Charlotte, Sanchia, Yolande, Adèle and Max waited on the platform for the train to open its doors. Beside them a trolley stood, loaded up with their bags. Max had originally tried to object to their bringing so much luggage but had finally relented under the chorus of protest he received in return.

Having been forced to wear regulation clothing for the past few weeks, the girls were eager to make the most of this opportunity to show off their own clothes. To their surprise, Max and Madame were all for them displaying their individuality on this trip. And adopting their own particular style of dress was a vital part of this, Madame told them. Hence all the luggage.

Though they were all dressed fashionably, each girl naturally had her own style. For the first part of their journey, Charlotte had opted to wear a long button-through dress in navy silk. She had knotted a navy-and-white spotted silk scarf around her shoulders and had placed her white straw boater at a jaunty angle.

'You look very nautical,' Max told her, coming to stand beside her on the platform as they were waiting to board the train. He demonstrated his approval by slipping his arm around her waist and hugging her lightly to him.

Charlotte immediately felt a thrill run through her at Max's touch. His embrace was innocent, yet it seemed a thousand erotic thoughts immediately raced through Charlotte's mind.

'More naughty than nautical,' she quipped lightly, reaching up on tiptoe to place a flirtatious kiss on his lips.

'Well, now, normally I would admonish you for that remark,' Max said. 'But I want you to be naughty on this trip. You can be as badly behaved as you wish.'

Charlotte's eyes rounded. 'Do you really mean that?' she said.

Max shrugged. 'I never say anything I do not mean.'

Once on board, Charlotte quickly discovered that the train itself was an absolute delight. Although she had travelled by similar modes of transport before, indeed with Cadell only a few weeks earlier, the very nature of their trip – the mystery, the excitement, the prospect of discovering new things – all added to her feeling that this was a 'first time' for her.

Certainly it was the first time she had ever travelled with Max. And the train itself was perfection. Not quite the Orient Express, it was nevertheless lavishly appointed. The individual sleeper compartments they had been allocated were wood-panelled and fitted out with luxurious soft furnishings in velvet and silk, while all the accoutrements, such as the light fittings and door handles, were gold-plated. Furthermore, each cabin had an ornate little porcelain basin set into a mahogany stand in one corner, which even had its own pumped water that jetted in a clear stream through gold taps fashioned to resemble spouting fish.

Everything was lavish and well designed, right down to the very last detail. And Charlotte discovered that, in common with the other compartments, her particular accommodation included a fold-down bed. In addition, there was a tall, necessarily roomy wardrobe for her clothes and another smaller cupboard. When she opened it, Charlotte discovered the small cupboard contained spare blankets, thick monogrammed towels – LS for 'Swiss-Ligne', the railway operator – and glassware from which to drink the complementary bottles of wine and mineral water. There was even a radiogram fitted into the wall at the head of the bed, so that she could enjoy either a little classical night music, the latest news, or some of the more popular tunes of the day.

'All designed to make our journey a relaxing one,' Max commented as he pumped his hand up and down on Charlotte's mattress to test its springs.

'Oh, I feel relaxed, all right,' Charlotte said with a blissful sigh. She stretched hugely, a smile of contentment on her face. 'Would you like a glass of wine, Max? I do believe it is late enough to have one.' She glanced at her watch to confirm that it was a decent hour to consume alcohol. She felt very grown-up, being able to offer Max a drink. Until now, it had always been the other way around.

Max nodded, a smile creasing his handsome features. 'I would indeed enjoy a glass of wine.'

He crossed the tiny cabin in a couple of strides and sat down in one of two club chairs placed either side of a small round table. The table was covered with a pale pink damask cloth. The cloth was clearly intended to complement the dusky rose velvet, which covered the club chairs and the pair of curtains which framed the cabin's one small window.

'I'm not usually a great lover of the colour pink,' Charlotte commented as she walked up to Max and handed him a glass of Sancerre. She sat down in the empty chair at the other side of the table from him and glanced around the cabin, a smile lighting up her face. 'But I adore the décor of this room. In a way, it makes me feel quite extraordinarily feminine.'

'Well, the fabric on the chairs is the exact colour of your vulva,' Max said, without batting an eyelid, although Charlotte spluttered into her wine when he said it. 'And the pink of the tablecloth rather resembles your nipples . . .' He eyed her chest thoughtfully until Charlotte blushed. 'What a shame the room does not feature puce,' he added lightly, 'to match the colour of your face.'

'Max! You – you!'

Charlotte felt beside herself with embarrassment. How could he talk so candidly about her private parts like that? Even worse, to look at her in such a blatantly lascivious way? She glanced around hastily, as though she expected a peeping Tom to be lurking somewhere about the intimate little cabin.

Max only laughed at her outrage. 'You should see yourself,' he said, taking a sip of his wine and reclining casually in the club chair. 'You look as though you are about to erupt. Like Mount Vesuvius.'

'Even an innocent volcano sounds sexual when you say its name,' Charlotte responded. She tried to sound disapproving, but failed to stop her lips from twitching. Considering he was so much older than her, Max Spieler really was quite incorrigible!

And so utterly desirable.

Beneath the thin fabric of her dress, Charlotte could feel her body warming to him: her nipples tightening into hard little buds, her intimate flesh moistening . . . And she doubted that it had anything to do with the wine. Why, she had only had a few sips.

'I cannot remember when I last felt this relaxed,' she said, changing the subject. Aping Max's casual pose, she reclined back in her chair and crossed her legs at the ankles. Letting her head drop back, she studied the wood-panelled ceiling for a moment or two, her gaze fixed to the rose-tinted cut-glass lightbowl that hugged the centre of the ceiling.

After a moment, Max followed her gaze.

'You know, Charlotte,' he murmured, surprising her with the use of her name – normally he used some kind of endearment, 'pink-hued lighting lends a particularly attractive glow to naked skin. It can be very flattering indeed.'

His words were as casual as his pose. So innocent-sounding that he might have been commenting on the weather, or the train timetable, or some such bland subject, Charlotte thought.

His casual air amused her. She already suspected where this might be leading and, without saying a word, put down her glass and stood up. First of all she went to the small window and drew the curtains together, blocking out the dying light of the sun. Then she turned on the light. Straightaway, she saw how the small compartment became suffused with a rosy glow, making the surroundings seem all the more intimate and womblike.

Her desire soared and, without a moment's hesitation, she reached up under her dress and began to roll down her stockings. She draped them over the back of her chair and sat down again. This time she did not cross her legs at the ankles but stretched one out in front of her, flexing her knee provocatively.

'You know, I think I agree with you, Max,' she murmured, glancing sideways at him under her lashes. The look she gave him was as seductive as the flexing of her bare leg. She moved her gaze to her foot and began to circle her ankle, describing small circles in the air. 'My skin does appear to have a nicer tone under this light.' Still apparently concentrating on her circling foot, she inched the hem of her dress up none-too-surreptitiously to mid-thigh. The time to be coy with Max was long past.

She didn't have to look at the man beside her to know he was watching her, visually taking in her every movement. His eyes were like strong beams of light, branding twin circles onto her skin.

'Mm,' she sighed, letting her head drop back again, but this time closing her eyes to block out the pinkish glow of the light. 'I really do feel so, so relaxed . . .'

Max was beside her in a flash. She heard him move and sensed his presence beside her. And when the first caress of his fingertips came, glancing across the sensitive flesh of her inner thigh, she hardly made a murmur but allowed her thighs to slip apart a little. Just enough for Max to allow his fingers to explore higher, if he so wished.

To Charlotte's slight dismay, his caresses travelled not to the apex of her thighs, where her ardent sex flesh dampened the soft cradle of her silk knickers, but in the opposite direction, down her calf toward her foot.

Max cradled her foot in his hands, his fingers deftly massaging the soft pads of flesh at the base of her toes.

This was blissful, too, in its own way, she thought, not bothering to open her eyes. After a moment, she forgot her disappointment and allowed herself to relax completely and enjoy his ministrations to her foot.

A knock came at the door, a moment later, startling them both. Charlotte opened her eyes to see one of the stewards standing on the threshold of the compartment. Dressed in the railway's uniform of white trousers and white jacket with gold buttons, the steward appeared very young, with light brown hair that flopped over one eye when he whipped off the peaked cap of his uniform and held it in front of him in a respectful manner.

He spoke hesitantly in Swiss, which Max translated for Charlotte's benefit. 'The steward wants to know if we require a table in the dining car, or if we would prefer to eat in our cabins? By the way, Charlotte, do you not think he is a handsome young specimen?'

Having just begun to consider the merits of dressing for dinner versus the less exciting but equally less stressful option of dining in her cabin, Charlotte was taken aback by Max's question.

She blushed immediately and flashed a nervous glance at

the steward. 'Hush, Max,' she admonished her tutor, 'he'll hear you.'

'I doubt that he can speak more than a few words of English,' Max replied, smiling affably at the steward. 'Tell me, young man, is there roast partridge on the menu tonight?'

The young man immediately looked confused. 'I – I sorry, sir,' he stammered, 'the English, she is difficult for me . . .' he allowed his words to trail off and shifted uncomfortably under Charlotte's scrutiny.

'You see,' Max murmured in an aside to Charlotte, before turning to the steward again. He spoke rapidly in his own language, to which the young man nodded and gave Max a grateful smile before fleeing.

'I told him we would prefer to eat here,' Max told Charlotte. 'I hope you do not mind?'

'Mind? I, er, no, I don't mind at all,' Charlotte stammered.

'Good,' Max said, sitting back on his heels and picking up Charlotte's foot again. 'Because I would rather spend time making love to you properly than fiddle with a bow tie and cufflinks.'

It wasn't often that Charlotte had the opportunity to enjoy time alone with Max. At least, she reflected some hours later, as she lay on her bunk with her head cradled in the crook of his shoulder, not in such an intimate way as this.

The past couple of hours had been blissful, interrupted only by the arrival of a different steward who had brought the dinner Max had ordered. Now the food lay congealing, untouched, on white china plates covered by two gleaming copper domes.

'Are you hungry?' Max asked, stroking Charlotte's hair.

She shook her head gently. 'No, not at all. But I would like another glass of wine.' Without waiting for Max to offer to pour it, she scrambled off the bunk and walked over to the table, where she had left the bottle and their glasses. She turned round, a glass in each hand and was startled to see the expression on Max's face.

'What?' she asked, forgetting her manners in her confusion.

He smiled, the stretching of his lips happening in a slow lazy fashion that turned Charlotte's knees to water. 'I was just thinking how beautiful you are,' he said, his gaze sweeping up and down her body, 'and how naturally and uninhibitedly you move without clothes, these days.'

Charlotte trembled and glowed inwardly in response to his compliment. Unable to help herself, she glanced down, noting the pert way her full breasts jutted out. It was true, she thought, nakedness did come naturally to her now. It hadn't occurred to her before, but nowadays she felt not an ounce of shame when she paraded around naked. Rather, she gloried in the sense of freedom that being without clothes gave her. The sexually confident woman she had become now was a far cry from the naive young girl she had been not so long ago. And she had Cadell to thank for that, and Max, of course, and to some extent Sanchia and Yolande.

Thinking about her friends made her feel instantly guilty. Since they had boarded the train for Paris, she had virtually ignored them and, perhaps worse still, monopolised Max.

'I ought to go and say good night to the others, before I turn in,' she murmured, thinking aloud.

'And so you should,' Max agreed, reaching out a hand to her. 'But first, come back and lie here beside me again. I want to drink my wine from your navel.'

With a giggle, Charlotte did as he bade her. At that moment, she felt as though she could refuse Max nothing. She had so much for which she should be grateful to him.

Much later, at around midnight, when Max had finally departed Charlotte's cabin for his own, Charlotte slipped on a nightgown and peignoir and went in search of her friends. They were not difficult to find. Max had seen to it that they were all allocated adjoining cabins. His was next to hers on one side and on the other was Sanchia's compartment, then Yolande's and finally Adèle's. Charlotte was glad about this. The further away from Adèle the better, she mused, making her way down the thickly carpeted corridor.

On her feet she wore eau-de-nil quilted satin slippers, like ballet shoes, which exactly matched the colour of her lingerie. Consequently, she made no sound as she padded the few short paces from her door to that of Sanchia's cabin. She knocked

171

lightly on the wooden door and, a scant few seconds later, the Spanish girl's dark head appeared around the edge of the door.

'Oh, Chattie, it is you,' she said, sounding inordinately pleased to see her friend. She held the door open wider so that Charlotte could enter her compartment.

'I just popped along to say good night,' Charlotte whispered. 'I must say, it will seem strange, sleeping in a room all on my own again.'

Sanchia winked broadly, her dark eyes twinkling with amusement. 'There is no need to whisper,' she said, 'and, by the way, I know you have not been alone. Max has been with you.'

Charlotte laughed. 'How do you know that?' she asked, raising the level of her voice only a fraction. Though she raised her eyebrows far more in surprise.

Her innocent question was rewarded by Sanchia's thick, treacly chuckle. 'These walls,' she said, walking over to the wood panelling and rapping lightly on it with her knuckles, 'are not all that thick.'

She threw a mischievous glance at Charlotte over her shoulder. Then she turned and tossed her head so that her hair settled around her shoulders in a thick dark cloud.

Watching the young girl, noting her unaffected gesture and the open way she smiled at her, Charlotte felt her breath catch in her throat. God, but she was lovely. So lovely that she ached to hold the young Spanish girl in her arms again. Moving swiftly, Charlotte crossed the room and hugged Sanchia to her. Then she held her at arms' length and studied the young woman's face for a moment, before allowing her serious expression to crease into a smile.

'You are incorrigible, do you know that?' Charlotte said. 'But I do love you!'

'I love you, too,' Sanchia responded simply.

The two girls hugged each other again, though there was nothing sexual in their embrace.

'I just want you to know that I have never had a friend like you before,' Charlotte said, moving to sit in one of the chairs on the other side of the room.

'Nor I you,' Sanchia said. She remained standing, gazing across the room at Charlotte.

There was such genuine warmth in her gaze that Charlotte felt a lump form in her throat. In just over a week, her time at Bad Alpendorf would come to an end and she and Sanchia would be forced to part.

'You won't lose touch when we . . .' Charlotte began.

Pausing only to gather up the front of her pale lemon nightgown, Sanchia rushed over to Charlotte and flung herself at her feet. She nestled her dark head in Charlotte's lap.

'No, of course not,' she declared vehemently, glancing up. The expression on her face was both honest and trusting.

With a fond smile, Charlotte put out her hand and stroked the young girl's hair.

'I am glad,' she murmured softly. 'Because you will never know how much I would hate to lose you.'

After sharing a cup of cocoa and a few girlish secrets with Sanchia, both girls moved onto Yolande's room.

'She might already be asleep,' Charlotte said, whispering again so as not to disturb the other passengers on the train. 'It must be very late by now.'

However, Yolande was very much awake and as exuberant as ever, the other two girls noticed. She flung open the door with characteristic abandon and greeted them both effusively.

'We could have been anyone,' Charlotte said, sounding shocked as she stepped into the room.

Charlotte gazed at the young woman through deliberately narrowed eyes. Yolande was clad only in a set of pink satin cami-knickers that contrasted wonderfully with the light brown hue of her skin, she noticed, feeling a fresh wave of warmth and camaraderie wash over her.

'I know,' Yolande giggled girlishly. 'That is the whole point. It might have been one of those handsome young stewards knocking at my door. But, alas, it was only you two.' She pretended to pout, then dissolved into a fresh bout of laughter.

'You are as bad as Sanchia,' Charlotte said, unable to help but laugh along with Yolande, her laughter was so infectious. 'You are both very, very bad girls.' She wagged her finger at them and gave them a mock glare down her nose in a way that was intended to be reminiscent of Madame. Obviously, her mimicry was accurate, she thought, feeling pleased, because the other two girls laughed all the louder and chorused, 'Yes Madame. No Madame. Three bags full, Madame.'

'Is someone taking our esteemed tutor's name in vain?' The acid comment came from the doorway.

Swiftly, all three young women turned their heads and Yolande clapped a hand to her mouth.

'Oops!' she muttered, 'I can't have shut the door properly.'

They looked collectively guilty as Adèle strode into the room. Like the rest of them, the young Englishwoman was clad in her nightwear: a long gown and matching peignoir of midnight blue satin, edged with ecru lace.

Each girl gawped as Adèle glared at them all. 'I do not think you should be in here, play-acting,' she said, sweeping a contemptuous glance over the trio. 'It is past one o'clock and we leave the train at ten-thirty.' She glanced pointedly at the gold Swiss timepiece which encircled her alabaster wrist.

'Is that new?' Yolande commented, changing the subject swiftly as she glanced at Adèle's wristwatch.

To everyone's surprise, twin pink spots formed upon Adèle's pale cheeks. 'It is. It was a gift,' she confirmed. She tossed her blonde head in a haughty manner. 'Though I fail to see what business it is of yours.'

The other three girls flashed quizzical glances at each other. It had been hitherto unknown for Adèle to blush, let alone appear as guilty as she did right at this moment.

'From Madame, no doubt,' Sanchia commented sagely.

Adèle blushed harder, answering the Spanish girl's question more effectively than words ever could.

Sanchia winked surreptitiously at Yolande and then Charlotte. 'May I see it?' she asked, walking over to Adèle and picking up her wrist. She pretended to study the wristwatch in great detail and made murmurs of approval as she did so. 'It is a fine watch,' she said at last, letting go of Adèle's wrist. 'You are lucky to have a patron like Madame.'

'She is not my patron,' Adèle retorted hotly, clearly recovering her composure a little. Wearing a rueful expression, she rubbed her wrist, as though Sanchia had bruised it in some way. 'I, too, gave her a gift. You see, I will not be returning to Bad Alpendorf after our trip to Paris. Madame agrees with me that I have nothing more to learn.'

Adèle spoke haughtily, as was customary for her, but it was clear to the other girls, from the slight tremor in her voice, that the decision had not been quite the mutual one she made it out to be.

'Well, well, so you have been kicked out at long last,' Yolande said, clearly unable to disguise her glee.

To her surprise, even though Adèle looked extremely discomfited by Yolande's remark, and didn't try to argue with it, Charlotte found she had no sympathy for the young woman. If this had happened to any of the others, it would have been different. But Adèle . . .

Charlotte swiftly recalled one of her father's favourite adages about making beds and having to lie on them. Then she smiled.

'So, you think it is amusing, do you, Charlotte?' Adèle snapped, rounding on her, eyes blazing. 'I might have known.'

'No, not at all. It wasn't that . . .' Charlotte tried to explain the reason for her smile, but Adèle wouldn't let her.

Instead, she cut in fiercely, 'Well, I'll have you know, Little Miss High-and-Mighty, Butter-Wouldn't-Melt-In-Your-Mouth, Madame has nothing but contempt for you. And as for Max . . .'

'Yes?' Charlotte enquired, a warning note in her voice.

'He told me that he thinks you are a silly little fool,' Adèle said, her thin lips forming a sardonic smirk. 'Apparently, he and Eduardo have no end of fun making jokes about you when you are not around. They both think you are a stupid little feather-brain, with no sense of sophistication, much less decency. After the episode with that blacksmith boy, I overheard Max saying to Madame that you were nothing more than a dirty little trollop, and that the best he can say about you is that you are not bothered about making your various orifices available to him whenever he wants to use them.' As Charlotte stared at the vicious young woman, open-mouthed, Adèle added, 'Oh, yes, and he was a little concerned that he might catch some dreadful disease from you. He said it was impossible

175

to tell who, or what, might have been inside you before him.'

'Why, of all the . . .' Both Sanchia and Yolande were quick to leap to Charlotte's defence.

'You take that back, Adèle!' Sanchia said, advancing toward the young woman, her expression menacing. Her eyes glowed like coals, all the passion of her temperament clearly surfacing and coming to the boil.

Apparently undeterred by Sanchia's fury, Adèle simply shrugged her thin shoulders. 'I will not retract a single word. It is all true. You can ask Max, if you don't believe me.'

At such a bold pronouncement, Sanchia wavered. She glanced at Yolande and then both girls glanced swiftly at Charlotte.

Charlotte's face was ashen and she stood stock-still, apparently devoid of emotion. Only the slight trembling of her shoulders and lower lip belied her true feelings. All at once, she swayed, like a willow. Fortunately, Yolande leaped forward just in time to catch her.

'Now look what you've done!' she shouted at Adèle as she cradled Charlotte in her arms.

Charlotte was shaking, but she hadn't quite fainted and, with the protective warmth of Yolande's arms around her, felt some of her old spirit return.

'I am all right, Yolande. Thank you,' Charlotte murmured, straightening up. After a moment she shrugged off the young woman's embrace and walked up to Adèle.

They stood a mere inch or so apart, Charlotte staring hard into the other girl's eyes.

'You are a liar, Adèle,' she said calmly. 'And a very nasty, catty one at that. Of course I shall not ask Max if what you say is true. I know already that it is not. He would not say such things about me, or anyone for that matter. He is too much of a gentleman.' Having said this, she paused, not for effect but to swallow the lump that obstructed her throat. With the greatest effort, she willed herself not to cry. 'I am glad you are not returning to Bad Alpendorf, Adèle,' she continued after a moment, when she had recovered her composure slightly. 'You are not a nice person to be around.'

'Nice – what has being nice got to do with anything?' Adèle's laughter was contemptuous. 'No one gets anywhere in this world by being nice. Nice is for silly little sugary girls like you, with candyfloss in place of brains –'

Adèle didn't get to finish her verbal attack. In a flash, all the anger and resentment Charlotte felt toward her compatriot erupted. She lunged at Adèle, her fingers clawing wildly at her pale-complexioned face and dragging at her hair.

'Ow – ow!' Adèle started to yell immediately. She fought back, trying to grab Charlotte by the wrists and pulling at her hair in return. With her hand swiftly raised, she slapped Charlotte hard across the cheek.

As Adèle's palm came into contact with her face, Charlotte felt first its sting as flesh connected with flesh, then stars seemed to explode in front of her eyes. Her head reeled and she staggered back a couple of paces. Unfortunately, she was still gripping Adèle's hair and thus managed to drag the other girl with her.

'Get off me, you bitch, get off me!' Adèle screamed. 'You're tearing my hair out by the roots!'

'Good, serves you right,' Sanchia said from the sidelines. However, she realised the whole train would be alerted to the uproar in a moment, if she didn't try to do something to stop her room-mates from attacking each other. With a huge effort, she hauled Adèle away from Charlotte.

Adèle screamed and immediately Sanchia saw why. Charlotte was left clutching a huge clump of Adèle's pale blonde hair in each fist.

Charlotte gazed at her hands, looking at the hair she was grasping but unable to assimilate it. It seemed inconceivable that she could have done such a thing.

'Get her out of here,' Charlotte muttered to Sanchia in a low voice. 'Get her out of my sight before I kill her.'

The Spanish girl paused for just a second. Then it was as though a light came on in her head and she glanced at Yolande. The other young woman nodded. It seemed the two girls had no need to communicate by using words; their thoughts were enough.

In moments Yolande had grabbed Adèle, too, and straightaway both young women began to systematically strip her. Adèle fought against them, naturally, but when Charlotte joined in the struggle, it was clear Adèle had lost the battle.

'What shall we do with her?' Sanchia questioned when Adèle was completely naked.

Yolande, who was still holding the struggling Englishwoman firmly, shrugged. 'I think we ought to leave that up to Charlotte,' she said, glancing in Charlotte's direction.

Stunned by the opportunity to get her revenge on Adèle at last, Charlotte simply stared at her friends. 'I don't know what to do with her,' she said. 'Throw her off the train? Let her walk all the way to Paris?' She laughed to show that she was only joking.

'Not a bad idea,' Sanchia murmured. She winked at Charlotte behind Adèle's back.

Immediately, Adèle began to struggle again. 'You cannot do such a dreadful thing to me!' she cried. 'I would be killed. And you would all be hanged for murder.'

'That is true,' Yolande said solemnly, making it appear as though the possibility of the death penalty were the only reason they should reconsider their options.

'Maybe we can't risk throwing her off the train, but we could eject her from this compartment,' Charlotte said, her eyes gleaming as a wicked vision began to take shape in her imagination. 'Just give me a moment,' she added quickly, 'there is something I must do first.'

Without offering any explanation to her two friends, she dashed out of the room. A few minutes later, she returned, looking triumphant. 'All right,' she said, rubbing her palms together decisively. 'Now we can throw her out.'

Chapter Thirteen

The fuss surrounding Adèle's ignominious expulsion from Yolande's carriage finally died down at around five in the morning. Max came to the compartment, looking for Charlotte and Sanchia. His facial expression told them he was clearly angry, yet something else lurked in his eyes. Looking at him, as he strode into the small compartment, his presence seeming to fill it, Charlotte hoped it was amusement.

Fortunately for all of them, it turned out that it was.

Max, it transpired, could not maintain his angry stance for long. His severe expression began to crumble as soon as he started to describe how he had received a knock on his door, only to find a harassed and very red-faced steward standing outside in the corridor, holding his coat around the shoulders of an otherwise naked Adèle.

'She screamed at me that I was a bastard as soon as I opened the door,' he told the three girls. He looked so bemused that they were each forced to smother a grin. 'I had been fast asleep and so I just stood there for a moment, trying to take everything in. Which I am sure just made poor Adèle all the more angry.' He paused for a moment, his expression becoming reflective.

'Poor Adèle, nothing. I wish I could have been there to witness it,' Charlotte countered, trying not to laugh aloud. 'Clearly you are reliving the scene in your head, Max.' She smiled broadly at him, knowing that her assumption was correct. Enigmatic though he could appear most of the time, sometimes Max Spieler was an open book. 'I hope you are not too angry with us – that is, mostly me,' she added.

Try as she might, Charlotte couldn't possibly look contrite. And all she felt was relief that her revenge for Adèle's nastiness to her, and indeed to all of them, was complete.

'Suffice it to say, Adèle will not be accompanying us to Paris, after all,' Max said. 'You are probably aware that she was not intending to return to Bad Alpendorf, in any event?'

'She told us,' Sanchia interjected. 'She said that she and Madame had reached a mutual decision about it.'

The way Max pursed his lips and muttered, 'Mm,' made it clear to all of the girls that their original assumption had been correct. Adèle had been asked to leave. She had taken no part in the decision.

'I hope you know that, while I may appear amused, I am not happy about your treatment of Adèle,' Max said. 'It was unkind and, above all, thoughtless. It could even have proved dangerous. What if she had been accosted by one of the other male passengers? My God, she could have been raped.' For the first time he looked truly horrified.

All three girls fell silent, each feeling guilty in the face of Max's reasoning. It was true. An attractive young woman abandoned naked and defenceless in the corridor of a train: anything could have happened to her.

'We did not intend that she should come to any harm,' Charlotte assured him, 'although I take your point, Max. It was stupid of me.'

'Yes it was,' Max agreed. Reaching out, he ruffled Charlotte's hair. 'Very stupid. But from what I understand from your friends, it was also entirely understandable that you should seek some form of retaliation. Speaking personally, I did not like Adèle either, but I thought her unfriendly way toward me was simply because she hated all men. I knew she was in love with my sister –'

'In love with her?' All three girls chorused, interrupting him. They looked shocked.

'We thought she was just sucking up to Madame,' Charlotte explained after a moment. 'You know, trying to be Madame's special pupil?' she added, when Max and her two friends gazed blankly at her, clearly failing to comprehend her idiomatic use of English.

'It was far more than that,' Max said. 'Adèle approached my sister and told her that she wanted them both to run the school together.'

'But what would you have done?' Charlotte asked, her brow furrowing in consternation.

'Exactly,' Max said. 'Which is precisely what my sister asked of Adèle. When she found out that Adèle couldn't care less what happened to me, naturally Birgitte – Madame,' he added hastily, 'said that she would not entertain her proposal for one minute. We are very close, my sister and I.'

'I know, and I think it is lovely. I wish I had a brother like you,' Charlotte said.

As she reached out and patted Max's hand, Charlotte was struck by the realisation that what she felt for Max was not love. At least, not the same type of love she felt for Cadell. The sort of affection and desire she held for Max was similar to her feelings for Sanchia and, up to a point, Yolande. Cadell was and always would be her first real and only true love, of that she now felt certain.

'Well, I think there is no real harm done,' Max concluded, getting stiffly to his feet. 'Adèle will leave the train at Paris and return straightaway to England. As for you three,' he paused and glanced fondly at their upturned faces, 'you should get some sleep. We have a long day ahead of us – and an even longer night,' he added mysteriously.

Yolande, Charlotte and Sanchia shared curious glances but agreed that yes, they badly needed to get their beauty sleep.

'Oh, I would not go as far as to say that,' Max joked, his eyes twinkling like the night sky as he gazed openly upon their loveliness. 'Your beauty could never be dimmed for want of a few hours' sleep. But all I can say is that you will need plenty of energy for tomorrow.'

'Max, could you please stop being so cryptic?' Charlotte begged him teasingly. She punched him lightly on the arm.

'No, I cannot,' he said. 'It is all part of my fun. Being a tutor to you girls is hard work, you know.'

In response to this, all three young women rolled their eyes.

'Ah, yes, how silly of me not to realise,' Charlotte quipped in a sardonic tone. 'Poor Max, your life must be such a trial.'

She giggled as Max slapped her behind in mock reproach, then skipped off down the corridor to her room. Once inside her cabin, she leant against the door and let out a happy sigh.

At last she felt truly at ease with herself. She knew what she wanted, or rather *who* she wanted. And goodness gracious, wasn't Cadell going to be surprised when he discovered what he could expect to get every night from her in return?

It was a groggy bunch who staggered from the train at La Gare du Nord station later that morning. Fortunately for them all, Max had arranged for a car to collect them and take them to their hotel, which was located in the heart of Paris.

'We will be staying on the Left Bank, close to Montparnasse,' Max told the three girls as they settled back on the plush leather seats of the Bugatti limousine. 'The hotel I have chosen is small but comfortable. You were to share twin-bedded rooms, but since Adèle has departed, it means you can either all share a room together, or one of you can have a room to herself.'

Charlotte glanced sideways at him and smiled. 'That sounds very bohemian,' she said. 'I mean, staying on the Left Bank.'

'It is intended to be.' Max flashed her a smile in return, then did the same to the other two girls. 'Our stay in Paris will be a foray into the more underground establishments.'

'Are you referring to opium dens?' Yolande was agog.

Max laughed. 'Not quite. But almost. I am particularly looking forward to witnessing your reactions to some of the more *avant-garde* aspects of this visit.' His expression was once again enigmatic, which piqued Charlotte's curiosity instantly.

'How do you mean, *avant-garde*?' she queried with a slight raising of her eyebrows.

'Oh, you will see,' Max said, apparently refusing to be led into revealing more than he intended. 'But, for now, I think we should concentrate on checking into the hotel and all of you getting a lot more sleep. I suggest we meet in the restaurant at seven for an early dinner, before we go out.'

Just as he spoke, the limousine pulled up outside a small, friendly-looking hotel. It was a tall narrow building with two black wrought-iron balconies to each floor. A profusion of brightly coloured flowers spilled from pots on the balconies.

'Oh, this is just lovely!' Charlotte exclaimed, clapping her hands together with childish enthusiasm. Her face was wreathed in smiles as she glanced up at the building.

When the chauffeur had, with the aid of a bellboy, finished installing all their luggage in their rooms, Charlotte, Yolande and Sanchia all bade a temporary goodbye to Max and trooped up the two flights of stairs to their room. Given the choice, they had opted to share one room and the concierge had been most accommodating about installing a third bed into one of the twin-bedded rooms.

'It will be more fun, like this,' Charlotte assured the others as she squeezed past the extra bed. In all honesty, the room was small enough already, without the addition of another bed.

'Claustrophobic, more like,' Yolande commented with a wry smile as she threw herself face-down on one of the beds. 'Oh, thank God, this is so comfortable.' Within minutes, she was snoring gently.

Charlotte walked over to the tall French windows that led out onto one of the balconies they had viewed from the street, then flung them open and stepped out. For a moment she stood, gripping the railing that ran around the top of the balcony and soaking up the unique atmosphere that was Paris. The sights and sounds were foreign yet, at the same time, familiar and a far cry from the stillness and peace of Bad Alpendorf. Just for a moment, she felt a wistful longing to hear the gentle tinkle of cow-bells. Then the moment passed and she turned to look back into the room.

Sanchia was lying prone on the furthest bed, the rhythmic rise and fall of her chest leaving Charlotte in no doubt that, like Yolande, she too had fallen asleep. Charlotte shrugged, a smile sweeping across her face. She felt tired, yet she knew she was too excited to sleep. Paris always did that to her. There was so much to enjoy about the city and, no matter how many times she might visit it, still so much to discover.

Brave enough to risk the wrath of Max if he were to find out, Charlotte picked up her bag and left the room, closing the door quietly behind her. She ran lightly down the two flights of stairs and, in a few moments, she was outside, standing on the narrow pavement. She had absolutely no idea where she was, or where she wanted to be heading, but decided to turn right up the street and see where that route took her.

Having made her decision, she began to walk decisively, her

arms swinging, cream leather clutch-bag in one hand and a smile on her face. Once again, Charlotte was on the look-out for adventure.

It was on the bank of the Seine, just a few kilometres from the Eiffel Tower, that she encountered the artist. Charlotte had walked a long way and was grateful to sink down on the lush springy grass and simply observe the artist as he worked.

He was seated on a low stool at an easel, his back to her, a sable brush loaded with green paint held in his left hand.

Charlotte hadn't seen his face, so had no idea how old the artist might be. She really wasn't all that interested in him, or in what he might be daubing on his canvas. In all honesty, she was too exhausted to care. With a sigh of contentment, she lay back upon the grass and flung one arm across her eyes to shield them from the uncompromising glare of the midday sun.

After a few minutes, she realised that she should have picked a spot that was in the shade. She was just struggling to her feet when the artist spoke to her.

'Afraid of catching too much of the sun?' He didn't turn his head when he spoke to her, but continued to paint. After a moment, he put down his brush and picked up a tube of blue paint from the box that lay by his feet on the grass. 'Are you deaf, or simply bloody rude?' he surprised Charlotte by asking. As he spoke, he squeezed the tube over his palette. A thin blue worm of paint eased out of the tube and onto the pallette.

'If you ask me, it is you who are rude,' Charlotte retorted, stooping to pick up her clutch-bag from the grass. 'If you must know, I would prefer to sit in the shade.'

'Too delicate, eh?' the man asked, still not turning round. Without saying anything else, he began to daub the blue paint in little spots all over the canvas.

'If you say so,' Charlotte muttered crossly.

She stood up straight, brushing stray blades of grass from the ankle-skimming safari-style dress she had chosen to wear that morning. In cream linen, the dress buttoned down the front to her waist, which was cinched in tightly with a snakeskin belt. The style of her dress was simple but flattering. With the top few buttons left undone, it showed off Charlotte's luscious cleavage to advantage, while the belt served to emphasise both the neatness of her waist and the generous curve of her hips.

'Don't walk away from me when I'm talking to you,' the artist said, just as she prepared to leave that particular spot.

'I beg your pardon?' Charlotte wheeled round. Her expression was at once incredulous and more than a little irate.

For the first time, the artist turned his head to look at her. He seemed fairly young, in his late twenties at the most. His features were regular, his chin obscured by a rather tatty beard the same colour brown as his hair. All in all rather unremarkable, Charlotte thought dismissively. Then she glanced at him again and happened to notice his eyes for the first time. They were a very surprising and intriguing shade of blue-green that she could best describe as teal.

When she realised she was staring blatantly at the artist, Charlotte looked deliberately away and raised her own eyes to heaven. She couldn't help wondering why God insisted on tempting her, time and time again, in this way. It seemed so unfair that so many of the men she had come into contact with lately had blue eyes.

Though, in this particular instance, she felt immune to the temptation. For once, her feelings of annoyance toward the artist outweighed her inherent attraction to the colour of his eyes. He was incredibly rude and would be quite impossible to like, she was sure.

All at once, the artist put down his brush and palette and turned round. He sat on the stool, boot-clad feet planted firmly apart. Then he leant forward, hands resting palm-down on his thighs to support the weight of his upper body. His facial expression was grave, the uncompromising look in his eyes impossible to shy away from.

'I asked you not to walk away from me. You English are very rude,' he said. Then he paused and shook his head rapidly, as though trying to dismiss an unwelcome thought before slapping a palm against his forehead in a dramatic gesture. 'Bah, but I don't know why I bother! I cannot hope to change the behaviour of an entire race just by talking to one person.'

'Do you mind not denigrating the English?' Charlotte

retorted hotly. 'It is typical of you French. You resent us for so many things, most of them to do with battles and war. I am not interested in history and refuse to take part in your silly prejudices.'

'Silly, eh?' The artist sat back and stroked his beard thoughtfully. For the first time, his hard expression appeared to soften and a twinkle came into his eyes. 'Well, all I can say is that I am not prepared to waste a glorious afternoon arguing with someone who is not academic,' he said. He waved his hand dismissively. 'Run along now. I am sure you have really pressing business, such as deciding what dress you should wear tonight, and I wouldn't wish to keep you.'

Charlotte stared at him, open-mouthed. His rudeness was quite incredible. As was his perception, she realised with a guilty pang. She had indeed been wondering what she should wear that evening.

'I shall go,' she retorted. 'Not because you tell me to, but because I wish it. I am certainly not prepared to stand here and be insulted by a peasant.' She paused and glanced contemptuously at his canvas, which was covered with indecipherable streaks and blobs of colour. 'Why, you cannot even paint. You are a fraud!'

At this, the artist surprised her by bursting out laughing. He threw back his head and let out such a loud guffaw that passers-by stopped in their tracks and stared at both him and Charlotte.

'What would a feather-brain like you know about art?' the artist said, at last. Taking a navy-blue handkerchief from his trouser pocket, he dabbed at his eyes where tears of mirth had formed.

'How dare you? Take that back!' Incensed by his insult, Charlotte lunged at the young man and slapped him smartly around the face. Then she took a step back. She felt not the least bit frightened or horrified by what she had done. Indeed, the satisfaction her action afforded her was mirrored by her expression.

'Such passion,' the artist murmured thoughtfully, appearing not at all angry or surprised by her outburst. If anything, he seemed awed by it. 'Now *that* has changed my opinion of you.'

'I couldn't care less what opinion you have of me,' Charlotte responded, glaring at him. 'You are nothing but an uncouth boor. Good day to you.' And with that, she turned on her heel.

She had barely made it a few feet across the grass before she felt a hand grab her by the elbow. The artist swung her round to face him. Then, to Charlotte's complete amazement, he pulled her roughly into his arms and kissed her hard.

When he finally let her go, Charlotte found herself gasping for breath. Her heart was galloping behind her ribcage and her face was flushed from being held so tightly by him. Furthermore, her mouth felt bruised, as though he had punched her rather than kissed her.

With a baleful glare, she passed the back of her hand across her lips and winced when she realised just how tender they felt.

'I should slap you again for that,' she said in a low voice, barely able to control her anger, nor her amazement at what he had done.

'And I should take you to a quiet spot and fuck the stupidity out of you,' the artist responded, matching her glare.

Charlotte's immediate response was to raise her arm to strike him again but, this time, the artist anticipated her reaction and caught her by the wrist. He pulled her arm down and held it by her side, grasping her other wrist and holding that arm down, too, just in case she should decide to use it.

Absolutely incensed, Charlotte tried to struggle, but to no avail. Her efforts were no match for his strength. And this alone amazed her. He appeared so thin and not at all muscular. What also amazed her was her body's reaction to his treatment of her, not to mention his threat. The adrenaline racing through her was translated into an urgent throbbing between her legs and an immediate tightening of her nipples which she found impossible to ignore.

'Come on – *allons-y*,' The artist said gruffly. He began dragging her, still holding her by the wrists, toward the bridge which spanned the river just a short distance away.

'What do you mean, come on? Where are you taking me?' Charlotte protested. When she saw the determination in the young artist's face, she immediately gave up trying to pull away from his grasp. She allowed herself to be led to a spot under the bridge, where they were shielded to a certain degree from the inquiring eyes of people passing by.

It was cold under the bridge. The rays of the sun were completely obscured by the thick brick walls which supported the bridge, and the air around them smelt damp and musty. When the artist pressed her back against one of the brick supports, Charlotte recoiled at the stone's clammy texture. She shivered and was almost glad when the young man's arms went around her briefly.

Looking up into the artist's face, she saw a gleam of desire in his eyes. He was panting, his breath coming in short sharp gasps. And there was no ignoring the fact that his body trembled almost as much as her own.

'I don't even know your name,' she gasped, after he had kissed her a second time. She arched her back, pressing herself ardently against him. She could feel the hardness at his groin digging into her belly and felt a continuous trickle of her feminine juices slide down the insides of her thighs.

'Christophe,' he mumbled gruffly, his fingers working deftly at the buttons that fastened down the front of her dress. All of a sudden, as the last button slipped through its hole, he ripped the front edges of her dress apart, making Charlotte gasp with arousal.

'Charlotte,' she muttered back, equally gruffly. Passion was coursing through her at an incredible rate, and she felt she could hardly wait until he had managed to free her thrusting breasts.

She aided him in pulling her camisole up to the base of her throat. It felt so wanton to be exposing her breasts to him in that fashion, and she gave a deep sigh of desire as his hands came up to cup them.

He caressed her breasts briefly, his fingertips tweaking urgently at her hard little nipples. Then all at once he groaned and began to fumble with his fly. His penis sprang free, hard and virile, making Charlotte whimper with longing. Sinking to her haunches she enveloped it in her mouth, licking and sucking, feeling it throb and swell between her lips until he grasped her by the hair and dragged her head away.

'Up,' he said, pulling her to her feet, 'up.'

His passion for her appeared to make him a man of little words but, right at that moment, Charlotte felt she could not care less. Her own body was responding to his ardour, the flesh between her thighs beating rhythmically to its own tune.

Without any attempt at protest, she allowed him to press her back against the cold clammy wall again and drag down her knickers. Then he slid his hands up under her dress, caressed her for a moment between her legs, then slipped a finger inside her.

'Nice and wet,' he growled, circling his finger.

Charlotte moaned and felt her legs give way slightly. Her whole body felt wet and open to him, and she ground herself urgently upon his knuckles as he thrust another finger and then another inside her greedy channel. His thumb toyed with her clitoris, pushing back the little hood of skin and caressing its tip in a circling motion.

'I need it . . .' Charlotte gasped, not making herself clear what she meant. Her whole body raged with desire and she literally leapt into his arms as he slid his hand from between her legs, cupped her buttocks and lifted her.

As she wrapped her legs round his hips, Charlotte positioned herself so that the tip of his penis was nudging her pouting vagina. She shuddered as she felt his hardness against the sensitive rim of her opening, then sighed hugely and with relief as he rammed himself hard up inside her.

For a small man, he appeared surprisingly strong. He manhandled her easily, supporting her buttocks with his hands and raising her up and down on his stiff shaft.

Charlotte bucked and ground her hips, moaning incoherently as she felt her arousal grow. He seemed to fill her so well, and her passion was further inflamed by their location. Just a little way off she could hear, quite clearly, a man and a woman talking. She thrilled at the thought that, at any moment, she and Christophe might be discovered.

As her mind whirled with such tantalising thoughts, she concentrated on rubbing her swollen little clit against Christophe's pubic bone. His beard tickled her naked breasts as she rode him and, at the last moment, just before they both came, he growled something in French to her that, although she couldn't understand it, sounded so deliciously wicked that it tipped her over the edge.

She soared and soared, then fell into oblivion as the fierce pleasure of her orgasm blotted out everything else. Now she no longer heard the voices of the French couple, nor felt her spine scraping the hard, damp stone of the bridge support. Everything was obliterated as she concentrated on the sheer pleasure of her climax.

As her pleasure gradually began to ebb, so she relaxed her grip. Her arms, which had been wound tightly round Christophe's shoulders, slackened, as did the fierce grip of her thighs round his hips.

With his hands still cupping her buttocks, Christophe raised her slightly, until his softened penis slipped out of her, then he lowered her gently, so that her feet were planted firmly on the ground.

Charlotte's legs felt weak and shaky and she had to remain leaning against the wall for a moment, until she regained some semblance of normality.

'I suppose that was intended to teach me a lesson,' she joked weakly as she gazed at Christophe.

If I look half as shell-shocked as he does, she thought, I shall have to take care to compose myself properly before I return to the hotel. All at once, she found herself wondering what the time must be, and glanced hastily at her watch.

'Are you late for an appointment?' Christophe inquired. As he spoke he stooped down and picked up the discarded scrap of white satin that used to be her knickers.

The fabric was damp, Charlotte realised, when she took her panties from him. As she held the scrap of satin in her hands, she realised she couldn't tell if the dampness came from the fact that they had been lying on the ground, or if it had come from her own body. More likely a bit of both, she mused, as she decided against putting her panties on again and instead tossed them into the river.

'That will set people wondering,' she murmured, a half-smile touching her lips as she watched the way the current picked up the scrap of satin and carried it rapidly down-river.

She glanced back at Christophe. 'No, I am not late, fortunately,' she said to him. 'I don't have to be back at the hotel for another couple of hours.'

She finished buttoning her dress and, once she had smoothed down her hair and righted her belt, which had become twisted, she felt more or less presentable again.

'In that case,' Christophe said, buttoning his fly and tucking in his shirt, 'would you care to accompany me somewhere close by for coffee?'

Chapter Fourteen

No one could possibly have guessed, from looking at her fresh appearance and bouncing gait as she walked into the hotel restaurant, that Charlotte had spent the afternoon having sex under a bridge with a complete stranger.

In fact, she hadn't yet had the chance to tell her two friends.

The three friends entered the restaurant, arms linked, with Charlotte in the centre of the trio. They immediately glanced around, looking for Max.

He was already waiting for them at a round table that was covered with a white cloth. The table was positioned right in the centre of the restaurant. But at this early hour, the room contained only a few diners. And Charlotte could barely disguise a smile as the two lone men who were dining there appeared unable to stop themselves from staring as she, Sanchia and Yolande unlinked their arms and sashayed in single file across the restaurant and over to where Max awaited them.

The men threw blatantly envious glances at Max, who rose to his feet as the delightful trio approached the table.

'Good evening, ladies,' he said genially.

Moving around the table, he drew out a chair for each of them. And when they were all seated, with Charlotte and Yolande flanking Max on either side and Sanchia seated opposite him, he inquired if they were all feeling well rested.

Sanchia and Yolande immediately responded that yes, they were, but Charlotte glanced hastily away and mumbled something about having been unable to relax.

For a few uncomfortable moments, Charlotte felt Max's quizzical gaze upon her as she concentrated on arranging her napkin across her lap. Feeling unaccountably embarrassed, she kept her own gaze firmly averted. She could feel a blush stealing across her cheeks and willed her heart to stop hammering. The last thing she felt inclined to do was blurt out what she had really been up to, that afternoon. It was hardly the time nor the place to reveal her indiscretion.

Thankfully, the waitress arrived just at that moment. She stopped at their table, pad and pencil poised ready to take their order.

'Nothing too heavy, girls,' Max warned them teasingly. 'You will need to be alert, later on.'

'Oh, Max, for heaven's sake!' Charlotte exclaimed as she turned in her chair to face him. Her expression was animated, her tone one of amused exasperation.

Alarmed by Charlotte's outburst, the waitress took a hasty step backward.

All Max deigned to do was smile enigmatically, which only served to frustrate Charlotte even further. However, she waited until their order had been dealt with, before she broached the subject of the coming evening's entertainment. She was too curious to let the matter rest.

Despite Charlotte's most ardent entreaties, Max still refused to be browbeaten; not even when Sanchia and Yolande joined in.

'All I will tell you at this stage,' he said, picking up his knife and fork and eyeing the plate in front of him, 'is that we are going to a little place I know, where we can enjoy a drink or two and some unusual entertainment.'

'How do you mean, "unusual"?' Sanchia butted in. While she waited for Max to speak, she speared a green bean with her fork.

'You will see,' Max said, tapping the side of his nose with his forefinger. 'Now, please, all of you, stop questioning me. You will find out for yourselves, soon enough.'

It was clear to all of them that Max could not, and would not, be drawn any further on the subject. One by one, the girls resolved privately to drop it and concentrate on the excellent meal they had ordered. While they ate, they shared a couple of bottles of Sancerre. The wine was mellow and fruity and soon had them all feeling slightly tipsy.

With cheeks flushed and eyes sparkling from the effects of the wine, they declined dessert and, after downing cups of dark aromatic espresso, went out into the lobby. Through the glass panels on the hotel's front doors, they could see the Bugatti limousine. Small puffs of smoke emerged from its exhaust as it purred patiently by the kerbside, clearly waiting to whisk them off to their destination.

A *frisson* of excitement ran through Charlotte as the four of them settled into the back of the car and began a sedate but purposeful drive through the more bohemian parts of Paris. The girls chatted with Max about inconsequential things, but inside they each felt a burning curiosity.

At last, it seemed, their curiosity was finally about to be assuaged. The car drew to a smooth halt outside a building that looked as though it should have been condemned. It was not quite the plush location they had been expecting.

Without exception, each girl stared out of the rear window of the car, mouth agape. At Max's bidding, they got uncertainly out of the car and stood on the pavement.

With expressions full of doubt they gazed up at the building. The walls of the three-storey building were crumbling. Huge chunks of plaster had fallen off in places, especially at the edges. It was clear that the decaying process was still going on, as smaller chunks of plaster littered the pavement below the building. Planks of wood had been nailed across the windows on the upper floors and, on the ground floor, the windows were barred.

At the right-hand side of the building a heavy wooden door stood, apparently locked and bolted. But as Max approached it, with the three girls following nervously behind, the door miraculously opened.

Charlotte, Sanchia and Yolande huddled closer together as they glimpsed the burly man who had opened the door. He was bare-chested, revealing a thick mat of black hair that sprouted at neck and wrists, making him appear as though he were wearing a particularly hairy jumper.

Yolande giggled nervously when she saw him and whispered to Charlotte and Sanchia that he probably had no difficulty staying warm under such a thick 'coat'.

195

'I agree. I doubt that he ever feels the cold,' Charlotte replied in a stage whisper.

Obviously Max overheard her, because he glanced over his shoulder at her and gave her a look of mock reproach. In return, Charlotte shrugged her shoulders and was tempted to stick her tongue out at him, but thought better of it. It was hardly the behaviour of a sophisticated woman.

The doorman admitted them and, as she squeezed past him, Charlotte caught a strong whiff of musk and stale sweat. She tried not to wrinkle her nose in disgust, and hurried all the more quickly after Max as he started to descend the long narrow staircase in front of them.

As they reached the bottom of the staircase, it seemed as though they had entered a completely different world. The air downstairs was smoky. The sweet jasmine and patchouli scents of joss sticks and oil emanated from small brass burners placed strategically about the room. The lighting was very dim, supplied only by thick beeswax candles.

As Charlotte's eyesight became better adjusted to the poor lighting, she stopped dead in her tracks.

Her first impression of the room was that it was small. But, as she walked further into the bowels of the room, she saw that it was in fact quite large, with various alcoves and other smaller rooms leading off at different tangents.

At one side of the room stood a long bar, behind which two dinner-suited young men waited attendance with studied nonchalance. The men were quite small and slight: one fair-haired and one dark. And Charlotte stared in undisguised admiration as they each carried a long ebony holder to their lips at precisely the same moment and puffed casually on black Sobranie cigarettes.

As they tapped ash in unison into one of the square cut-glass ashtrays, which were placed on the polished wood bar-top at regular intervals, she couldn't help noticing too how slender their fingers were, the finely tapered ends tipped with short but perfectly manicured nails.

'Come along, Charlotte,' Max murmured to her, disturbing her reverie.

Charlotte hesitated for only a moment before following Max

and the others. A sense of acute anticipation burned inside her as she resumed the survey of her surroundings.

Around the rest of the room were scattered huge mounds of cushions, which were covered in a variety of fabrics, from silk and satin to tapestry and velvet. Elegant *chaises-longues* and low two- and three-seater backless chairs, in the style of Louis Quinze, were the only substantial form of furnishing.

'What is this place, Max?' Charlotte whispered. She drew Max aside and tried to look nonchalant, reaching up on tiptoe so that she could speak directly into his ear. Low music played but she didn't want to run the risk of being overhead. 'Is it a bar, or a nightclub, or someone's home? I really cannot tell.'

'Ostensibly it is a drinking club,' Max told her, making no effort to lower his voice. 'But, as you can see, it is also a little bit more than that. These people are all bohemians – artists, musicians, actors, artist's models and the like. They are also hedonists. People devoted to the pursuit of pleasure. This place is called Halcyon.'

'I can see why that is,' Charlotte said, giving the place another sweeping glance.

At that moment their attention was arrested by a trio of people, a man and two women. The man carried a large tapestry cushion in one hand and a strange-looking musical instrument in the other. The instrument looked to Charlotte like a cross between a guitar and a harp.

'That instrument is called a sitar,' Max told the three girls, in response to their questioning looks – by this time, Sanchia and Yolande had also clustered round Max to hear what was being said. 'It is from India and has a unique sound, which you will no doubt find out for yourselves, in a moment or two.'

He paused as the man – who was of indeterminate age, long-haired and bearded – set down the cushion and sat down cross-legged upon it. He positioned the base of the sitar in his lap and rested the neck of it against his right shoulder. Then, with his left hand, he began to pluck at the strings.

Charlotte listened in rapture. The sound the instrument made was like nothing she had ever heard before. It was sweet and mystical, the melody haunting and uncontroversially eastern in origin. It spoke to her of the Mystic East, an area of the world which fascinated her and which she hoped she would visit one day. Perhaps, she mused, Cadell could be persuaded to take her with him on one of his business trips there?

She had been so caught up in the music that she had hardly noticed what the two girls who accompanied the musician were doing. Now she saw that they were swaying side by side to the music. Slim and tall with long dark wavy hair, they were dressed very strangely, in diaphanous pantaloons of sheer white gauze. On their breasts they wore just the tiniest triangles of gold silk, decorated with sequins. But the strangest and most alluring sight of all was that of the brightly coloured jewels which they wore set in their navels: one an emerald and one an amethyst.

Apparently oblivious to the interested stares they received, the girls swayed in time with the music, their hips circling slowly, first one way and then the other, their slender arms marking sweeping paths. As they danced, their faces wore oddly beatific expressions, as though they were caught in the grip of something strange and mesmerising that no one else in the room could sense.

Their hair swung about their delicate faces as they began to increase the pace a little, and when the beat slowed, their hair settled like silk curtains around their shoulders and hung down their backs, the fine dusky ends brushing the upper swell of their buttocks.

In an instant, as one girl turned slightly and seemed to gaze straight at Charlotte – her dark eyes as glazed as the rest of her expression – Charlotte suddenly experienced a sharp bolt of desire that almost knocked her to the ground. Both girls were beautiful, but this one seemed as though she had been especially created for Charlotte's pleasure, such was the connection she felt with the young woman.

Charlotte's arousal was instantaneous and all-consuming. Once again, she experienced a slow burning sensation that started in the pit of her belly and spread like wildfire to encompass her whole body. Under the soft silk-jersey fabric of her ankle-length dress, Charlotte felt her nipples swell and tighten.

The dress was a deliberate choice, in sophisticated black and completely plain at the front, with a modest neckline.

However unassuming it might appear from the front, the back of the dress was intended to shock. The neckline was draped in soft folds and scooped low, just skimming the base of her spine, revealing the start of the cleft between her buttocks. The whole of the dress was superbly cut and flattered Charlotte's figure to perfection, clinging gently but deliberately to her luscious curves and displaying the full sweep of her spine to flawless advantage.

Max's approval, as she slipped off the opera cape she wore over the top of her dress, was made obvious as she handed the cape to an attendant and turned to watch the dancers again. His compliment was a sharp hiss of warm breath that glanced across her shoulder blades, making her quiver.

Charlotte glanced over her shoulder at him and smiled coquettishly. 'I thought you might like the surprise,' she said.

Max's immediate response was to grasp her by the shoulders and place a kiss at the top of her spine, right between her shoulder blades, his kiss dampening the skin that his breath had just warmed. Then he ran a single finger down the full length of her spine. At the edge of her dress, his finger did not stop its journey, but continued downwards into the cleft between her buttocks.

With a nervous giggle, Charlotte wriggled her hips. 'Max,' she hissed, sounding shocked, 'people will see –'

A sharp burst of gruff laughter interrupted her protests. 'That is the most innocent caress most people here will witness tonight,' he said, sounding mysterious again. But, before Charlotte could think of a suitable retort, he took her by the arm and led her over to the bar. 'I think you need a glass of champagne to loosen you up,' he said.

One of the waiters – the fair-haired one – came over to them and Charlotte had to look twice . . . three times . . . Then her jaw dropped. My God, she thought, her eyes widening with shock, the barman is a woman!

It took her a few moments to recover her composure.

The waiter was indeed a woman. Though from a distance she made a very passable attempt at looking like a man. With her blonde hair cut short and slicked back from her face, no make-up, save for a thin moustache pencilled across her upper lip, and a neat boyish figure, it was very difficult to tell the difference.

'Androgyny is very fashionable at the moment,' Max told Charlotte. 'Here in this secular part of Paris, you will find many women dressed as men and men dressed as women.'

'No!' Charlotte was unable to contain her disbelief.

'It is true, I tell you.' Max paused to order two bottles of champagne and four glasses. 'There is nothing you can do or say here that would shock anyone. You could walk into here stark naked and no one would bat an eyelid.'

As he spoke, Charlotte noticed that the dancers had taken off their minute tops and were now dancing bare-breasted. Every so often, they danced up to each other and rubbed their naked torsos together.

Feeling another pang, Charlotte quickly averted her gaze. She was starting to believe Max. And the atmosphere surrounding them was beginning to affect her in a very strange way. She felt a churning of excitement inside her that she couldn't quell. Nor did she want to. She sensed that there was a lot of potential here for experiencing new things and was eager to find out what form they might take.

She helped Max carry the champagne and glasses over to a spare mound of cushions, positioned not too far from the dancers. Charlotte lowered herself gingerly, arranging the hem of her dress neatly around her legs as she curled them under her. Then she leant back against the cushions behind her, letting her elbows support her as she watched Max pour the champagne.

Sanchia and Yolande came over and sat down. They smiled happily and in unison as Max handed them each a glass of the effervescent wine.

Charlotte took a couple of sips from her own glass and immediately felt herself relax a little. The bubbles in the champagne danced delightfully upon her tongue and burst upon the back of her throat as she swallowed. For a moment, she closed her eyes and simply savoured the coldness and dry fruitiness of her drink. Then she opened her eyes again and resumed her observation of the dancers.

The two girls were now dancing very close, their half-naked

bodies swaying together in perfect time. Their backs were arched, forcing each pair of breasts to thrust toward each other, their jutting nipples brushing. Their nipples were rouged, Charlotte noticed, feeling her stomach tighten perceptibly at the sight. And their areolae were huge dark rings.

The girls were clearly of Mediterranean origin. Their skin was olive-toned. It gleamed under a thin sheen of what Charlotte guessed was some kind of body oil. Beneath the diaphanous trousers, she could see the outline of their buttocks clearly. And the dark triangles of hair at the apex of their thighs appeared all the more tantalising for their scant amount of cover.

Their mode of dress was as shameless and abandoned as their style of dance. Their hips gyrated and their bodies swayed with the grace of tall reeds. Presently, the girls began to caress each other. The caresses were glancing at first, almost accidental. Long, graceful fingers touched bare skin at shoulders and breasts, then swept tantalisingly down arms and spines. At one point, the girls turned and danced back to back, their arms by their sides, fingers entwined as shoulder blades brushed each other and buttocks melded together.

'Ah, *Dios mio*, this dance, it is arousing, no?' Sanchia breathed. She sat next to Charlotte, her legs – clad in cream silk wide-legged trousers – crossed in the same fashion as those of the sitar player.

'Very,' Charlotte murmured back in agreement.

She hardly glanced at Sanchia. The truth was, she felt unable to take her eyes off the erotic spectacle taking place in front of her. The dance was innocent, yet incredibly arousing. And she found her level of desire mounting to an unbearable degree.

'Have you noticed how some of the other people here are reacting to the dance?' Yolande queried from the other side of Max.

It was only then, in response to her friend's question, that Charlotte felt able to tear her gaze away from the dancers and look around her instead. The sight that met her eyes, in every conceivable corner of the room, was shocking and, in some ways, far more arousing than that of the entertainment she had been witnessing.

All around them people had started to disrobe. Bare breasts, stomachs and bottoms could be seen everywhere Charlotte happened to glance. And those who were seated around them were caressing either themselves, or each other, quite openly; women with men, men with men, women with women . . .

Charlotte could hardly believe her eyes, particularly at the sight of the men together. It was the first time she had ever encountered male homosexuality. And she watched in awed amazement as one man close by them knelt between his companion's outstretched legs and took his penis in his mouth.

Burning with embarrassment, she looked quickly away, only to meet Max's amused stare.

'Are you disconcerted by what you see, my little one?' he asked gently. His hand came up to stroke her hair, his caress continuing down the back of her neck and the exposed sweep of her spine.

In response, Charlotte shivered. Max's fingers felt like tiny icicles glancing down the hot flesh of her naked back, yet in reality she knew his skin would be warm to the touch.

'A little,' she admitted, giving him a sheepish smile, 'but more intrigued than anything else. I didn't realise men did it in the same way with each other as a man and a woman,' she added as she watched another man slide his hard shaft between the buttocks of another.

Without meaning to, she winced.

Max laughed. 'Almost, but not quite.'

Charlotte blushed. 'You know what I mean.'

'But men and women can do it that way, too, can they not, Max?' Sanchia butted in.

To Charlotte's surprise, Max seemed taken aback by Sanchia's question.

'Can they?' Charlotte pressed him, her eyes widening at the thought.

Max looked uncharacteristically awkward as he cleared his throat. 'Yes, but it is illegal,' he said. Picking up his glass of champagne, he drained it in a single gulp.

'Why, Max, I do believe Sanchia has managed to embarrass you,' Charlotte said teasingly. 'I would not have thought it possible.' She flashed an amused glance at her Spanish companion, whose dark eyes glittered with undisguised wickedness.

'Never. Not I,' Max protested, although Charlotte deemed his protest a little feeble.

Fortunately for Max, his embarrassment was saved by one of the dancers. She came over to them, still swaying in time to the music as she moved. As she neared them, she stretched out her hands. Her gaze was fixed on Charlotte, making it clear that Charlotte was her target.

The girl said something in French which Charlotte translated as, 'Come dance with me?'

'Does she want me to dance with her?' Charlotte asked Max, unable to trust her own ears. It seemed too good to be true that the dancer was the one she had felt instantly attracted to: the one with the amethyst embedded in her navel. And yet she felt nervous about getting up and dancing in front of a roomful of strangers.

She quickly explained this to Max.

'I hardly think too many people here will be taking notice of you,' Max said, glancing around the room then smiling at Charlotte. 'They seem otherwise occupied, to me.'

It was true, Charlotte concluded, as she followed Max's glance. She still felt hesitant, though she got to her feet and took the girl's hand. Glancing sideways, she gave the girl a shy smile. 'I am not a very good dancer,' she said in French.

'It does not matter,' the girl replied. 'This is simply a form of free expression. There is no right or wrong way to demonstrate how you feel.'

At that moment, Charlotte felt as though her legs were made of lead and that she had two left feet. To begin with, her dance was more of an awkward and ungainly shuffle. Gradually, however, her love of music took over and she began to feel a little more relaxed. She copied the other two girls, simply allowing her body to sway in time with the rhythm.

After a moment or two the other dancer drifted away. She went to join a group of people sprawled on cushions on the far side of the room.

'Is she disappointed that I am dancing with you?' Charlotte

asked. She understood that lesbians were just as capable of jealousy as heterosexual couples.

The girl laughed sweetly. 'No, not at all. She has simply gone to join her friends, that is all. I am Eugenie, by the way.'

She held out her hand once again and Charlotte took it, repeating her own name. They did not shake hands, however, but simply gripped each other. Small tingles, like shockwaves, rippled up Charlotte's arm and for once she found it difficult to smile. Indeed, her expression was frozen as she tried hard to ignore the powerful wave of desire that swept over her.

Once again, it seemed, she was destined to experience a new encounter.

Chapter Fifteen

Somehow, during the course of the evening, Charlotte found herself shedding most of her clothes. As she continued to dance with Eugenie, her dress started to feel unbearably cumbersome.

After a few more glasses of champagne, she felt uninhibited enough to remove it.

Next came the half-slip she wore under her dress, which left her clad only in a pair of black silk-and-chantilly-lace French knickers, silk stockings and shoes. Her stockings were opaque and secured at mid-thigh by black satin garters, while her shoes were medium-heeled, in black calfskin, with narrow straps that crossed her high instep and were secured by tiny black pearls.

The deep ebony, in contrast to her pale skin, looked amazing, she thought immodestly as she glanced down at herself. And the delicate rose shade of her jutting nipples exactly matched the colour of her lips, both upper and lower. A flush spread over her at the thought of that secret flesh between her legs which swelled and chafed gently against the soft silk of her underwear.

In her head, she felt it was only a matter of time before that, too, was revealed. But when? And to whom?

Swiftly, unable to bear the torment of the unknown, she turned her thoughts back to the present. It felt superbly decadent to be dancing in front of so many people, while wearing such little clothing. Her wantonness appalled and thrilled her in equal measure. Her breasts swung freely as she swayed to the music and, even if she managed to ignore everyone else present, there was no way she could deny the arousing knowledge that the eyes of her two friends and Max were fixed upon her as she moved.

For all their professed boldness, both Sanchia and Yolande appeared envious of her abandon and moved restlessly on the cushions on which they reclined.

But it mattered not who was watching her, or what they thought. In truth, Charlotte thought, she felt as though she had been taken over by the music and the hedonistic milieu of the club. The atmosphere was as mesmerising as the erotic gyrations of Eugenie, who swayed gracefully in front of her.

Every so often, Eugenie's steps would bring her so close to Charlotte that their breasts touched. The sensation was spellbinding. And there was no way Charlotte could resist reaching out to feel the silky texture of Eugenie's skin for herself. Her fingertips skimmed the satin sheen of Eugenie's bare shoulders and upper arms, and presently she felt daring enough to risk stroking a breast.

Eugenie immediately arched her back when Charlotte touched her. She thrust her willing flesh toward her, silently urging Charlotte to caress her more boldly.

With such lusciousness presented to her in this licentious way, Charlotte couldn't resist cupping Eugenie's small pointed globes in both hands. Her caresses were gentle but eager. The young woman's breasts felt wonderful: firm, yet malleable. The bold nipples were cone-shaped, the rouge that enhanced them leaving Charlotte's fingertips coated with a faint blush.

As Charlotte stroked her fingers over the stiff buds Eugenie gave a moan that was loud enough for Charlotte to hear above the music. Liquid desire trickled through Charlotte when she heard that sound. The firm warmth of Eugenie's breasts in her hands and the sight of the young woman's wet and slightly parted lips almost drove her to distraction. More than anything, she wanted to grab the young woman by the hand and drag her off to a secluded corner somewhere.

With her heart beating rapidly, Charlotte glanced round. It wasn't long before she noticed that one of the *chaises longues* had become free on the far side of the room. The yellow brocade-covered *chaise* was not in a particularly isolated spot, but at least it was positioned in a corner of the room that was draped in heavy shadow.

Seizing her courage and Eugenie's hand, Charlotte pulled the exotic young woman in the direction of the *chaise*. With only a brief backward glance at the sitar player, Eugenie went willingly with Charlotte.

Obviously realising that he had now lost both his dancers, the sitar player shrugged and put down his instrument before sauntering over to the bar.

'I could not carry on dancing. Not when I want you so much,' Charlotte gasped ardently, as she urged Eugenie to sit next to her on the *chaise*.

In response, Eugenie said nothing, but gave Charlotte an enigmatic half-smile. Leaning forward, she hooked her thumbs under the elasticated waistband of her sheer pantaloons and wriggled out of them. Afterward, she did not sit upright like Charlotte, but draped herself across the *chaise* and rested her head in Charlotte's lap. Wearing a seductive expression, her dark eyes afire with barely suppressed desire, she reclined, entirely naked, the languid sprawl of her wanton body clearly an open invitation.

As she gazed down at the young woman, Charlotte felt everything galvanize inside her. Her desire for Eugenie was so extreme it shocked her. Passion surged inside her with such potency she could hardly stop herself from trembling as she stroked her hands in wonder over the young woman's shoulders and across her breasts. The nipples hardened immediately and, in an unconscious gesture, Charlotte licked her lips.

Just as she bent her head to take one of those delicious buds in her mouth, a man approached them. It was the same one who had been playing the sitar, Charlotte realised.

Eugenie gave him a sideways glance then smiled at him, the casual wave of her hand an open invitation to him to join them.

'Do you mind?' Eugenie asked Charlotte, her question seemingly an afterthought.

For a moment Charlotte hesitated. She had hoped to have Eugenie all to herself, yet it seemed impossible to refuse the beautiful young woman anything. And in any case the young man – who introduced himself to her as Marcus – had already seated himself on the floor beside the *chaise* and had begun to trail his fingertips lightly across Eugenie's torso in a meandering caress.

The young Frenchwoman's body strained to Marcus's touch. It was clear to Charlotte that the two of them were lovers and that Eugenie very much wanted her boyfriend to join them in whatever pleasures they decided to explore. To deny either of them would be churlish, Charlotte decided. And if she were to do so, she might run the risk of losing Eugenie to Marcus completely.

She couldn't bear to let the opportunity of making love with the dusky-haired young maiden pass, and so she smiled and whispered softly that she had no objection at all to Marcus joining them.

Throwing a hasty glance of gratitude at Charlotte, Marcus immediately got up onto his knees and began to caress Eugenie in a more intimate fashion.

Charlotte watched the movements of his hands with fascination. The hair at the apex of the young woman's thighs was lush and dark, completely obscuring the delicate petals of her intimate flesh. Yet, as Marcus began to stroke the profusion of glossy curls and comb his fingers through them, Charlotte couldn't help but notice the way Eugenie's outer lips swelled, gradually revealing the moist rose-hued flesh of her inner lips.

Eugenie was panting slightly, her lips wetted and parted. The pointed tip of her tongue kept flicking out to stroke across the sullen fullness of her bottom lip and her eyelids were half-closed, the expression in her eyes hazy with lust.

'Please to kiss her breasts,' Marcus said to Charlotte in broken English. 'She love the woman's mouth on her nipples.'

'Oh, I would love to,' Charlotte responded eagerly, feeling a fresh rush of desire.

Dropping her head forward, she cupped both Eugenie's breasts in her hands. Forcing herself to take things slowly, she allowed the ends of her hair to trail seductively across Eugenie's torso as she stroked her tongue around her breasts and over the hard buds of her nipples.

As she tongued and suckled the young woman's breasts, Charlotte sensed that Marcus was watching her. When she raised her head, she saw that her assumption was correct. The expression on his face was a mixture of reverence and undisguised desire.

'Ah, you women,' he said, sounding full of awe. 'I love you all. So beautiful. So natural.'

Charlotte smiled warmly at him. Marcus was not the most handsome of men, yet he had a certain way about him. It was a charisma that she couldn't deny was very attractive. He carried with him the air of an artist and she thought Eugenie extremely lucky to have such a man, while Marcus was even more fortunate for having a girl as beautiful and seductive as Eugenie.

With only a slight amount of hesitation, she told them what she thought.

Both Eugenie and Marcus smiled, firstly at each other and then at Charlotte.

'You will stay here for a while with us, yes?' Marcus asked, looking directly at Charlotte.

Even though she wanted to very much, for a moment she hesitated. She felt she ought to ask Max if it was all right for her to do so, but she could not see him anywhere. Nor could she immediately spot Sanchia or Yolande.

Then all at once her searching gaze alighted on her two friends who – judging by their state of undress and uninhibited actions with a small group of men and women Charlotte had never seen before – were clearly not giving a moment's thought to what Charlotte might be getting up to.

'I am not planning to go anywhere, just yet,' Charlotte answered Marcus, hoping that he would get the message.

'Then perhaps you would care to taste Eugenie for yourself,' Marcus responded. So saying, he spread Eugenie's outer labia wide apart with his fingers and made Charlotte an offering of her pouting sex.

With mounting excitement, Charlotte got up carefully and placed a cushion beneath Eugenie's head, before moving to the opposite end of the *chaise*. Then she knelt on the seat between Eugenie's thighs.

As she glanced down and her gaze alighted upon the pouting pink flesh in front of her, she felt her breath catch. A slow trickle of moisture soaked into the silken crotch of her knickers and she had to clench her thighs together tightly to help assuage her arousal a little.

Moving closer, Charlotte dared to touch and study the flesh laid out before her, as enticing as any banquet. As always, she found the discovery of another woman's body absolutely fascinating. Eugenie's outer lips were dark, olive-toned like the rest of her flesh, their colouring providing a beautiful contrast to the rosy petals nestling between them. And while Charlotte was helplessly seduced by such beauty, she managed to force herself not to rush things but to take them as slowly and sensuously as possible.

Her fingertips began a journey that her tongue was destined to finish. As she parted the soft lips that pouted so beguilingly at her, Charlotte was delighted to encounter Eugenie's moist honeyed core. Charlotte slid a couple of fingers gently inside the young woman, the slippery walls of Eugenie's vagina aiding their smooth passage.

Charlotte glanced up as Eugenie gave a little moan and began to churn her hips. She shared a conspiratorial, almost loving smile with Marcus. It was clear that he delighted in Eugenie's responses and in witnessing her pleasure.

This realisation caused Charlotte to experience a sudden surge of happiness. All at once, she understood that this was how Cadell would treat her. That this level of unselfish and abandoned giving and receiving of pleasure was what he had envisaged for their future together, all along. It was clearly the reason he had insisted on enroling her at the school at Bad Alpendorf.

Her thoughts were interrupted by the whispering glance of Marcus's fingers on her shoulder. 'I want to touch you, too. Do you mind it?'

Charlotte's sideways glance met his eyes. Dark like coals, they seemed to smoulder with undisguised desire. She smiled as she shook her head lightly. 'No, I don't mind,' she murmured. 'I would love you to touch me.'

Still kneeling between Eugenie's legs, Charlotte got to her hands and knees, to enable Marcus to slip her French knickers over her hips and down her legs. She kicked them off with hardly a second thought, then arched her back and let out a sigh of pleasure as he immediately pressed his lips to the split plum of her sex.

It aroused her still further to realise that the three of them were joined in pleasure, her lips pressed to Eugenie's sex, Marcus's mouth exploring hers. She gasped, her tongue flickering wildly over the young woman's flesh as she felt Marcus's tongue do the same to her flesh in return. The hard bud of Eugenie's clitoris was clearly discernible. It seemed to pulse under Charlotte's tongue and swell to twice its original size as she lapped gently at it.

Then, all at once, Eugenie began to buck her hips. Her movements were so uncontrolled that Charlotte was forced to grip her hips, in an attempt to hold her still and to stop the hard bud of the young woman's clitoris from escaping the relentless caresses of her tongue.

'Aiee . . . !' the French girl cried out suddenly. The muscles in her flat belly tensed and bowed outward and she began to shudder.

Still gripping her hips, Charlotte kept up the sensuous rhythm her tongue had begun to beat against Eugenie's clitoris. It was only when the girl began to flinch each time Charlotte touched her with the tip of her tongue that Charlotte realised she had taken all she could for the moment.

She had been so intent on Eugenie's pleasure that she had barely noticed what Marcus had been doing to her. Now, though, with all her concentration redirected to the tingling flesh between her thighs, she felt the first dark waves of her own climax wash over her.

The cries and whimpers which she uttered with total abandon as her passion reached its crescendo were greeted by the sound of a slow handclap.

'Bravo, little one,' a familiar voice murmured in her ear.

As she glanced sideways, Charlotte felt her heart turn over. Then her stomach clenched. What a position to be discovered in! And why was he here, of all places? The last person on earth she expected to see.

'Cadell?' she said in a wondering voice.

His slow smile warmed her, as did the clear picture of love and desire in his blue eyes.

'Did you miss me?' he asked, sounding amused. 'Or is that a stupid question, under the circumstances?'

Charlotte didn't hesitate for a moment. She jumped up, heedless right now of Eugenie – who still lay in a blissful state upon the *chaise* – and Marcus. Then she threw her arms around Cadell and hugged him to her with all her might.

'Miss you?' she said, tears of joy glistening in her eyes. 'Of course I've missed you.' Suddenly her face fell. 'But . . . Oh, my darling . . . What must you think of me?' Her crestfallen glance fell on Eugenie and Marcus.

To her relief, when she looked back at Cadell, she saw that he was smiling broadly.

'Come with me, little one,' he said gently, taking her by the hand.

He led her, naked save for her stockings and shoes, to a tiny room off the main bar area. Already seated in there were Max, Sanchia and Yolande.

Charlotte's eyes widened in surprise when she saw them, and noted the expectant looks on the two girls' faces.

'Cadell . . . I . . .' she began.

With eyes that twinkled with amusement, Cadell pressed a finger to her lips. 'Hush, my darling. There is no need to explain a thing, nor to look so guilty. If anything, you are to be congratulated. Max here has been telling me that you have applied yourself to your lessons extremely well. And, of course, I have just had the pleasure of witnessing the proof for myself.'

Then, without a moment's hesitation he kissed her, his tongue plunging ardently into her mouth, which was still open in surprise.

Buoyed up by pleasure and passion for her future husband, Charlotte embraced him eagerly. She returned his kiss with abandon, her tongue entwining avidly with his.

When they finally broke apart, she gazed at him with sparkling eyes. 'I can't believe that you are really here,' she murmured as he led her over to an empty *chaise* which stood at right-angles to the one where Max and her two friends sat.

The *chaise* was luxuriously upholstered in deep green velvet. As Charlotte sat, she felt her bare skin respond with sensual delight to the texture of the rich fabric. Filled with happiness and contentment, she squeezed Cadell's hand and let out a huge sigh.

Max ordered a fresh bottle of champagne and some canapés, though Charlotte hardly noticed what she ate or drank. She only had eyes for Cadell. It seemed inconceivable that he should be there, seated next to her. If it were not for the unmistakably masculine scent of him, and the seductive warmth of his thigh pressed against hers, she might have thought she was dreaming the whole thing.

Gradually, she became aware of the incongruous nature of her predicament. There she was, wearing next to nothing save her shoes and stockings, and seated in a Parisian bar dedicated to hedonists. It was a far cry from the innocent setting of her childhood home, where she and Cadell had first met. And where he had first proposed marriage – if not to her directly . . .

A quickening of excitement thrilled through her as she remembered the circumstances of that day: the way Cadell had spanked her, and afterward had taken her so passionately . . .

She leant into the crook of his arm and turned her face up to gaze directly into his eyes. 'Cadell,' she began, her face alive with mischief, 'you do realise that I have been behaving in an extremely outrageous fashion?'

Her smile widened as Cadell nodded. She could see by the expression in his eyes that he already understood where this conversation was leading.

'In that case,' she continued, hardly able to stop herself from climaxing just at the mere thought of what she intended would happen next, 'do you not think it would be right and proper – as my future husband, you understand – to punish me, as you see fit?' She ended on a hopeful note.

Cadell's answer was to raise his right hand and massage it in a thoughtful manner with his left. 'You know, my darling,' he said, his expression one of mock gravity, 'I think you may be right. Not only that, but I feel sure such bad behaviour should be dealt with as soon as possible.'

Almost delirious with anticipation, Charlotte threw a glance of unashamed delight at her friends, then allowed Cadell Fox-Talbot to lead her, naked, from the club and into a waiting limousine.

A Message from the Publisher

Headline Liaison is a new concept in erotic fiction: a list of books designed for the reading pleasure of both men and women, to be read alone – or together with your lover. As such, we would be most interested to hear from our readers.

Did you read the book with your partner? Did it fire your imagination? Did it turn you on – or off? Did you like the story, the characters, the setting? What did you think of the cover presentation? In short, what's your opinion? If you care to offer it, please write to:

The Editor
Headline Liaison
338 Euston Road
London NW1 3BH

Or maybe you think you could do better if you wrote an erotic novel yourself. We are always on the look-out for new authors. If you'd like to try your hand at writing a book for possible inclusion in the Liaison list, here are our basic guidelines: We are looking for novels of approximately 80,000 words in which the erotic content should aim to please both men and women and should not describe illegal sexual activity (pedophilia, for example). The novel should contain sympathetic and interesting characters, pace, atmosphere and an intriguing plotline.

If you'd like to have a go, please submit to the Editor a sample of at least 10,000 words, clearly typed on one side of the paper only, together with a short resume of the storyline. Should you wish your material returned to you please include a stamped addressed envelope. If we like it sufficiently, we will offer you a contract for publication.